SPIRIT DANCE

SPIRIT DANCE

E.L. CHAPPEL

Spirit Dance

Printed in the United States of America.

For information,
E.L. Chappel
1611 S. Utica #201
Tulsa, OK 74104

www.elchappel.com

ISBN-13: 978-0692456552
ISBN-10: 0692456554

Second Edition: August 2016

Dedication

To Debra, for guiding me on the path to be better. I'm forever grateful.

CHAPTER 1

Tana

Smash.

Rat-tat-tat-tat-tat. The sound of machine gun bullets shatters glass.

I leap from bed just as the perimeter alarms sound.

Grab a lamp from the nightstand. Drop to the floor, crawl to the doorjamb and hug my knees to my chest.

Who is it this time?

I rock. My heart pounds in sync with the screeching siren. I wait for the signal.

My lips quiver.

A weighted fist bangs once, and I lift from the floor. The doorknob jiggles.

Oh, please… not again.

Trembling, I lift the wooden lamp shaft overhead.

"Tana."

I exhale, relieved to hear a familiar voice. Twitch, and fumble with the makeshift weapon in my hands. Scrambling to my knees, I reach to unlock the latch.

Hesitating, I curl my fingers over the lock.

"Now," my security detail barks.

I flip the thumb latch.

Cree-eek, the heavy door edges open. I peek through the crack until my eyes connect with Eddie's.

"Let's go." He reaches in and grabs my arm. Feet slipping beneath me, I scurry out into the hall. "Keep your head down," he adds, sounding calm despite the fact that a full tactical team of armored guards is sprinting up the main stairs.

Pacing a step in front of me, Eddie acts as a human shield. "This way."

Following embassy emergency protocol, he avoids the obvious way out and ushers me to the end of the hall. We push through a faux-wainscot panel to a hidden exit. Disappearing down the spiraling stairwell, we descend until we reach the cellar.

Another guard joins us and assumes the post position. His cheek glued to an AK rifle, he sweeps the barrel side to side, clearing our path of any intruders.

"Where are my…" I start to ask, but Eddie puts a shushing finger to his lips.

He points around the corner and holds up two thick fingers.

His partner nods and shuffles ahead. At the back door, he squares his stance, ratchets a knee and kicks through the wood slab.

Instantly, bullets fly again. Eddie and I recoil.

I squat. He bends over me, protecting like a Kevlar blanket. I cover my ears.

"Look away," he shouts.

It's too late. I can't tear my eyes from the horror. The first body to rush the threshold jerks, convulsing with each *rat-tat-tat* of the rifle.

Chest, neck, stomach, *rat-tat-tat*. A chunk of flesh blows from his cheek.

"Ahhhh," I gasp, as blood and skin splatter the shooter's visor.

The firing subsides, and I know this is our one shot.

Boldly stepping through the doorway, the guard spins in a circle, and with a continuous *pop, pop, pop* of shells, unloads what remains of his thirty rounds of ammunition.

"Move," Eddie belts, reloading a second magazine. He grabs my collar, yanks me upright, and we move forward as one, me, as close as his shadow. Gun to cheek, the guard scans a narrow stretch of stepping-stones that lead to a storm shelter.

Once outside, mist coats my cheeks. The air is cool and damp. So much so that I can see my panting breath.

My stockinged feet graze the ground as Eddie drags me across heaps of lifeless corpses, strategically weaving back and forth so we don't present a steady target.

As we approach the in-ground shelter. Two doors push open. Gun barrels appear.

We round the steel panel, pass the crouched soldiers, and leap onto a concrete stairway, skipping every other step. Footfalls chase behind us until we are safely in the bunker.

Heart pounding, I slow from a run and glance over my shoulder. The guards have followed, and after securing the entrance, position themselves, weapons trained, at the only way in or out.

"Dear..."

My head snaps forward to see two panicked faces.

Eddie halts, releasing my arm.

"You okay? Mom asks.

"Cold?" Dad strides forward and wraps his warm arms around me.

I release the embrace. Back away and gnaw a fingernail. Mom straightens my shirt collar and I smooth my wrinkled jeans. Bury both hands in my hoodie's kangaroo pocket and say, "I've started sleeping in my clothes."

CHAPTER 2

"Tana Lyre," Mom yells from upstairs.

Rough night? I'm tempted to quip, but know better than to get too real before she has had her ten-mile run.

Instead, I pretend. Act as if nothing has happened. The way my family always does the morning after attempted break-ins.

Keep up appearances. I rehearse our mantra. My head throbs, stomach rumbles. *Keep up appearances. If it isn't said out loud, then it didn't happen.*

It's sort of the same approach we use to handle the daily death threats. As if, left unread, the hundreds of emails promising to end my dad's life will miraculously disappear.

This sort of thing is a consequence, I guess, of being the daughter of high-profile diplomatic mediators determined to change the world.

Deny, deny, deny… I repeat, until my memory of last night fades.

Luckily, having not just one, but two parents that work for the United Nations also has a few advantages. Heavy emphasis on *few.* Top of the list is June, my savior and our cook. If I had to rely on my mother for meals, I'd undoubtedly live on drive-thru.

"In the kitchen," I shout back to my mother, as June slides sizzling eggs and bacon onto my plate. "Never learn to cook," mom always says. "Once you do, you're forever labeled domestic."

I watch June, humming as she fries sausage and bacon. Funny, June doesn't seem to mind being a homemaker. Actually, she seems happy.

"You better get going before I change my mind," Mom's scratchy voice echoes from the second floor.

"Are you going to meet us at the airport?"

"No dear, way too much work to do. I have conference calls all morning."

"Bummer," I murmur.

"You best hightail it out of here." June shoos. "After a cup of coffee, she'll come to her senses and put a stop to this flying business."

I stuff the fried eggs in my mouth, wolf down the ketchup toast and pass on the juicy bacon, which is thick as a slice of ham. I carry my breakfast plate to the sink and rinse off any remnants. "Meet me on Bond Street later?" I whisper to June.

"We'll shop for a dress at Liberty, then go for a mani/pedi afterward."

I kiss her lightly on each cheek and then hear my mother holler, "Tana."

"Out the door," I say, with puffed cheeks, certain I look like a chipmunk stockpiling for a long winter.

I push away from the table, scoop up my flight bag, and bust through the bullet-ridden screen door. Outside, I jog across the uneven cobblestones and past the lilac hedges to a heavy iron gate. Gripping the pointed rods, I hook my feet on the toe-kick and glance over at the stone guardhouse. After a series of short chimes, I ride the security fence as it swings open.

"Morning," I grunt, mouth still half full, and leap from the iron rail.

Eddie hustles across the driveway and climbs into the waxed sedan. It's only distinguishing markings are a set of government-issued license plates. When the gate is completely shut, I drag my duffle across the cobblestone drive to the left side of the car, climb in, and plop behind the passenger seat.

Eddie cranks the big-block V8 engine and shifts into gear. Idling, he eyes me in the rearview mirror. "London City Airport?"

I don't bother answering. Eddie knows exactly where I'm going, and what's about to happen.

Only the most exciting moment in any fifteen-year-old's life. I collapse against the cushy seat, close my eyes, and think back to how long it took me to get here.

An entire year.

"It's finished." Dad had said as we stood that morning and looked over our masterpiece.

"Done," I sighed, gliding my hand over the slick wing.

"Hard to believe that a year ago this airplane was nothing more than a bunch of pieces in boxed crates and now it's certified to fly through the air."

"It looked like two seatless canoes," I smiled. "Remember?"

"Blimey."

"And the sanding: the wings, the body, the tail; I was pretty sure my arms were going to fall off."

Dad walked over, took my wrist and lifted my arm above my head. "Nope, it appears that this one is still attached."

I giggled and straightened my headband. Stepped back and admired our teamwork. For the last year, we'd spent five evenings a week and weekends building this plane that reminded me of a blown-up version of a toy model in a hobby store.

"Have to admit, I didn't think we could do it."

"Ye of little faith," Dad hung an arm on my shoulder. "Happy early birthday, Tana,"

"What?" I squealed. My hand flew to my mouth. "But my birthday isn't for two weeks." I spoke through split fingers.

"Yes, love."

"It's mine, for real?"

"How we going to save the world without a set of wings and wheels?"

I hugged him as tight as I could, wishing I'd never have to let go.

"Just one thing," he said as we separated. "Don't tell your mother. She's bound to have a bloody fit."

"She doesn't get it, does she?"

Dad looked like he was searching for something on my face. "Ah, T, your mother understands the importance of helping others. She just thinks it's best done with feet firmly on the ground, seated at a negotiating table. But you and I… Well," he flicks my ponytail, "we belong out on the front lines, don't we?"

"Yes," I agreed, even though I hated keeping secrets from my mother. I touched my heart as a twang of guilt pinged in my chest.

"You ready to learn how to pre-flight this bird?"

"Beyond ready," I leapt in the air and bounced in a circle.

"Lesson one: Always start at the tip of the left wing."

Wide-eyed, I shadowed his every move.

"Put your cheek to the front edge and look for any dents or dings. If its not smooth it won't go as fast."

I matched an eye to the curved edge and walked the entire length of the wing. Stopping where the wing attaches to the body of the plane, I pointed to the cabin. "The fuselage," I say.

"So you weren't sleeping during ground school." He looked at the hangar ceiling. "A miracle. While I still have your undivided attention, check that the fuel cap is secure."

I stood arm's length from the cabin and bent over the top of the wing. Pushed down on the cap lock and confirmed it closed. "Checked."

"When pre-flighting a plane, you have to think in 3D."

I immediately crouched down and inspected the underside of the wing. Duck-walking, I moved beneath the canopy, squeezed the landing gear tire, and wiggled the panel door that sealed flush once in the air.

Dad squatted beside me and passed a clear plastic cup with a spike in the middle. "It's imperative to drain fuel from the tanks before each flight, Tana. If there's water, rust, or paint in the fuel, the engine will quit mid-air."

"I never want to have an engine failure, Dad," I shuddered.

"It's the pits, and since our plane only has one motor, if it seizes, you'll wish you had taken a course on how to fly gliders."

I shoved the pointed spike into a pinhole on the underside of the wing. Pushed the cup up like a plunger until a cupful of gas drained out. Once the cup was filled to the brim, I released the tension and raised it against the bright white paint on the wing.

"No water bubbles or floating particles," Dad said.

"Is aviation gas—"

"AVGAS," Dad corrected. "Have to know the lingo."

"Is *AVGAS,*" I repeated, emphasizing the acronym, "always blue?" The wing's pearl paint highlighted the liquid's pale, sky-blue color.

"Always," he said. "So it doesn't get confused with jet fuel; the big guys' gas is clear." Dad took the fuel strainer from my hand and dumped the contents into a small drum marked "Flammable."

"We can use the leftovers to fill up the tug," he said. I glanced over a shoulder at the push mower with a t-bar attached to the front. The bar hooked onto the nose wheel to help us tow the airplane in and out of the hangar.

Dad strode to the airplane's nose. "The engine cowling should be secure. Do you remember how many cylinders?"

"Six," I said. "Three hundred fifty horsepower, right?"

Dad stood taller and squeezed my shoulder. Back to business, he popped a wallet-sized hatch on top of the engine cowl. Twisted a cap and slid the dipstick from the oil reservoir.

"Eight quarts," he yanked a rag from his pocket and wiped the pencil-thin piece of aluminum clean. Angled it back into the sleeve, sealed the cap and closed the hatch.

"Same deal here," he bent to confirm that the nose tire was inflated and had no gashes. He ran his hands over the propeller blades. "No nicks or dents." His fingers felt both blades' sharp edges. "Who knows, next year we may even add some racing stripes."

I grinned, knowing that painting a pair of white stripes near the prop tips would be more for him than for me. Still, I played along. "That would be cool."

He took a second rag from his back pocket. This time, it's microfiber instead of a paper rag. Polished the spinner, the pointed metal cone that keeps the propeller blades attached. "Fingerprints make a bird look chintzy," he said. "This girl is anything but cheap."

"Girl?" I ask.

"Ships and planes are always girls, women. I'm guessing in the old days—"

"When you were a kid?"

"No," his eyes bugged and he slugged my shoulder. "When your mother was young."

We both belly-laughed.

"Seriously though, thousands of years ago, I suspect men at war missed their women waiting at home."

"I kind of like that our plane is a girl. It's super strong."

"Made of a carbon fiber composite, strong as steel."

"Holds her ground under intense air pressure."

"No oxygen required all the way up to twenty-four thousand feet."

The pearl-white paint seemed to tingle beneath my palm. "She's fast."

"Three hundred fifty mph."

"Can beat most other single-engines in a race."

"Not most, T, all."

I put a second hand on her belly and sensed raw, pent-up power. "Off the charts. Rad."

Mirroring the same steps on the right side of our dad-daughter project, we checked the remaining tire, sumped fuel from the tank, rounded the wingtip, and continued to the backside.

"What are these for?" I asked, holding one of two finger-length wicks sticking out from the trailing edge.

"Static dischargers," Dad said. "They help shed electricity build up—"

I pretend-snored.

"Ixnay the ecturelay. Got it. Think of it like how you use hairspray to calm your curls."

"Kills the static."

He twanged the wick. "Exactly." He lifted and then lowered the rectangular panel, called an aileron, spanning the outer third of the wing. "Looks like we'll have free range to turn left and right. Test the wing flaps, Tana." I jiggled a wider panel that ran from mid wing to the spot where the wings disappear in the plane's body.

"Locked and flush." I reported.

"We'll use flaps on take off in order to get off the ground sooner."

"Also in-flight if we want to slow down."

"Like brakes."

"Air brakes." I giggled again and fell in line behind my father, who moved down the back of the plane and bent his neck to examine the tail. He circled around, eyes glued on the plane, until we arrived back where we began—the back of the left wing.

"All that's left is the cockpit check. Climb aboard."

I stepped on an L-shaped peg and bounced myself onto the wing. Dad followed, joining me on the wing walk. He squatted, unlatched two handles, and the gull-wing door lifted overhead.

"Opens like that Ferrari you had your eye on."

Dad winced. "Ferraris are known for their scissor doors. These remind me more of the DeLorean from Back to the Future."

I got what he meant.

"Red toggle turns electric power on," he touched the lower part of the instrument panel. "Not-so-cleverly named the master power switch."

Master of the cockpit. I made note. My own memory jogger.

"Go ahead, get in. Grab that clipboard and Velcro the notepad onto your thigh."

"Pilots are all about the lists, aren't they?"

"You have no idea. Here are the keys." He tossed a ring with a mini-key that looked similar to the one for my bike lock.

"Planes need keys?"

"Only if you want to start the engine," Dad teased. Dropped into the seat beside me and glanced at the list attached to my kneeboard.

"Read off the Before Starting Engines Checklist."

"You okay?" Eddie asks interrupting my memory. My eyes pop open. "I mean, after last night?" He sighs. "Heck of a way to end your birthday."

"Not bad," I lie.

Deny. If I admit I'm terrified to fall a sleep at night, I'll be sent straight back to another one of those face-your-fears shrinks.

Fake it 'til you make it. I shrug, remembering the advice from the last counseling session. "Instead of focusing on the break-ins, think about all the uninterrupted evenings you spent safe in your bed," the counselor said.

Sound advice, I suppose. If I lived in a petrie dish. But not in my world. This month, the count stands, woken by the perimeter alarms—twenty-one, full nights of sleep—seven."From what I heard," I say evenly, aware of Eddie's ulterior agenda, "they didn't even make it in the house this time."

"Tana, being awakened by gunfire in the middle of the night is enough to put even the most experienced aviator on edge."

Don't you dare.

I lock my jaw and sit as still as a seized propeller. I avoid crossing my arms, blinking, or inadvertently looking at the floor. Tell-tale signs of anxiety or deception. Or so I've learned. Interrogation by interpreting body language is one of Eddie's many areas of expertise.

Fiercely fighting the urge to chew my fingernails, I remain still, staring blankly ahead, giving his trained eyes absolutely nothing to interpret.

Even if I am still upset, there's no way I'm copping to feeling shaken. If I do, Eddie will be obligated to report back to my mother. Then, without a doubt, my first attempt at flying solo will be delayed.

Again.

A moment, by the way, I've been anticipating for over a year.

"Gunfire?" I play stupid, maintaining solid eye contact, hands loosely folded on my lap. "Must have slept through it."

My bodyguard's jaw clenches, but he accepts my press-release-worthy recollection. Not wanting to get into it, I'd guess. Eddie picks his battles.

Stay on guard, I remind myself. Although the muscular nape of Eddie's neck appears normal, I'm certain he has had an additional set of eyes surgically implanted beneath his Caesar-style hair cut. Believe me, nothing gets past that haphazard shag.

"First solo?" He shifts gears, checks for cars and pulls from the curb. "Your mom finally gave in?" His eyes drift to me for an instant and then return to the busy London traffic. Luckily, the diplomatic compound is only fifteen minutes from the airport.

"I'm sure you had nothing to do with that?" I say, aware that without Dad's and Eddie's lobbying, I'd still be cooped up in my bedroom flying the likes of a desk chair.

I love to fly airplanes. More than I love target practice, living in the city, dining with royalty, and people that monopolize global TV. Flying is what I live for. If I had the choice—which I don't—I would do nothing else. Forgo food and sleep and like a robot, plug myself into a wall. *Zap*, a few hours later I'd be charged and back to soaring high and far away. Free as an uncaged bird.

But it wasn't love at first sight for aviation and me. Not even close. The first time I flew on a plane, I puked.

Never eat two scoops of bubblegum ice cream before getting on a private jet. Take my word for it. Regurgitated pink milk stains the carpet.

Despite the soggy mess I made in the cabin, our assigned pilot and security detail, Eddie Stiles, still decided to make a grand gesture. He took me and my temperamental stomach under his seasoned wing. After that, during every trip my globetrotting parents dragged me on, he invited me into the cockpit and explained the hundreds of switches and dials that clutter instrument panels on transcontinental jets.

Week after week, he toggled circuit breakers, allowed me to push every button, and eventually even arranged for me to do brief stints in the copilot's seat.

That's when I first felt it. The tingle. The aviation bug, buzzing in my gut.

Eventually, my body didn't fight the thrill anymore. In fact, I began to feel euphoric in the air. I asked Eddie if someone like me—a puking, pink girly-girl—could actually become a pilot.

In less time than it took a turbine to spin, he said something I'll never forget: "You're wearing pink?" He removed his mirrored glasses and smiled. "Didn't notice."

So, my passion for the air crept up on me. The kindling ignited into a perpetually-burning flame. A fire that, without Eddie's help, would have been stomped out by the Safety Patrol—aka my mother.

When Eddie's grimace reflects back at me I know I guessed right, and he has lobbied my mother on my behalf. Although he'd never admit it.

"You earned this all on your own, T," he said. "Don't let anyone tell you any different." For someone who works for the government, Eddie isn't a very good liar.

With my legs tingling from sitting so straight, I give a little ground and shift in my seat.

"I earned this on my own? Or is it because Dad is leaving for the States tomorrow and yesterday was my birthday?" I drop my guard, really wanting to know the answer. Eddie is one of the few people I can trust.

"So you didn't hear the news?" he asks.

"You mean the same old," I exhale. "One side claims they were wronged, the other says it wasn't their fault." I say, sick of listening to the lawsuit's back-and-forth tactics. "Regardless of who gets hurt, in the end defendants and plaintiffs will stop at nothing to win."

"And the fact that the drug company conceded?"

"Really? They settled? Because last I heard, Dad was about to lose his first mediation."

"Call came in this morning."

"Didn't see that coming. What changed?"

"Not sure, but your dad won. Victims got justice. The drug company's going to be held accountable for their actions, that's all I need to know."

Cool. Case closed. I have no idea how my parents can stand their jobs. I reach down and untie the laces on my chunky utility boots.

"Your dad plays by the rules, and the truth always prevails." Eddie's smile gleams.

You get what you give. The rules according to Dad. Blind faith that the Universe rewards those who do what is right and just.

I fight the urge to roll my eyes and nod in agreement.

"Not only did the good guys claim victory, the bad guys will be forced to pay for their crimes," he says. "Billions."

As my protector's grin widens, it's safe to assume he's reminiscing about the old days. A time, I hear, when he also fought for those who couldn't help themselves.

"Since when are you a skeptic?" I watched Eddie's brows bunch in the review mirror. "By starting the TLF initiative, aren't you following in your parents' footsteps?"

"Creating an international database for missing girls makes an immediate impact."

"Stopping a company from making pills that cause kids seizures doesn't?"

"Of course it does." I blow my bangs in the air. "That's not what I meant. The mediation process just takes forever."

"Be polite, Tana. Use your filter," I hear mom's voice ring in my ears. *"It's impolite to discuss business and politics outside the family."*

"Be a steamroller, or tread lightly? Which one is it, Mom?" I mutter to myself.

"What?" Eddie says.

"Nothing." Just a parental mind-bender.

I clam up, as my folks insist I do, while secretly wondering what it would be like to open my mouth and blurt out whatever comes to mind.

How would it feel? Eating dinner with the itty-bitty dessert fork. Without a single thought about the consequences. No image to maintain. No need to impress. Forgetting all about being appropriate and correct.

Or… A streak of excitement raises goose bumps across my skin. I envision the next black-tie dinner: seated properly and surrounded by a table full of VIPs. After slurping my soup, I'd climb to my feet, thrust a fist in the air like Lady Liberty and scream at a decibel level I've never been allowed to use: "Why can't we all drop the charade and just be real?"

My hand flies to my lips, concealing a defiant grin.

As Eddie turns into the general aviation terminal, my fantasy fades. The surge of wildness simmers down, and I settle into an appropriate disposition.

Oftentimes, I consider that it might be easier to be mute. Occasionally, I do hear how others perceive me. They use words like "privileged," "inaccessible," and "fragile." Not to mention far harsher adjectives. But the truth is, most of the time I'm scared. Terrified of the death threats. The vendettas. Afraid of the people who are desperate to hurt my dad, my mom, Eddie, my family.

I know I should feel lucky.

I glance out the window at the sea-blue sky, the ramp full of airplanes, and then turn to my friend Eddie. Aware how close my life is to being perfect.

Why, then, am I so afraid that at any second it will all disappear?

From behind the car's tinted window, I see a familiar group of kids. Airport junkies—aspiring aviators who hang around outside the gates, hoping to bum a ride in an open seat.

"After I get my license, I think I'll offer to take them for joy rides," I say, and reach to open the window and share my exciting news. Their heads turn as we roll to the curb. The bulletproof glass winds down and the trio stares.

"Oh, looky who's here." The tallest boy nudges his friends. "No way you'll ever be able to fly on your own, scared little rich girl."

They straighten their arms like wings, angle them down, and then aim into the ground. "Crash and burn, princess," they chime.

I swallow the lump scaling my throat and smash the window-close button. Turn away and allow my eyes to drift to the floor. *Is there somewhere, anywhere, some group where I fit?*

"Never mind them, T," Eddie grumbles. "You weren't meant to be in crowds."

Tortoising, I hunch my back, chin to chest, and slide down in the seat until my thighs touch my abdomen. Any fight I had in the tank was used up last night during the break-in.

My driver turns in his seat and starts our pre-flight chant: "Given the chance..."

I hug my legs tight and shake my head.

He closes an eye, cocks his neck, and lolls his tongue from the side of his mouth like a mental patient off his meds. "Given the chance..." he slurs.

A glint of sunlight shoots through the tinted window and I raise my sightline to the endless horizon.

Perhaps up there is where I belong.

Eddie points at the kids rolling in the dirt and then makes an universal arm gesture undoubtedly handed down from his Sicilian roots. Instantly, I crack up. My hands unlatch, my knees extend, and I scoot back and sit tall, grinning.

"Those who can't," I chant, "buy bomber jackets and aviator glasses."

"Heads tilted upward," we say together. "Gazing longingly into the air."

CHAPTER 3

"Is that a future aviator?" Dad shouts as I climb from the black sedan. Eddie hands the car off to the lineman and trails close behind. "You ready to fly solo?"

Lingering outside the security fence, I drag damp palms over my loose-fitting pink jumpsuit. *This is really going to happen.*

A cross between terror and excitement ripples over my chest.

Watching Dad pre-flight our single-engine airplane, I hang my fingers through the chain links as he inspects the underside of the home-built's wings.

"Leave no rivet unchecked," the Eagle Scout in him boasts. He pushes from a grasshopper squat and stands over the top of the wing tank to check the fuel caps one last time.

My smile widens.

Finally, the opportunity to show him. Prove I'm capable of doing something epic all by myself.

From behind, Eddie's shadow casts over me, and I notice my dad look past me and give Eddie a curious nod. Releasing the fence, I grab my flight bag and sprint to the front of the airport terminal building. Two sets of metallic blue doors split open and I toss my black duffle on the security X-ray belt.

"Morning, Malcolm." Anxiously, I unhook two dangly, cross-shaped earrings and then set my sturdy hiking boots in a plastic bin.

"Good morning, lovely." The security agent glances overhead, waits for a green light and then ushers me through the metal detector.

Eddie follows, casually, like he doesn't notice the screech of the alarm. He carries a gun. At least one that I know of, and he is never required to disarm for security checks.

"Malcolm?" I teeter, awaiting his permission.

"All clear, Miss Lyre." He foregoes the electric wand. I skip forward. "I hear today's the big day."

"Yes." I hurry to the X-ray bin and shove my feet into my all-weather boots. Sturdy, waterproof, and fire-rated. The only reasonable choice, being the daughter of a scoutmaster extraordinaire. In a rush, however, I forget to tie the laces.

"A couple of practice landings with Dad, and then he gets out and I'm off, away, free." My hand slices through the air mimicking a soaring eagle. Scooping my headset from my duffle's mesh side pocket, I beeline for the ramp access door.

"Forget these?" Malcolm calls out. I whirl around to see the cross earrings swaying from the security guard's fingertips.

"Not my…" I push my hair back with a thick fabric headband and pinch an earlobe. "My birthday earrings."

Flushed, I backtrack, pluck the hammered metal from his palm and press a thin hook through each ear. *Ugh*, less than twenty-four hours and I've nearly lost a family heirloom. The turquoise crosses Grandma wore in the Miss Oklahoma pageant.

"Thanks, Malcolm." I say aware I've just dodged a lengthy responsibility lecture. "You saved my life."

"What made Mrs. Dr. Lyre change her mind?" Malcolm asks. "Allow her number one girl to fly alone?"

My eyes drift to Eddie. Standing off to the side, a few steps away but never out of arm's reach. He flashes a strong, serious look, seeming to say,

"Don't let my efforts go to waste." I run over and wrap my arms around my best friend.

"Thanks for believing in me, Eddie." Tears fill my eyes. "I won't let you down."

I let go, dab my eyes, and stretch my neck tall. Refocusing on the screener, I cup hands around my grandmother's earrings. "First chance I get, these go straight back to my mother."

A look of concern tugs on Malcolm's jolly expression.

"Make no mistake," I reassure. "I'm all grown up, responsible."

He winces.

"Except, of course when it comes to jewelry." *Divert and distract.* "Which really has no practical use in the cockpit, anyway." Not bad, I think, hardly recognizing my own voice. The way it rings with absolute certainty makes me wonder—*is this what it feels like to be an adult?* I grin, realizing that in a few short months I won't be alone anymore. I'll have a license and be flying all over Europe, reconnecting with my long-distance friends. *Freedom.*

Without the slightest bit of hesitation, I turn and stride out the door.

The sun edges a hair above the horizon and casts an iridescent glow over the ramp, highlighting tiny pools of engine oil and AVGAS. I snake in and out of the tie-down ropes to the edge of the parking area, shading my eyes to check the windsock.

The orange funnel hangs limp. Calm winds and clear skies. Just as forecasted.

My insides tingle. The aviation bug stirs. Things are definitely going my way.

A dainty yellow butterfly playfully loops inches above my face. I pause and trace its whimsical flight path with my index finger. Appearing dizzy from the series of twists and barrel rolls, the butterfly drunkenly zigzags, levels, and then drifts across the quiet airfield. I watch with admiration. Hoping, someday, to navigate as gracefully through the air.

Spinning to take a step, I trip over my untied laces. My ankle rolls and I timber to my knees. Midair, the contents of my unzipped flight bag scatter across the ramp. As the ground approaches, my hands fly up to break the fall. On all fours, oily liquid covers my palms.

There goes the readiness patch. Settling on my heels, I drag damp palms over my thighs. *Slow down, Lyre. You have plenty of time.*

In one arcing pass, I stretch sideways and manage to corral a kneeboard, headset, and electronic chart pad. Crawl forward a few feet and reach for the lanyard holding my medical certificate. Then, as if someone yanked my ponytail, my head jerks up, startled by a curious sound.

Three equally-paced beeps hack off like the last seconds of a game clock. I climb to my feet. An eerie silence settles.

What was...Squinting, I whirl around.

A thundering *kaboom* explodes. The ground shakes. Blinding light sparks. A thrust of scorching heat blasts, knocking me flat on my back.

A piercing ring echoes.

Excruciating pain tears through my ears. My neck jars. Twists. I feel Gran's earrings unhook as my head ricochets off the pavement. A second explosion fires.

CHAPTER 4

A fiery orange flame mushrooms into the air.

I stumble to my feet and face the thick cloud of billowing smoke. Sizzling embers crack into ash and fall to the ground.

My eyes water. Burn. I blink. Squint and scan the charred blaze for any sign of our red-and-white plane. "Daddy," I scream.

Coughing, I try to shout again. But my throat is bone dry, as if I swallowed a mouthful of sand. The toxic stench of burning gas scalds the inside of my nose. My eyelids roast. I blink again. Stare into the flickering flames engulfing the shattered fuselage.

Adapt and adjust.

Survival skills 101. Although I have no voice, my sight remains intact, and I search the inferno for any sign of my father.

His tall silhouette is nowhere to be found.

Tears flood my eyes. Partially a reflex, but mostly from fear of the truth I saw with my own eyes.

No. My heart heaves, aching with the facts my mind resists. I rally. *Dad is still alive.*

Stretching my thick headband over my nose and mouth, I suck in a huge breath and run into the sooty fog.

Inside the gray smoke, I stumble in darkness. Choking waving my arms, struggling to feel my way. Out of the darkness a massive pulse of oven-like air blows. Lifts me from my feet and I fall backwards. Thousands of pieces of razor-sharp metal puncture my skin. Burrowing, the blades slice my flesh the way a knife cuts a stick of warm butter.

When I no longer feel the sting of the sword-like edges, I sense something damp puddling on my chest. Flat on my back, my eardrums ring. Throb. I cover both ears. Attempt to scream again, to no avail.

A dull buzzing begins. Muted sirens wail.

"Over here," an unfamiliar voice calls. I feel calloused palms grip my wrists. My arms fly overhead, and I'm dragged from the intense heat. Still, my skin burns as if on fire.

A second responder arrives. Grabs my untied boots. My body lifts from the ground, swinging side to side like a waterlogged hammock. If the coolness in the air is any measure, we are no longer in the sooty fog. A sharp sound cracks and my ribcage erupts in agony. I gasp for air.

"On three." The first responder's voice sounds miles away. The buzzing is so loud, I'd swear my skull is wedged in a hornets nest. He counts down, then lowers me onto a stretcher.

Once secure, I crane my neck to see men in fireproof Kevlar, and others in white epaulette shirts sewn with emergency patches. I hear numerous voices, none of which I recognize.

Eddie. Where's Eddie?

Tears sting my eyes. I attempt to twist to the opposite shoulder in an effort to locate my protector.

"Don't move." Gloved hands steady my skull. I feel their fingers tense. "Raise her feet up twelve inches," the EMT says. "I need cold water. Now."

Two firemen leave my side and take off toward the water cannon soaking the blaze.

Skin scorching, I reach for my face, feel for my headband, and touch the lobes of my ears.

"Easy," the EMT says, moves my hand away and caresses my palm. Meanwhile, he puts his ear to my mouth and listens. After a light tap on my stomach, the responder touches my collarbone.

"Ahh," I writhe on the gurney and unleash a lioness roar. By the time it reaches my tongue, however, it comes out no louder than a mouse squeak. The tech winces sympathetically and continues his examination.

Another siren sounds. This one is different, like the firing of a toy laser gun.

In less time than it takes to inhale, a man in a white lab coat leans against the stretcher. "Update?" he says with a heavy accent.

"Third degree burns, shattered collar bone, ruptured eardrum, punctured lung, Doc Ong."

"Shrapnel?"

"Multiple superficial entry wounds in the hands, face, forehead, and neck. Collarbone appears to be the most concentrated area."

"Accident?"

"No idea what caused the explosion."

"We don't know what type of metal struck our patient, then?"

The EMT shrugs and retrieves an IV.

"Other casualties?"

His name is Benjamin Lyre. British envoy, human rights advocate for the UN. Eddie. Please. Tell them the man is my father.

A foul foam fills my mouth, numbing my tongue.

Dr. Ong puckers his lips, appearing to survey the scale of the blast perimeter. Then, like a distance runner who finds his pace, he settles into a rescue rhythm. "Administer fluids immediately. Get her in the ambulance stat, and cut off this singed leather jacket. Where's that cold water?"

The pulsing siren of the EMS vehicle beeps, and after the gurney rolls a few feet, I'm loaded in the back. A medical tech inside pulls the doors shut. I feel a prick in my arm.

The sirens stop wailing and I can suddenly hear voices outside the ambulance.

"How is she?" a voice asks.

"Better now that she's sedated," Ong says. I fight off drowsiness and concentrate on their words. "She'll have a lot to process when she wakes up."

"Any other injuries?"

"Just one. Man, late forties, not yet identified. Deceased."

"He's not dead." Glacial tears flood my eyes. "No, Daddy." My heart shatters. "*Please* come back. I can't. Won't," I wail. "How will I save the world without you?"

"Shhh, poor girl," the EMT strokes my head.

A cool sensation climbs my arm.

"I promise," I bubble and cross a throbbing hand over my heart. "I'll never fly without you."

"This isn't water," Ong's voice echoes from beyond the sealed doors.

"What is it, then?"

"Evidence," Dr. Ong interrupts. "This was no accident. It's murder."

CHAPTER 5

One year later.

"I refuse to leave London," I shout at my mother. She stands as sturdy as a hundred-year old oak tree, blocking my bedroom door with her arms layered. "My entire life." I push past the empty moving boxes and match my shoulders to hers. "The so-called stability of staying in one place for high school?" Hot as a firecracker my temper explodes. "And the TLF foundation? How am I suppose to help lost girls thousands of miles from here? I'm the founder and we're headquartered in London." Despite my heated tone, Mom's expression remains unaffected. Glassy-eyed, as if her mind is somewhere else.

"You've been talking about expanding the charity's reach," she says, her voice even. "The US is as good of a place as any for a satellite branch."

Shift tactics, I think, noticing that the only unpacked boxes left in our Hyde Park flat are scattered around my feet. Desperate, I reach for her heartstrings and question the one thing she may still remotely care about.

"And the UN? Your life's work? What about being on the front lines? Privy to what's actually happening, not just the stories on twenty-four-hour news. The security escort, private jets, the perks… June. You can't just walk away from the things you love." Purposely, I leave out Eddie, since after months of investigating, I'm certain he's the one who ignited the bomb that killed my father.

Mom's eyes widen and she sighs. "Are we talking about me or you?"

Trancelike, her gaze darts around the room, pausing momentarily on various objects—the hand-carved headboard made in Italy, the plush rug from our stint in Dubai, the Murano glass chandelier, the Austrian cuckoo clock—as if taking inventory.

Her chin drops. "I should have held my ground." She touches her upper lip with a finger. "Despite our best intentions, we surrounded you with superficial things. Didn't we?" When I don't respond, she continues. "We believed that our work would be enough to show you… and ourselves… that helping others is the only thing that really matters. Your dad was mistaken. Our words meant nothing and our actions prove that."

"Please." I blow out, lifting overgrown bangs. "Is that why you haven't deleted the prime minister's number from speed dial?"

For a second I think I see her cheek twitch. Low blow, I know. Playing the career card. But like Mom always says, there's no room for pleasantries in heated negotiations. Smart move, if I do say so myself. Deflecting the focus from me to her. With the taste of victory swirling in my mouth, I'd wager that under different circumstances Mom might even be proud.

I watch as the headstrong negotiator seems to be weighing a hefty decision.

When her sealed lips split, I know she's decided. "The *one* thing I love has just barely recovered from eleven months of surgeries, skin grafts and hours of physical therapy." She closes the gap between us and then runs her fingers over the thin scars hashed across my forehead. "Our life…" She cradles my chin. "My line of work is no place to raise a sixteen-year-old girl." Her bony fingers slide down my neck and skim the steel rods replacing my collarbone. "It's the way of the world."

"Which world?" A fierce surge of anger rages, rattling every single bone in my spine. "The one governed by these invisible so-called rules?" Heat flushes my skin. "Where what you put out comes back twofold?" I stomp a furious foot on the wood floor. "How did following the 'rules' work for Dad?"

Mom shrinks as if she's seen a ghost. Her eyes mist. Her skin dampens, paling to the color of the drippy, London fog. "It was an accident, Tana." Her voice crumbles.

"Accident?" I clench my fists. "You can't be serious?"

Mom cringes. A hand flies up to cover her ear. Lingers there for a moment before easing to her neck. "An unfortunate chain of events that led to…" she rasps, repeatedly caressing her throat. "…that led to an untimely death." She closes her eyes, breathes in, and exhales. As quickly as it came, my mother's vulnerability disappears. The hardcore negotiator resurfaces. "Perhaps when you're older," she says, strong and assured, "you'll understand. Doing the right thing, Tana, is all that matters. Reality is…" Her jaw barely moves. "We're not safe here."

"It's been a whole year," I belt, my lungs now fully functional. Although they were initially damaged from the explosion, Dr. Ong and his team of specialists replaced the dead tissue with samples grown in a lab. "Look at me." I pull my shirt off my shoulder. "Completely healed."

My mother chuckles politely as she does after hearing a lame joke. "If that's the case, then why are you yelling?"

She has a point, I guess. Although I'll never admit it.

The sutures are gone. Scars healed. But the wounds inside are open and tender as if freshly cut.

Right as usual, Mom. I haven't moved on a bit, and you're crazy if you think I'll ever tell you what's really going on. Even though you've given up, I'm still searching for evidence. Proof—so that when I track down Eddie, he will spend every last minute of his lying, deceiving, two-faced existence behind bars.

This tidbit of information, however, I'll keep to myself. Because if Mom found out the real reason I'm desperate to stay in London, the fact that I spend every spare moment searching for potential leads, she'll never let me stay.

Suddenly I have an idea. A wild, crazy-cool, irresistible counteroffer. "If London has too many memories," I say, quashing the flame of pain burning in my gut, "How about someplace we've never lived?

Somewhere she'll really admire. Prague, Italy... *Hold on, I've got it.*

"How about France?" I fire, hoping again to catch her off balance. *Paris is only two hours on the Eurostar.*

"France?" she asks.

"To live. If we have to move, I'm willing to try somewhere else in Europe."

Before the words leave my mouth she is already shaking her head. "Divert and distract," she sighs. "Just like your father. You always avoid the facts in order to serve your own agenda." Absent any expression, she folds a pile of hot-pink t-shirts.

"What facts?" I snap.

"The notion that you have a say in the matter." After straightening the last shirt collar, she corners the pile with the edge of my bed. "It's decided. I'm taking us somewhere safe to live, near people I can trust. Not negotiable. We're going to Oklahoma."

"But... Tulsa? Come on. Anywhere but there." As if doused with lighter fluid, the fire monster inside erupts. I lunge at the corner of the bed and bat her folded stack to the floor.

Mom's jaw tightens. I'm certain she's about to issue one of her famous ultimatums, but I am saved by the doorbell. Her head whips around and she darts for the laptop on my desk. Her fingers fumble over the keyboard as she switches to the security camera images. Her chest heaves, lower lip quivering, as she zooms in on the frame of the front door. A tall man in a raincoat is rubbing his galoshes on the stoop.

Mom blows out and hurries to the door. "Uncle Hugh is here with the movers."

Nearly in the hall, she hesitates and turns back. Even though her eyes shoot daggers, her voice is soft and sweet. Slow-paced like a kindergarten teacher. "You might want to hurry, dear." She glances at the empty boxes scattered around my room. "Whatever isn't packed in the next sixty minutes stays behind."

CHAPTER 6

I hate heat. Hate Oklahoma even more. I've been here for a month and still haven't gotten used to it. Despise the boots, the hats, and all the Southern pleasantries that every citizen seems determined to extend.

Incredibly annoying.

As I stare out the window of the leased SUV at the dry Arkansas River, I can't help but long for the churning waves of the Thames or the fluid beauty of the Seine.

Anywhere but here.

I hate my mother, too. Can't stand the fact that in less than a year, she, the top mediator at the United Nations, quit her job and uprooted us from the buzzing hum of London to the quiet, sleepy, molasses flow of the Sooner state.

Of all places, why Tulsa? I pleaded with her even as we boarded the international flight from Heathrow.

"It's a safe place to raise a family," she replied for the hundredth time.

I heard the conviction in her words, but was well aware of her ulterior agenda. What she didn't dare voice—her hope that a 4,500 mile distance from our past might help us move on. Maybe even forget.

Tulsa proved to be exactly as advertised. Pleasant, peaceful, and an ocean away from our life "BLD." Before the Loss of Dad.

Conveniently, however, my mother skipped over the part about it being tiny—rural even, —in comparison to all the exotic places we have lived.

Bor-ing.

I'm convinced the second largest city in Oklahoma is quite possibly the edge of the universe. And besides, who needs a place to grow up? Officially sixteen, I'm fully grown. Twelve months, two days and six hours have passed since Dad was murdered. Blown to bits in front of my eyes by a homemade pipe bomb. The detonation bore no specific signature and with all the evidence incinerated, the killer responsible for his death has never officially been found. Privately, though, the British police admitted to my mom that only a person highly trained in explosives could build such a targeted blast. She doesn't know that I heard that part. Doesn't think I'm mature enough to handle the truth. But I have my ways of finding out the things she doesn't want me to know.

Even though our so-called "trusted head of security" possessed these rare skills and disappeared immediately after the event, I overheard the inspector say there wasn't any proof to pursue an arrest. Legally, anyway.

Fact is, Eddie used us. Pretended to be part of our family and then destroyed the very thing he pledged his life to protect. He didn't play fair. Nor will I, going forward.

Despite my mother's lame attempt to change the landscape, hide out, start over, I remain lingering in a smoldering cloud of unanswered questions. Regardless of how friendly the community, how exceptional the cutting-edge school, and how infinite the supply of unconditional love from my grandparents, I can't let go. Need to know the truth. Vow to spend every spare minute searching for the answer to one question: Where is Eddie Stiles?

"Living on Tulsa Time" plays on the satellite radio as Mom passes the leisurely drivers cruising along Riverside Drive. I'm living in a honky-talking, cow-toting, neon nightmare. I don't bother hiding my disgust. I exhale and squint at the sparse skyline. Four tall buildings surround what looks like a miniature World Trade Center tower.

Why is the sun here so bright?

I clench the door handle as my mom, speed racer, whizzes past the entrance to the National Prep School.

Fantastic mediator? Probably. Good driver? Not so much.

Mom hooks her index finger around the steering wheel and flips a U-turn. As we cut across traffic, the back tire catches the grassy median and the SUV jumps the curb. My chest laps against the shoulder belt.

So much for being safe.

She floors the accelerator and glances in the rearview mirror. "You're going to be late."

Driving like she's training for NASCAR, Mom skids into the turn lane and climbs the winding drive up to the main administration building.

And that would be the end of the world, right? Being late for the first day of solitary confinement in this impostor of an international high school?

I sit silently, having absolutely nothing to say to my mother.

As we weave around the tree-lined path, I wonder if the campus has changed since my mother graduated thirty years ago. I search her face for hints of nostalgia but see nothing but the paranoia that's been thinly veiled on her face since my dad was killed. She's constantly on guard. Double-and triple-locking the doors, checking the rearview mirror every five seconds to make sure nobody is following. She says Dad died in an accident, but her actions prove that she believes something different. And she thinks I'm stupid enough not to see through her.

Rays from the morning sun bend around gothic gargoyles that seem to watch as the freshmen track across the lawn of freshly cut fescue. Intense August heat burns every ounce of moisture from the air. At the peak of the circle drive, Mom slams the brakes.

"Repeat the plan," she quizzes.

I roll my eyes. "For the thousandth time: no texting while walking, pay attention to my surroundings. Don't loiter out in the open, go straight into the orientation building."

"And..."

My voice wanes, sounding like a scolded child. "If I hear gunfire, head to the nearest tornado shelter and call security with my cell."

"Button one," she demonstrates on her own screen. "I programmed the number on speed dial. What else?"

"Two bars of lead ballast are in my bag. If attacked, hit them with my pack and sprint a hundred-yard dash."

Mom bows her head, approving. "Most importantly," she tags on, "keep your guard up. Don't talk to anyone we haven't met."

"Yeah right, that shouldn't be a problem, starting a new high school and all."

"Go," she barks. "Wait for me inside; I'll be right behind you."

Fantastic. I swipe gloss across my lips.

First day of high school. With my mother. Can someone please remind me why I'm here?

I sigh again, loud and dramatic to make sure she hears, and then search the grounds for other parents.

Can you say "new kid?"

I blow my jagged bangs from my eyes and consider begging her to stay in the car. But since the explosion, I'm rarely allowed out of my mother's sight, never mind left on my own. Orientation at National will be the first time we've been apart in twelve months.

A non-negotiable frown spreads across my mom's lips.

All right, I know, not a chance.

She toggles the door locks open and taps the accelerator. There is no sense in arguing, since stubbornness runs deep in the Lyre family. That is, if you can still call what we've become a family. We're more like two quarter horses who stick together for survival. Luckily, I can still count on my grandparents to be somewhat normal.

Without a word, I grab my battering ram backpack and climb out of the car. The SUV revs and then tears toward visitor parking.

Standing on the curb, I calculate exactly how long before I get my driver's license. Twenty-eight days. An eternity. Assuming, of course, I survive that long riding shotgun with my mother. I shuffle a loose pebble between my canvas high tops and kick it across the sidewalk, when from behind, I feel a touch on my arm and leap at least a foot in the air. I stutter-step, readying to thrust my backpack at the threat. Whirl around to see a wispy, auburn-haired girl who stands at least a head shorter than me.

"Sorry."

"You're fine," The mousy girl sneezes, straightens an arm in front of her, cringing. "Don't touch people you don't know." She knocks her head as a memory jogger. "I'm not the best at observing social cues."

And I'm the worst at making new friends.

After a closer look, I estimate the waif opposite me to weigh less than a hundred pounds. Not remotely close to being a threat.

Red-faced, I lower my bag.

"New kid, huh?" she asks.

"That obvious?"

She points to the disheveled woman adjusting her skirt as she trots up the drive. "The parental escort is a dead giveaway." Her freckled nose wrinkles, mashing edgy purple frames against her brow. "KC McKenna, Okie, born and bred," she says, extending a hand.

"Tana Lyre." I take KC's narrow palm. "Contemplating boarding school."

Reluctantly, I look back toward my mother, who moves closer, spastically waving her arms in order to get my attention. When I don't respond, she shouts my name.

"Yours?" KC whispers through pursed lips.

"Unfortunately."

"You want to go inside?"

I quickly nod and we sling our packs over our shoulders and bolt up the stairs.

CHAPTER 7

"Welcome back, KC." A bubbly blonde wearing an orientation leader badge meets us at the door.

"Brooklyn Dehavilland," KC faces me. "Meet Tana Lyre; she's new this year."

"Wait, Tana Lyre?" The tall girl opposite me squeals, running fingers through her flat-ironed hair. "The Tana Lyre who started the TLF foundation featured in *Rad* magazine over the summer?"

"Guilty," I say. Raising a hand in the air.

"You started a charity?" KC sneezes.

"OMG, what a fantastic cause." Brooklyn bounces closer and throws her arms around me. "I saw your name on the roster, but wow," she lets go and looks me over. "You don't look anything like in the feature."

Just kill me now.

"Anyway," she says. "O-kay," her hand slaps on a hip as if starting a pep cheer. "What's your track?" She clasps her hands together.

Let me guess, a cheerleader.

The National School is unique. So I'm told. One of the few prep programs that guarantees placement into what most consider high-flying careers. That is, if you believe the brochures. The curriculum focuses on specific areas of interest instead of the typical grab-bag of general subjects. Teachers are industry professionals, claiming to be experts in their fields, who take semester sabbaticals from work to come and guest-instruct in their area of expertise. Carte blanche, according to Gran, to give students unlimited amounts of homework.

Whatever.

"Science/Tech, Business/Finance, Language/Human Resources, or Art/Politics?" Brooklyn tilts her head and giggles.

"Definitely Science/Tech," KC answers.

"Me too," I say, even though I have no idea what she is talking about. I fake a grin and swing a thick canopy of bangs over my eyes to hide out.

"Killer." Brooklyn's bright smile gleams as she scrolls down a list on her tablet and searches for class assignments. "O-kay," this time she side-steps, moving her feet shoulder width apart. "First tech module is Aerodynamics and Fundamentals of Flight, taught by a highly decorated fighter pilot, Professor Lamar Flough."

"Fundamentals of Flight?" A flash fire rips through my body. Its fumes push against the top of my skull, vibrating like the lid on a pressure cooker.

"You two will need to report to the hangar at Jones Airport first thing tomorrow morning." The volunteer hugs the template to her narrow midsection. "Eight o'clock, prompt." She claps.

A red patch of prickly heat blisters my forearms, instantly itching like crazy. I rub stubby nails across the rash and scan the hallway, searching for the traitor. Just beyond the crowd of incoming freshmen, I spot the queen of manipulation leaning against the wall, talking to a man in a navy blue uniform.

Brooklyn turns and matches my sight line. "Actually," she squeals, "the man standing with that menopausal hottie in head-to-toe black is Professor Flough."

"My mom is hot, all right." I grind my molars and consider that maybe her fiery temperament is genetic. Pushing my way through the sea of newbies, I storm toward my mother, sensing KC's willowy presence close behind.

Inches from the professor, the enemy turns and smiles. A sappy, phony, you-better-not-make-a-scene-or-else grin. The pressure building in my skull pounds against my forehead. My temples throb, and I'm fairly sure if I passed a mirror I'd see smoke shooting from my ears.

"Dear." Mom pushes my bangs behind my smoldering earlobe. "Don't you have one of those headbands you used to like to wear? You're prettier without all that hair in your face."

I shake my bangs back over my eyes.

Don't you get it?

My skin burns.

That girl is gone.

I roll my shoulders back and stand tall, hoping to show, once again, how much I've grown. I breathe deeply, steady myself, and then speak like a robot through a locked jaw. "I am not flying airplanes."

My mom's cheek twitches and her face flashes *the* look. Not the stone-cold, non-negotiable look from the car, but the other look. The single expression that has convinced presidents, dictators, and heads of militant groups to reconsider their uncompromising positions.

No way, Mom. Not going to work this time. Your accommodating pink princess died alongside Dad on the ramp in London.

Despite the fact my mom used to intimidate powerful world leaders, her glare doesn't scare me a bit.

Perhaps sensing WWIII brewing in front of him, the man in the navy military uniform steps between me and Mom and introduces himself.

"I'm Professor Lamar Flough. The guest Fundamentals of Flight instructor for this semester. You must be Tana," he says, and snaps his chewing gum. "I was getting acquainted with your mother."

I drag my own glare to examine the professor. His porcupine buzz cut spikes four or five inches taller than my mom, making the professor over six feet tall. Between his deep-sea eyes and the troughs in his leathery skin, I'd guess Lamar Flough is no stranger to hostile circumstances. And if the layers of pins coloring his lapel are any indication, he's probably survived countless tours of duty, received medals of valor, and is responsible for more kills than he's allowed to mention.

I, however, am uncertain of his track record in mouth-to-mouth combat. The weapon of choice in mother-versus-daughter conflicts.

As his reputation predicted, Professor Flough doesn't back away from the challenge. Instead, he plants two pointed boots well into my personal space. "So, I hear you've logged quite a few flight hours." His drawl drags like blackstrap molasses.

I nod so as not to be totally rude, swing my bangs and wait for the fringe to settle front and center. Covering my eyes. Exactly the way I like them.

"Fifteen or twenty hours, is that in the right ZIP code?" The professor asks, angling his gaze to attempt a glimpse through my jagged hair.

I don't respond.

With his face inches from mine, I get a closer look at the supposed living legend. His skin is covered with scars, the most noteworthy being a bite of skin missing from his middle ear. An injury, I'll bet, that came from provoking another unwilling young aviator.

Undeterred, Professor Flough presses on. "Well, that would be around the hours most pilots solo."

I lift my chin just enough to make sure my mother can see my glare. A signature look of my own that says, "How dare you tell this stranger our personal business?"

Feeling a volcanic event building in my ribcage, I clench my teeth in order to contain my spooling tongue.

"Hmm, not too keen on sharing with grownups?" Flough rubs his deformed ear. "So be it…" He winks at my mom and then faces the orientation leaders. "I know someone you might want to meet. "Trigger," he hollers, then releases a sharp whistle.

No sooner has the sound left his lips, then KC and I spin and look.

Stare.

Gawk. At a boy with tanned skin, his father's deep eyes and a strong jaw that appears to have been forged from steel.

"Snap." KC starts.

"Crackle." Involuntarily slips through my lips.

"Pop." KC's jaw drops onto my shoulder.

When the young man standing opposite Brooklyn lifts his head, something inside me stirs. His big, sky-blue eyes stare longer than what is considered polite, his focus so intense, it's almost as if we know one another.

"Have we met?" I say under my breath. Sensing an invisible force tugging at my chest.

"The offspring of some Greek sun god, if I had to guess," KC says.

Son of a *sky* god, to be more accurate. I see KC's point, though, since he's gifted with lean muscles and a head of thick, blond hair. Our gazes mingle a little longer before his lips stretch into a "hang loose" surfer smile.

I feel light-headed. The inferno burning inside me smolders, volatile lava simmers leaving me struggling to remember why I'm mad. Within seconds my pounding pulse settles into a rhythmic reggae beat. A riff rings in my head: "Every little thing is going to be all right."

The pull of the sky god's tractor beam yanks harder.

Trigger breaks away, and his hand wraps around Brooklyn's elbow. When he whispers something in her ear, she giggles. She lays a hand on his chest, nods yes, and then they separate. Grinning, he struts in our direction.

"Crossed wires," I twist my neck, attempting to get blood flowing back to my brain. Must be still suffering the effects of the six-hour time change from London.

As the fly-boy approaches, KC whispers, "I'm not so sure."

"Mrs. Lyre, meet T. Xanthus Flough." The professor introduces, patting his son's collar. "He helps out with my Fundamentals of Flight class."

Panic flicks across Mom's eyes, although her expression remains steady. "Kind of young, isn't he?" Mom taps a finger on her upper lip. "To be a teacher's assistant?"

"Trigger's fifteen." Flough defends, and trades his gum for a toothpick. "The darn most responsible kid I know. He's been flying longer than he's been walking."

"Fifteen and three quarters." Trigger adds.

"I'm sure he's excellent for his age." Mom puts a hand on the professor's forearm. "But *you* will be the one flying with my daughter, correct?" Mom continues to grill Flough, and I tune out the conversation.

KC's quick breaths land on my neck. "If he's in our aviation module," she fans herself. "I definitely think you should reconsider the no-fly ultimatum."

"Trigger." The sky god's offspring moves to offer a hand.

KC steps from behind me and removes her glasses.

"Kellan—" she sneezes. "Catherine—" achoos. "McKenna." After seven rounds of "Gesundheit" and "Bless you," she dabs the tip of her nose with a tissue. "Welcome to National."

"Glad to be here, Kellan—"

"Call me KC." Her nostrils flare, signaling she may still have one sneeze in the tank, but after two quick sniffs the tickle appears to pass.

"KC, it is." Trigger skips the handshake.

Professor Flough eyes me. "This young lady is reluctantly enrolled in our Fundamentals course."

"Reluctantly?" Trigger's eyebrows arch.

"Rumor is, her heart's not in it anymore."

I dust the protective awning from my eyes and tuck loose strands behind either ear.

"Nice to meet a fellow aviator, reluctant or otherwise." Trigger says with a firm grip. I can't help but notice his eyes glint like an ever-burning star.

His thick calluses prick my palm, and when he doesn't let go right away my throat tightens.

"Um, oh, I don't know, maybe, well…" *Gulp.* "I guess I could… just come and listen." The invisible tug returns, urging me towards him.

Trigger squeezes my thumb. Hard. "So Miss Reluctant is now curious?" He hovers like a smug cat about to lure a canary from the safety of her birdcage. "See you at the hangar. Zero-eight-hundred."

CHAPTER 8

"Oooh, right rudder, more right rudder," my father shouts from the copilot's side of the cockpit as the nose of our single-engine airplane zigs across the white stripes painted in the middle of the runway and arrows toward the blacktop's edge. "Bottom part of the right pedal. Step on it."

Heels grazing the floor, I use my toes and jam the car-brake-like pedal. The tip of the propeller darts in the opposite direction.

"That's it," Dad coaches as we zag across the centerline to the opposite edge of pavement. "Left rudder to counteract." He clenches the eyebrow dash in front of him and extends his knee for encouragement. "Easy."

I push half-strength on the left pedal. One wheel drops off the pavement, spins in the grass, and corrects towards the middle of the runway pointing south.

"Gingerly on the right," Dad grips the armrest. "Look way down the runway and once the spinner matches the white dashed lines, add a little left."

Shooting less like a rocket and more like a sling-shot, we snake over the center target. "That's my girl, find a rhythm. Like you're stepping on that stair thingy your mom works out on."

Picturing the motion of what's commonly known as the StairMaster, I settle into a back-and-forth rhythm. As advertised, the plane tracks straight down the centerline.

"Hand back on the throttle," Dad coaches, and my eyes shoot to my palm resting on my thigh. I reach for one of the three colored handles mid-panel and clench the round one that reminds me of a rod on a Foosball table.

"Not that one," Dad peels my hand from the red handle and shifts my grip two shafts to the left. "Red is the fuel shut-off."

Well, I had three choices—black, blue and red.

"Crap." I make a mental note as the landscape rushes by. *Don't touch anything red.* "It was the prettiest," I explain. Remembering that the black handle is for power, while the blue controls propeller speed.

"Eyes forward," Dad says, and I tear my gaze from the trio of levers. Sit tall in the seat and look over the dash.

"Five hundred feet of asphalt left," Dad calls out. From my periphery, I notice a black sign with the number five whiz by on the runway's edge.

"Check airspeed, Tana."

"Eighty knots," I read the number from the screen in front of me roughly the size of my portable tablet.

"Light pull on the side stick, honey." Dad looks like he's rowing a boat.

With my left hand, I cock my wrist and I lift the joystick.

The front of the plane lifts from the ground.

"Woo-hoo. Cheers!" Dad celebrates. "Less sky showing on the windshield means we're climbing, more blue means we're ground-bound. Keep easing the stick back. Oh, yes, that's it. Once the airspeed reaches 100, move the black handle back an inch."

"Roger," I say. Feel myself grinning ear-to-ear. My view alternates from outside to scanning the instrument panel.

"Time to retract the landing gear."

I hesitate. With one hand on the side stick and the other on the black throttle lever, I am out of limbs. "How?"

Dad laughs. "It's okay to move from the power handle to adjust a radio or the map, or change configuration. Check the speed again, release the throttle, and lift the lollipop lever to raise the wheels into the belly."

I take a deep breath, flick my hand over to the gear handle, lift it, and then quickly move my fingers back to the throttle.

Dad puts his ear to the window. "Listen for the hydraulic motor. Once the whining stops, the green lights above the gear lever should all go out."

After a quick scan in and out, I glance at the triangle of lights. One for the nose wheel and one for each main wheel.

"Wing flaps next," Dad adds. "Do you remember what they're for?"

"The panels on the back edge of the wing, that, uh... shorten the distance needed to take off. And they can slow us down in the air."

"That's my girl," Dad nudges my shoulder.

Slightly more confident, I verify airspeed and then release the throttle and cycle the flat paddle handle. "Flaps up," I say, mimicking the way I've watched Eddie call out on the jet.

"Three thousand feet," Dad answers, his eyes trained on the altitude indicator. "Lower the nose until the horizon line cuts the windscreen in half."

I relax the tension in my fingers, and the control stick rests against the meaty part of my palm. The plane levels and glides through the air.

"Tana and Benjamin Lyre, off to save the world."

My alarm clock rings. My eyes pop open. My thoughts swim. Unaware that I was dreaming. It's seven in the morning.

The memory of my first flight whisks away.

A tear tracks my cheek. I don't wipe it away.

Barely awake, I roll over in bed. *Cripes.* Forty minutes until I'm supposed to be at school.

I wiggle from the soft sheets twisted around my legs and stare at the cracks in the plaster ceiling. Fractured, sprawling, warily forging ahead. One of the veined lines splinters from the main fault and branches off toward the house on the corner like the wobbly needle of a compass. I don't need to look out the window to track its elongated path. It points a half-block away to my grandparents' colonial. The house where my mother grew up. I'm told I visited often as an infant, but I have no recollection. Just photo memories from Gran's holiday scrapbook.

My eyes focus hard on the hundred-year-old ceiling. Damaged, in desperate need of repair.

Kind of like my life.

My gaze sinks and drifts across the room to the National School uniform, hanging from the closet door that stands ajar. Cargo pants, a white pressed blouse and a navy blazer dangle over a pair of leather loafers, boxed on the floor.

I trace the wood planks from the shoebox to the doorjamb and catch a glimpse of stacked plastic bins packed with prissy, pink clothes. The thick casing does nothing to conceal the bright and optimistic remnants from the past. They no longer fit my life; that's why I left them in London. I have no idea why mom brought them here.

Blinking the reminders away, I refocus on my uniform.

Doesn't matter what she says, I'm not going to school.

My time is far better spent searching the web for new leads on Dad's murder than sitting in some tired classroom, listening to a teacher drone on about being prepared for what will happen in three years. My future is now. Beyond that, who cares?

The alarm sounds again. Seven-ten.

The mission begins.

A springy, double pillow-top mattress makes me almost three feet above the floor, so I hang my legs over the edge, hop down, and slide into the chair opposite a refurbished desk. With my fingers drumming on the leather inlay, I consider the stay-home-from-school options.

Pinkeye, migraine, or the go-to stomach bug.

Pinkeye is tough to fake, and I've used stomach bugs so many times that Mom forced me to get a flu shot. That left one excuse.

I hit the space bar on my laptop and search for migraine symptoms: sharp pain, throbbing in front temple, nausea, light vertigo, and very little tolerance for strong odors.

Perfect.

The floor creaks as I tiptoe into the bathroom. Standing in front of the pedestal sink I stare into the mirror.

Migraine it is.

But I need to be convincing. Animated. Dramatic. All characteristics I dread. Because even though my mom is distracted and paranoid, obsessed with protecting us from all things bad and dangerous, she isn't stupid. Not even close.

I reach for a puffy brush and dust my face with pale, loose powder. Mat my hair against my scalp and practice a few painful looking winces.

Three, two, one… ignition. Lift-off.

With the poise of an Oscar-winning actor, I leave my pseudo-dressing room, pull a black sweatshirt over my PJs, and head into the hallway.

I creep down each oak stair, descending deeper into my role. When I reach the last rickety step, my head even pretend-throbs. Then I see it.

A show-stopper. My flight bag carefully packed by the front door. A long charred tear in the duffle allows my noise-canceling headset to spill from a pocket.

My breastbone thrusts against my sweatshirt and then caves against my spinal cord.

No longer in character, I hear an exploding sound and cover my ears.

Spiral back. Feel the heat from the flames. Choke smoke as if I'm standing on the London City ramp.

My knees buckle and I collapse on that final riser.

Sooty tears soak my eyes.

"Tana, is that you?" my mother shouts from the kitchen.

I stumble to my feet and peer around the corner.

"If you have a headache, there's aspirin in the medicine cabinet." A strong garlicky smell drifts from the oven.

How does she…?

"Your grandfather came over and upgraded our wireless network. Each computer in the house mirrors the others." Mom's voice is stern, sharp; the seasoned negotiator returns. "Better hurry or you'll be late for school."

"First the perpetual chaperoning and now you're spying on me. What did I do to deserve this?" I belt. "If you're so eager to get in the air, Mom, why don't you take the stupid flight class?"

"Nothing good comes of being afraid, Tana. Believe me, I know."

My legs shake, my stomach cramps. I wipe the stinging sadness from my face with my sleeve, steadying on the handrail. Cowering, I focus on the black duffle. The burn marks, the shrapnel tears, my dust-covered flight gear. A black, billowing cloud appears from nowhere.

It's not real.

I gasp three times, trying to catch my breath.

An overpowering rage erupts. After two quick, stuttering steps, I run full speed, swing my leg back, and punt the bag into the air.

CHAPTER 9

My toes hurt.

They're killing me, actually. Not that I'll ever admit it.

Odds are good Mom would just repeat a variation of one of Gran's tough love sayings: "Kick a bag filled with gear and you'll get what you deserve." It's no wonder Mom was drawn to my father. Any sort of nurturing in my family came from the Lyres.

As Mom winds the car around the ring road on the south side of the airport, I rub the top of my boot and wiggle each sore toe. Ten minutes until first period. Professor Flough's flight course.

Joy.

"Is the weather going to improve?" Mom says glancing at the sky.

A thick blanket of charcoal clouds blocks all sunlight. "Don't know."

"The forecasts were unclear?'

I shrug. "Didn't check."

"Aren't you required to get an official briefing before planning a flight, dear?"

"No need."

Mom's index finger taps her lip. "Did the rules change?"

"Doubt it," I snap. "I don't need to check weather because I'm not going flying." I roll my eyes and look out the window.

"Tana, I asked you a question."

Near the middle of the airfield, a lighthouse-like tower turns, shooting two beams of light. First a green. Then a white.

"The weather isn't going to improve," I say.

"If you didn't read the reports, how do you know?"

"The beacon is on."

"The rotating light?"

"Yes, Mother," I sigh. "Lights on during the day mean you need to fly using instruments."

"Instruments?"

"All you need to know is the weather will be crap for the rest of the day."

Mom's hands tighten on the steering wheel. She glances in the side mirror. Her eyelid twitches. "KC seems nice. You guys appeared to hit it off. What do you think? Is she possibly friend material?"

Truth is, I don't have any friends. It wasn't always this way, though. Not so long ago, before my parents became the UN's mediation dream team, my social calendar was booked out months in advance. These days, however, I consider cultivating relationships a colossal waste of Earth minutes. Invaluable time better spent focusing on the only thing that matters. Catching the man who killed my father.

I did like KC. Have to admit I was relieved to have someone to hang out with during orientation. For being local, she didn't appear to have a set group of friends. On this rare occasion, I actually agreed with my mom. "Yeah, I hope we'll have classes together."

"And Trigger, I don't mind saying he's a looker."

"Now you sound like Gran."

Mom shudders. "It's okay to be scared, Tana. Anyone in your position would be. New school, no established friendships… I understand."

I spin in my seat and shoot eye daggers at her. "You were Miss Oklahoma, right? Grew up here, went through school with all the same kids. Class president, Junior League, a debutante, and graduated Valedictorian your senior year," I blow my bangs in the air. "Can you tell me how you have any clue what I'm going through?"

"You're right, I was heavily involved, so I could secure scholarships to go away to college. That doesn't mean high school went smoothly for me. I did what I had to do to get by." Mom exhales. "Besides, half that stuff isn't what it's cracked up to be." She checks the rearview mirror. "What I'm trying to say is that you have every opportunity. Choices. Resources. Girls your age can do anything they want."

Except live in London without a husband. Just as fast as the mental quip comes, a chaser of guilt follows. *I'm sorry, I didn't really mean that. It's just you're always saying one thing and then doing another.* I refocus on the beacon tower. Before I say something I'll regret.

"Just hang in there, dear," Mom reaches for my arm and then stops. Since moving to Oklahoma, she has fallen back into the no-public-displays-of-affection rule.

My heart tightens. *God, I miss my father.*

"Things will get better, Tana," Mom pats my forearm.

The SUV wheels squeal as we approach the security gate. A guard steps out and Mom cracks the window.

"National School's Hangars," she says through the inch gap.

"Those two," the officer smiles and points behind the control tower to a two-story rectangular steel building with an arched roof.

"Would you like to see our IDs?" Mom says.

The guard's friendly expression sours. "Lyre, right?" he snarls, squinting until all that remains of his eyes are two narrow slits. From his expression, I gather he'd like to demonstrate a place to put our IDs where the sun won't shine on them. "I ran your license plate as you approached the airfield," he grumbles, firm and official.

"Perfect," Mom rubs her lips together. "All access points are surveilled." Still, she presses her driver's license flat against the glass.

The security officer raises his view to match mine.

I know. Crazy lady, I transmit with another eye roll.

He blinks away, reads Mom's ID and clears us to Hangar 10. Mom stops at the curb.

"Do you have your pepper spray—" she starts to say, but I've already climbed out of the car and slammed the door.

Hurling my loaded duffle over one shoulder, I stride to the steel door marked "NA Aviation."

In front of the entrance, a small yellow butterfly playfully loops, barrel-rolls and then hovers over the access keypad. "Shoo," I gulp, swatting away the flitterbug, and then key in my student ID number, committed to avoid anything with wings.

The electronic lock clicks open, and I enter a cavernous, unlit hallway.

"Hello," I holler into the darkness, only to hear my own voice echo back. "Anyone here?"

Cautiously, I pass by a vacant dispatch desk. Creep past series of abandoned conference rooms. Look behind, and when I realize the corridor is empty, glue myself to the wall.

"Professor Flough?" I slide against the wall, the leather on my bomber jacket scratching against the textured paint. I'm half-expecting someone to spring from the shadows.

"KC… Trigger?" I call out, not much louder than a whisper, and dig for my pepper spray. *Crap.* My hands tremble. *It's way down in my cargo pants pocket.*

Where are they?

My throat tightens. Goosebumps rise on my skin. I tiptoe along the carpet runner to an opening tall and wide enough to accommodate a giant.

Reaching forward, I twist the cold knob, and the weighted door creeks open.

Edging around the corner, I stop and my hand flies over my mouth.

"Oh," I hardly believe my eyes. I gape at the state-of-the-art training center that rises in front of me.

Passing through the enormous opening, I touch my collarbone and caress the raised scar to soothe my racing heartbeat.

Sure didn't see this in the brochures.

More curious than afraid, I forge forward.

Two space-age simulators, a wind tunnel, turbine engines and a weather station circle a massive computer center covering the polished floor.

And…

My view juts to a gutted jet fuselage. Then to a pool the size of a small lake. Exactly like the one I've read about at NASA's astronaut training center.

Is this real?

From the outside, the four corrugated gray walls and the bi-fold door appear typical. *But inside.* I see stars.

The hangar holds enough edgy tech to qualify it as world-class.

Walking wide-eyed through this aviation wonderland, I think about what other things I don't know about National High School. I continue down the roped center aisle and search for my classmates.

In the far corner, Professor Flough's commanding voice reverberates from behind a line of lockers, outlining what sound like safety procedures for the course. I trace the sound, and when his drawl gets louder, I round the last metal cabinet.

Sixteen students crowd the tight corridor, leaning on their assigned cubbies. Trigger stands front and center at his dad's side, dressed in a baggy flight suit, looking far hotter than I remember; Air Force blue is undoubtedly his color. His invisible tractor beam pulls me towards him.

When he looks up, I quickly turn away and notice KC sitting cross-legged on the floor, diligently typing on her tablet.

"Tana," Professor Flough breaks from the briefing and waves me into the group. With each step my body grows heavy, as if I'm trudging through freshly poured cement. "Glad you came." Flough steers me to a gunmetal locker with a duct tape tag marked "Lyre."

"You can store your flight bag and any personal belongings there."

I drag concrete-block feet to my assigned station, lift the latch and open the door. The hinge screeches like fingernails on a chalkboard. I shudder. Inside, I see a flight suit hanging.

My stomach cinches.

"Jumpsuits are required during this module." Professor Flough reaches around me and dangles my uniform from his finger. "Hate for you to ruin your…" He scans my mourning garb: grim cargo pants and matching black pullover. "…clothes."

The class laughs. I suspect I should be embarrassed. Obviously, I'm in gross violation of National's strict dress code. But the truth is, I really couldn't care less.

My shoulders shrug and I take the suit, pull the zipper, and climb into the canvas one-piece. Pea-green. Like the soup. I'm certain I don't look nearly as good as Trigger.

Almost as if she senses my discomfort, KC scoots across the polished floor and straightens my pant leg. I squat next to her and mouth my thanks.

The safety briefing resumes.

"Flying is inherently safe," Flough says. "You have a better chance of being hit by lightning than being in a plane crash."

On cue, a thrashing bolt booms from the weather center across the hangar. KC throws her hands over her head.

Trigger grins.

The class laughs again. I can't help but join them.

"All right," Professor Flough says, "enough horsing around." He shouts over the divider, "As I was saying, in-flight accidents are very rare."

Although I can't see it, I'm certain my skin pastes, the way I'm told it does right before I throw up.

"Incidents involving airplanes on the ground are even less likely." The professor pulls a checklist from his cargo pocket and holds the quick reference spiral notebook for everyone to see. "If you follow procedures, you'll never get into trouble."

Despite the cool air in the hangar, sweat beads on my forehead. My hands become clammy and I swallow the nausea scaling my throat.

"Each of you will be assigned a partner." I hear Flough's molasses voice, but I can barely make out the words, "You'll be a team, a crew for the entire module. In charge of each other's lives."

Unable to quash the gag reflex, I grab my stomach and run toward the exit.

CHAPTER 10

Heaving, I barge through the ramp door, duck my head between my legs and vomit. Chunks of frozen waffles and stomach bile spew from my mouth.

I collapse into the fetal position, shivering.

If he had followed the checklist carefully… Professor Flough's words ring in my ears.

If Dad had gone to work that morning. If I'd never begged him to teach me to fly. Then he would still be here, safe, alive.

If, if, if…

I pound fists against my knees. If I could just do that day all over again.

But my dad was the ultimate list maker; Mr. Safety above all else. Quite possibly the most cautious person on the entire planet. Followed the professor's revered procedures to the letter. The fact remains, the checklist did nothing to prevent his death. Only reinforcing my belief that the accident wasn't an accident at all.

A brisk wind blows and laps against my tingling cheeks.

It's okay, you're okay.

I squeeze my shins. Rock.

In fairness, the professor's advice did resemble the perpetual guilt track looping in my head. *BOOM!* Inside, anger bubbles against my scars.

Arms, legs, neck, forehead, the obvious and the hidden. Everywhere the shrapnel left its mark. The stitched wounds throb. Sweat-soaked bangs glue to my forehead.

The steel door whines and my head snaps up as Trigger's sturdy boots tromp onto the ramp. Shaking my bangs loose, I peek through the matted strings.

Initially, he arcs wide, avoiding my stomach contents. And when I stay completely still, he hurries forward and squats to meet my fixed stare.

"You okay?" he asks, while splitting wet strands with his index finger. The elongated green beam of the rotating beacon lights his face; a single white glint chases a half a second later.

Tenderly, Trigger's knuckle dusts across my forehead. I flinch and knock his hand from my temple. Then wish I hadn't. His warm skin felt so good. *Why did I do that?*

After widening the gap between us, he offers an opened palm. I accept, and he pulls me to my feet. He steps back, hooks a thumb through a belt loop, and waits, seemingly unaffected by the fact he found me curled on the ground surrounded by vomit.

He waits. Patiently, like someone who has no other place on Earth he rather be at this moment.

Although the answer to his question is simple, I struggle to respond. Sure, an "I'm fine," or even "yes" will do. But for some reason, one I can't explain, I feel like saying more.

"I lost someone in an accident last year," I say in one breath.

"In an airplane?" Trigger asks, looping a second thumb on his belt. "Acquaintance?"

I shake my head.

"Friend?"

Tears flood my eyes.

Trigger volleys a stone between his boots. "Family." His voice trails off.

My lower lip quivers, and when my chin gives way, all I can say is, "Father."

Trigger shoves his hands deep into his flight suit pockets. "I'm really sorry, Tana." His words soothe like the hum of a well-timed engine. "In a plane crash?" he asks.

Yes. The three-letter word chokes in my throat. Even though I say nothing, Trigger's head bobs like he can completely relate. I assume he's no stranger to loss. After all, he comes from a long line of fighter pilots.

He passes the small rock between his feet and pauses. I notice his face flush red. "Then there's my dad. Champion of the checklist. Worshiper of the rules. With his infallible procedures." He launches the stone across the tarmac.

Forcing the pain back where it came from, I swallow until my airway is clear. "It's not his fault." I say.

"Yeah, the Wing King is never wrong."

I laugh. Picturing Professor Flough downing a plate full of extra-spicy buffalo wings.

"Wing King?"

"His highness." Trigger bows. "His nickname when we lived overseas."

"Not Ace of the Base?"

Trigger cracks up. "He didn't see the sign…"

I join him, holding my gut. "Adults seem to think that lists are the answer to everything."

"Yeah," Trigger agrees. "Why is that?"

"Control, I guess." I sniffle. "At the end of the day, if every line item has a check next to it, then they're doing a good job."

I look into Trigger's ocean blues. They've paled to the color of glacier ice.

"Your dad is a veteran, a hero, a legend." I say.

"Benjamin Lyre is true patriot, a lifesaver, gladiator of the underdog," rings through my ears.

"Probably the best pilot ever to grace the skies."

Best human rights mediator of this time, perhaps ever.

Tongue-tied, I pause. Suck saliva through my parched throat. "Odds are, the Wing King has some idea what he's talking about."

"Probably why two grade schools were dedicated in his name." Trigger stares straight up at the sky and systematically scans like he's measuring the distance between the clouds and the ground. "Looks like the weather is clearing," he says, sniffing the air.

"Really?" I search the dense, drippy overcast sky, showing no signs of sun. The green and white streams of the beacon tower continue to spin. "You're a half-fuel-tank-full kind of guy, aren't you?"

Trigger's wide surfer smile returns. His icy gaze softens. "Tell you what. How about I take you flying?"

"Oh," I mumble, cotton-mouthed. "I-I don't know." My limbs shake like a rain stick. I glance at the sky, half-expecting the soupy clouds to split, affording my father a clear shot to strike with an electrified promise breaker bolt non-stop from heaven.

I layer both arms over my head. "Haven't piloted since my dad... passed." Guilt ridden, I close my eyes, hoping to hide from the deathbed vow to never fly again. Too late. The memory replays.

"You know I love you, right?" Dad said as we wiped bug guts off the wings.

"Yeah dad, jeez," I spritzed water on the front edge and then rubbed with a soft cloth. "Why are you being so weird?"

"What's the verdict?" Dad rounded the wing tip and buffed alongside me. "You like how she flies?"

"Love it," I leapt in the air and hopped in a circle.

"Bloody good, T." Dad stared at me for a long time.

I tossed the soiled rag on top of the wing and looked back. "What?"

"I'm just happy, tickled, that you like to be up in the air. When Eddie told me you were interested, well, quite frankly, I was surprised."

"How come?"

"You ride horses with your mum, and shop with June," he scratched his head. "I never really got on much with my father… and, well, the hours your mom and I put in at the UN…"

"It's okay, Dad, I know what an impact your work has."

"Well, yes, but, blast it." He shuffled his feet. "What I'm trying to say, failing miserably, is that I'm happy we have something we can share together."

I moved closer, sucked my breath in and buried my head into his chest.

"Me too, Dad." I breathed.

"Flying is our thing."

"A dad-daughter crew."

"Promise me we'll always share the cockpit."

"Pinky-promise."

"Earth to Tana," Trigger snaps his fingers. "The mother ship is calling."

"Sorry," I shake off the memory. "I was just remembering something."

Trigger replies with a surfer grin. "We'll go up. Maybe even have a little fun. What do you think?" The vastness of his ocean blues churns, and I hear the "every little thing" reggae jam in my head. "No pressure." He finds another pebble and lobs it between his boots. "Honestly, you won't have to do a thing."

Apparently Trigger takes my silence as agreement, because before I know what's happening, he has set a time and place. "Meet you here tonight at six." His tone sounding more like a statement then a question.

Long seconds pass before I answer. Minutes, probably. I'm not stalling, I'm worrying, wondering what's the right thing to do. A ride, that's all. I look at the sky and plead my case.

We're still a dad-daughter crew.

Trigger walks back to the hangar and holds the steel door open. "You coming?"

Torn, my heavy boots drag against the asphalt. I plod ahead, aware of my choices. Quit or go against my word. And I've never been a quitter.

CHAPTER 11

Holding on for my life, I lean against the passenger door, head bouncing on the window.

For the second time today, I ride shotgun to the Jones Riverside Airport.

Our pearly, metallic SUV barely escapes being sideswiped as my mother rocks the road rumbler to pass a car observing the speed limit. I guess she figures if we're going to early graves, it may as well be on our own terms. Once back on smooth pavement, the SUV accelerates and snakes around the ring road on the south side of the fenced field.

"After I drop you, I'm going directly to your school's fall fundraiser," my mother says and then rambles on about how much she hates crowds, big groups, you know, being a such a massive security risk.

Tuning out her voice, I consider if the UN is aware their former heavy hitter now suffers from daily anxiety attacks. I could understand if she were someone else. But the woman seated next to me is the uber Linnea Lyre. Ball-breaking, tough-as-steel-rails, marathon-running, super mother who taught me to never back down and more importantly, to never give up. Whose morning affirmation is, "When the bridge is blown, find a rope." Believe me, I've read the sticky notes on her bureau mirror. I just don't understand. What has happened to the legend that used to be my mother?

Five minutes to five. I read the clock on the dash, remembering Trigger set our meeting for six.

Right on time.

Moments later, the car rolls through the security gate and mom suddenly abandons her fifteen-minute rant. Almost as if she has just realized her daughter actually volunteered to return to the hangar.

"What's going on tonight?" she asks in a light-hearted, girlfriend tone.

But we're not friends, not even close. And if the same blood didn't run in our veins, I'm positive I'd choose someone else to be related to. Someone who made me feel safe instead of scared. Unfortunately for me, we're bound by DNA.

"Uh, can you say 'homework?' "

Instead of acknowledging my disrespectful tone, mom does something unusual. No lecture, no condescending finger, no threat of perpetual grounding. She remains calm. Uncharacteristically cool.

"So you're meeting a study group?" she probes. Trying to act casual, failing miserably, seemingly out of practice. So much for the negotiator's renowned poker face.

As I gather my flight bag, I exhale. Loud and dramatic. Until there's no doubt in my mind she realizes how much I detest her phony tactics.

"Trigger offered to take me flying," I mumble and stare at my lap. "But I don't know."

"Tana." Mom reaches over the armrest and pinches my tattered sleeve. "Your dad would be so happy if you soloed and finished your flight training."

"How would you know," I roar. "You never came to the hangar. Flying was something we did together. A dad-daughter thing."

Our thing.

I knock my mother's hand from my bomber jacket. "Don't even pretend to have a clue about what he wanted."

"Is that what you think? That I didn't want to participate? Your father was obsessed with the plane—and that antique compass. While Dad was out at the airport being your buddy, I was setting boundaries, enforcing the rules, protecting you. Being a good parent."

Fumbling for the latch, my jittery fingers finally clasp the handle. Once the door flies open, I stumble out on the sidewalk and without a word, stride toward National's flight dispatch.

Inside, I cross the massive hangar. Stomping, arms swinging, adrenaline dripping from every pore. My father was a great dad. I mean, where is it written that in order to be a good parent you have to be distant and rigid? He just didn't believe in being so hardcore. And why is she so resentful about that old magnetic compass? Seething, I straight-arm the steel door and barge through the ramp exit. Dusk's final streams of sunlight splash across my face.

Outside, the weather is CAVU—Clear And Visibility Unlimited—just as Trigger forecasted.

Marching forward, I notice the son of the living legend draining fuel from the wing tanks. Trigger holds the clear plastic strainer filled with blue AVGAS against the white wing and inspects for water bubbles and other contaminants, checking off the pre-flight boxes as his dad instructed. The fuel must be clear, because he removes a cap on top of the wing and pours the contents of the strainer back in the tank.

He doesn't see me yet. My anger shifts to fear.

I shake, picturing the propeller turn over, the wheels roll. The engine grind as the airplane breaks ground and lifts into the air.

Faintly, I hear a clock tick. Far away at first, but in no time, the seconds click off louder. And louder.

Pulsing black spots fill my view.

My hands cover my ears.

"You can't go without me." Dad's sturdy voice trumps over the tick-tocks. "You promised. Only to fly together. Remember?"

The ground beneath my feet rumbles, and a fiery flash of heat roasts my skin. Bursts of smoke flood both nostrils.

No, no. I gulp air. *It's all wrong; not safe here.*

Trembling, I spin on a heel. Run, full-speed for the refuge of National's hangar.

"That's my girl," the familiar voice follows. My arms swing faster.

Besides, I rationalize, *Trigger's way too young to have a license.* I lower my chin and pull the re-stitched shearling collar tightly around my neck.

Arriving at the hangar entrance, my finger tips have barely touched the metal door handle when Trigger shouts, "Hey, Tana, you forget something?"

I freeze, exhale and squeeze my eyes shut, wishing I could blink three times and disappear. Fully aware there are no such thing as genies or magic, my hand falls to my side and I turn to respond.

A courtesy, Dad.

I owe him that, at least, since he's gone to the trouble of readying the airplane. I'll make up some excuse. Tell him I'm not well or have too much homework.

The cords in my throat tighten as if I've choked down a bitter pill. Even the thought of offering such a lame explanation upsets my already-queasy stomach.

I hear it again. Not the ticking clock, but the easygoing beat that seems to echo anytime Trigger's around.

"Don't worry," rings impossibly in my head, "about a thing." The nausea begins to subside. "Every little thing is going to be all right."

How does he do that?

What if… I shuffle forward and rub the scar on my collarbone. *Could I…* I bite down and churn my cheek. *Possibly…* I settle on flat feet, hips weaving in time with the imaginary steel drums. *Tell him the truth?*

"*You can only trust family love,*" my father's memory screeches in my mind, killing the music as if a needle scratched over a vinyl record. "*Have you forgotten how many outsiders tried to hurt us? Your mum, me, Eddie. We're the only ones you can count on.*"

At once, I lose my breath. As if some Herculean hand smashes through my rib cage and clenches my heart within its crushing grip.

Scratch Eddie. I shake my bangs angrily across my forehead. *You have no idea what he did.*

I take in air.

You're right, Dad, my mind volleys.

I barely know Trigger. He was kind when I needed it. Consoled me while I puked. Compassion he'd probably extend to any struggling stranger. Chances are good that he'll wind up hurting me in the end.

Dad doesn't reply. His words fade from my head. The spots in my vision vanish.

My swimming thoughts clear and rewind to orientation. "Of course he's old enough." Professor Flough said confidently. "Trigger's been flying since he's been walking." The certainty in the remembered words eases my jittery limbs. A hair. Besides, what school would allow Trigger to assist his dad if he weren't an excellent pilot? I swallow again. The tremors return.

"So, what do you think?" He straightens from over the wing, flashing that surfer smile, and my brain scrambles. The swirls in his ocean blues erase any recollection of why I'm so amped.

Trigger stands, chest puffed as if showing off his prized long board collection.

Now nearing the left wingtip, I actually notice the aircraft.

Awesome. My jaw slacks. *Truly.*

I drop my bag on the tarmac.

So what's it going to be, Lyre? The dormant aviation bug awakens from a year-long nap. *Fear or curiosity?*

In that moment all the horrors from the past whisk away with the speed of a running river; the voices, the memories of heat and flames, and the shakes disappear with them.

I choose curiosity, I think, staring at the home-built plane. A single-engine model very similar to the one Dad and I built.

"Composite frame, super-charged engine, three-bladed propeller." Delicately, I skim my palm along the wing and feel the superior workmanship that undoubtedly came from hundreds of hours of hand-sanding. Tedious grunt work that is all too familiar. Work necessary, however, to make the plane fly wicked fast.

A tiny tingle flutters about my compressed chest. I smile. Apprehension transforms into excitement. I touch the plane's nose and a burst of electricity ignites every nerve ending. My fingers tingle, remembering how it feels to handle the control stick.

Trigger's lips purse. "So, you know more than you let on, Miss Reluctant Flyer."

Unwilling to break the connection, my palm skates across the slick surface and rounds the body towards the tail. Out of habit, I check the baggage door and the oil cap, then stand a few feet back from the plane.

"My dad and I built a kit just like this." The edges of my mouth lift, but quickly sag.

"She's pressurized to fly as high as twenty-six thousand feet and can go about four hours before running out of gas." Trigger uses his sleeve to polish the propeller. "Tulsa to Arizona nonstop, flying as high as most propeller-driven airliners."

"Fastest six-cylinder in the skies," I add.

Trigger jogs around and unlatches the gull door. Exactly like the one on Dad's dream DeLorean. "Ready to go?" he waves me ahead.

Again, a question that's not really a question. "You do realize that eye contact doesn't necessarily mean 'yes,' right?"

Trigger's mouth curls into a cocky grin. With a smile like that, I'm sure he typically gets anything he wants.

Stepping back, I take one more glance at the four-seater. Two wings, three wheels, one engine. Looks like it will fly.

Out of excuses, I complete one final inspection lap and then pause next to the self-assured aviator.

"I have a question," I say, sounding impossibly like my mother.

"Shoot."

"Aren't you fifteen?"

"Fifteen and three quarters." Trigger buries his hands in his pockets and tilts back on his heels. "I know what you're thinking—have to be sixteen get a recreational pilot's license."

"Seventeen for a private," I nerd out and quote the age requirements from the Federal Aviation Regulation's handbook. From memory.

His weight teeters for a moment and once flat-footed, his hands leave his pockets. "I handled the flight controls alone at eight, flew in formation with my dad at ten." He rubs his palms together. "Grew up on military bases where rules are slightly different than in the civilian world."

A proud, steely posture, the kind soldiers assume before saluting, stiffens over him. Except he doesn't salute. He stands steady, certain, confident. Solid as an armored Hummer.

I can relate. Not about the military or the unwavering confidence but the part about being outside some of the restrictions put on regular citizens.

"Sort of like being the daughter of two diplomats."

He stares at me, tractor beam drawing like metal to a magnet. "By fourteen I had logged a couple thousand flight hours. Built an airplane and practiced more combat maneuvers than most enlisted pilots," Trigger quotes his qualifications. "After all, my dad wrote the manuals," he adds, as if his long list of accomplishments isn't grand enough and he needs to tack on his dad's for credibility. Little does he know that at fifteen, his resume already rivals any high schooler's I've met. Globally.

Trigger scratches his neck and then dusts the front of his shirt.

He's nervous.

In that moment, I see the sky surfer in a different light. Responsible and grown up in flying, but also unsteady, wanting to cast a grand image of being more experienced in the ways of the world. Something else, it seems, we have in common. I take a mental snapshot of my new acquaintance. Making note of a tear in Trigger's anti-gravity pressure suit.

"Do you have a license or not?" I ask.

Trigger lowers his head. "My dad convinced the FAA to give me a special exemption." His foot taps. He points to the metal stair trailing the wing. "Time to go."

Every muscle in my body clenches. "It's only a joyride, Dad. Nothing more," I say under my breath.

Unassisted, I place my right boot on the L-shaped peg, press against the asphalt, bounce once and propel myself up. Turning on the wing walk, I face the youngest certified pilot on the planet. Arms layered, legs shoulder-width apart, his feet firmly planted on the ground.

"I guess having a world-class reputation has its advantages."

"One advantage," Trigger climbs the stair and braces the door. "Try being the ever-dependable son of a living legend."

After a stretch across the left side of the cabin, I reach my leg over the black, blue, and red handles and then plop into the right seat.

Trigger lowers in next to me, reaches over, and pulls the door closed.

Wedged in the tight cockpit, we sit shoulder to shoulder. His pristine blue flight jacket rubs against my soiled bomber. Surges of pins and needles bounce back and forth between us.

Does he feel it, too?

Trigger grips the dash, sighs, and after a couple of awkward seconds, he twists. "No pressure, right?" A bitter laugh chases his mocking words. He adjusts his headset over his ears and flips on the master power switch.

Following his lead, I cover my head with the spare set of noise-canceling muffs, all too familiar with the daunting expectations that come along with having exceptional parents.

Focusing forward, I scan the instruments, eyes holding on the dash mounted compass.

What are the odds?

I hunch closer and examine the airplane's compass. Instead of the sleek black version typically seen on the windshield, this backup instrument was made from weathered steel and screwed to a shiny brass plate.

An exact match to the one Dad put in our plane. "Cool compass," I say. Curiosity overpowering politeness. Trying to recall where Dad found a similar antique for our instrument panel. "Where did you get it?"

"Don't know. Found it buried in the pile of junk otherwise known as my dad's tool box." He centers a notepad-sized clipboard on his thigh and wraps the Velcro strap around his leg to hold the kneeboard in place. "Probably traded for it at one of those crazy hangar sales he's loves going to." Trigger clears his throat. " 'Be alert, son,' " he says in Professor Plough's drill sergeant tone. " 'You never know when you're going to stumble across a tactical advantage.' " Trigger shakes his head and puts the key in the ignition. "Funny, for being career military, Dad's becoming kind of a packrat."

Craning his neck, he checks out either window, making sure the ramp is clear. "Have to admit, though, I was kind of surprised the relic actually worked."

I nod, struggling to recall where our compass came from.

Neither my father nor my uncle served in the military, making it unlikely government-issued. There was a good chance I'd heard the compass's story during one of Dad's and my late nights at the hangar. Back then, though, his stories seemed boring and long-winded. So much, I frequently zoned out. At this moment, however, I'd give about anything to hear his voice.

"How do you hear?" Trigger's voice echoes over the intercom.

My attention snaps back to the present. "Loud and clear," I reply.

He adjusts the foam-covered mike, moving it closer to his lips.

I notch my seat forward and fasten my seatbelt, hoping his flying skills match his reputation.

Shoving the checklist under the kneeboard's clip, Trigger runs the to-do items.

Once satisfied, he yells, "Clear," and cranks the propeller.

CHAPTER 12

The propeller spins.

Trigger taxis the plane to the end of the north-facing runway. Tests the engine and then inches to just shy of the lines painted on the pavement equivalent to stop signs.

"The Riverside Airport's identifier is RVS," he reads from the map clipped to his kneeboard. He twists the airport's three letter address into the GPS mounted on the instrument panel.

"Now, when we want to return all we have to do is push the 'direct to' button and the direction needles will show a straight path back. Since it's getting dark," he points to the tablet shaped screen on my side of the instrument panel, "I like to have a backup view on the moving map."

"Sounds good," I say, relieved. Dad and I used the same procedure.

After one last scan of the instruments, Trigger looks out the window and checks for landing aircraft. "The departure end is clear," he says aloud.

He keys the radio's mike. "Tulsa tower, Experimental N111X, is ready for takeoff Runway One Left."

"Cleared for takeoff Runway One Left," crackles over the intercom.

Trigger makes haste matching the nose to the center of the active runway. Releases the brakes, adds full throttle and, as a blast of hot air rushes over my legs, the airplane rolls across the blacktop.

Although sweat beads on my forehead, my heart thumps with excitement.

"Fifty knots, sixty knots." He reads the airspeed.

The plane motors forward like a bullet train.

"Seventy knots… Rotate."

With a smooth pull backwards on the side-yoke, the plane breaks ground.

Landmarks start to shrink as the engine gulps the cool evening air. Cranking, lifting the plane past one thousand feet.

In a blink the altimeter reads 3,000 feet. Trigger rolls the plane on its side and eases the throttle an inch. After the laboring roar of firing cylinders settle into a steady hum, we glide listlessly through the smooth air.

Bright lights from Tulsa's twinkling skyline fill the side window, reflecting my face, beaming with with delight.

"See." Trigger dips the wing further to get a better view. "What did I tell you?" Adding throttle, the plane climbs higher. "Watch this."

Soaring thousands of feet above any traffic or obstructions, Trigger shows off his skill. He effortlessly maneuvers the nose. First above and then below the horizon line, outlining the shape of a lazy number eight. With each smooth loop, my body relaxes, pulse slows, stomach butterflies subside and quickly disappear.

Leaning against my shoulder straps, I gaze admiringly over the dash. Apparently, the rumors are true. Trigger is an excellent stick.

"Not bad," I say, fighting back a grin.

From the corner of my eye, I catch him watching as I search the inky sky for familiar star clusters.

He grins. "Take the controls." His reassuring hand touches my shoulder.

"Take the controls?" I mouth the words and glance at the skilled pilot sitting beside me.

Me? Fly? Now?

My molars start to chatter.

The dim cockpit lights blur and smear Trigger's sculpted features.

My eyelids bat, desperate to clear my view. And when I finally refocus, a new face appears.

My father's.

"What are you waiting for?" Although it's impossible, Trigger's voice speaks from dad's lips.

I'm dreaming.

I shake my head, hoping to clear the shape shift. But when the Dad-Trigger hybrid remains, there's no denying I'm wide awake.

"Go on, then," he repeats.

The image nods, encouraging me to take the control stick. So I do. I clench the yoke on my side. Instinctively, my remaining hand wraps loosely around the throttle.

Trigger must have released his stick, because the pressure on my side weighs heavily in my palm. Seconds later, the plane begins to rock. Side to side, up, then down. To make matters worse, I clench my hand and chase each sharp oscillation.

"Don't over-control. Smooth corrections." Again my father's words channel through Trigger.

I exhale, relax my grip, and try to manipulate the stick with fingertips. The choppiness dampens and the wings settle to level flight.

"That's my girl," Dad's coaching celebrates over my earmuffs.

A tear trickles down my cheek as I slowly turn and face my dead father's head atop Trigger's sturdy shoulders. In this moment I realize I can't go on without him.

Out of thin air, a dainty yellow butterfly appears and floats across dad's ghastly features.

"How did you get in here?" I ask the beautiful creature I saw seconds before the explosion. "More importantly—why are you here?"

The spirited flitterbug hovers in my face, as if it has something to say.

"What is it?"

I squint. Its wings fan faster. Vibrate and suddenly burst into flames.

"Please, no," I shout, as Dad's memory spontaneously combusts.

Burns.

Smokes.

And melts away all over again.

Inhaling the heat from the vision, my nose hairs singe. I squeeze my eyes, hoping to escape. In the dark, my thoughts wander. Desperately searching for a time, a place, a moment without pain.

Then, as if a match is struck, I'm able to see a room—a square table, four chairs. I breathe in a hint of fresh lavender.

Our old kitchen in London.

My vision settles on the closest wooden seat. My chair.

Plantation blinds diffuse the dawn's rays, warming my goose-prickled arms. Soaking in the whitewashed space, I relish being where my family ate and shared our daily stories. Incidental and mundane events that bonded us together.

Comfortable, safe, happy, secure.

I remember those feelings. Distantly, however, almost as if they, too, were only part of this vivid dream.

A cool breeze whisks through the blinds. I shiver. The warmth from the golden light dims, the picture pales, and the sense of my family fades and disappears.

When my eyes reopen, I know what to do. Something I should have done twelve months prior.

I jam the throttle full forward.

Yank the control stick to the rear stop and hold it there. Tightly. Desperately. Urgently. My bicep throbs as I hold my wrist near my shoulder. The nose of the airplane pitches straight up like a rocket aiming towards the stars.

"Hey, Tana, you okay?" Trigger's voice edges with concern.

I ignore him. Squeeze my grip on the side-stick and pull even harder.

My vision narrows, focusing solely on the glow of the sky's most resilient star. As hoped, my dad's face reappears.

I'm coming, Daddy.

The plane's airspeed slows. Eighty knots, seventy knots, sixty...

The controls become sluggish. Sloppy and unresponsive.

Trigger tries to intervene. Grabs the stick on his side of the cockpit in order to fight my back pressure. But he's too late.

I have leverage, and determination. Nothing will get in the way of being reunited with my father.

Hunkering down, I don't give an inch. The dwindling speed slows further.

Wing tips buffet. On the verge of a stall, the nose wanes, moving side to side over the horizon.

"Tana!" Trigger screams, flexes his balled bicep and ratchets harder.

I feel him pushing forward. Against my resolve.

He's much stronger than I am, but I'm committed. With nothing to lose, adrenaline shoots through my arm, amping my strength. My yoke holds steady. Solid as bricked mortar.

The engine coughs. Hesitates. Sputters. The nose oscillates from side to side, then falls to the left.

Next to me, Dad's image grins.

"We're going to stall," Trigger pleads, his panic resonating over the intercom.

"Almost there," I whisper.

My burdened limbs lighten. Numb, I stare into the darkness.

"Whatever it is…" Trigger rallies against the backward force. He props one foot against the instrument panel, anchoring his positive position. "This-is-not-the-answer," he grunts.

The plane sinks.

Trembling, I murmur, "Not much longer, Dad."

"You won't be able to see him," Trigger wails. "Not this way."

My eyes mist. Not from fear or regret. I feel no sadness or guilt, just peace at the thought that I won't be lonely anymore.

"It's not your time, Tana." Booming words pierce my death fog like a clap of thunder. "Your dad was taken. Had no choice in the matter. But you," Trigger says with a tsk of disgust. "You…" His laugh crackles like a bonfire. "You're nothing but a coward. A chickenshit quitter."

Quitter?

A sharp pain strikes my side.

Did he just call me a quitter?

As if poked with a cattle prod, a of sting of anger zaps my insides. *And chicken? If I'm such a coward, why was I learning how to fly?*

Out of control, my emotions erupt. "You don't know me." I growl through a locked jaw.

Reeling, I feel Trigger's damp hand slide on top of mine. His fingers drape over my clenched fist, tighten, and then linger.

"I know that you have your whole life ahead of you," he says, a reggae riff somehow intermingles with his words.

Intertwined, our hands slowly edge the throttle aft.

Surprisingly, I don't fight him. Not one bit.

The blanket of his warm palm makes my fingers mushy. Trigger throttles back, eases the stick to the left and banks the airplane over ninety degrees. Gracefully, the nose arches and falls through the horizon like an unmanned rocket returning to earth.

While the g-forces on the wings unload, the plane quickly gains speed.

My hand falls from the stick. I eye Trigger and then stare into the night sky.

Dad's image has vanished. His presence, his security, his love, gone with it. Any sense of comfort I feel fades. I am truly alone.

The airflow rushes over the wings like a tidal wave and the flight controls activate.

"You know," Trigger says while using smooth but precise hand movements to maneuver the plane back to level flight, "as long as I'm around, you'll never be alone."

Trigger's words shock. How could he say that? Claim to stick by my side despite the fact I just tried to kill him?

Oh, I get it. He's doing whatever it takes to keep me calm. I'm being handled by another person who will do anything to keep the peace.

Do I blame him? No. If put in a similar situation, I'd do the same. Deflect, divert, and distract. The proven approach my dad also used on difficult, irrational people.

In this case, me.

I hang back and wait, knowing I will find out his true intentions once we get back on the ground.

Trigger clears the airspace before turning to a westerly heading. "I understand you miss him."

From the look on his face I sense he knows how I feel. "Growing up around pilots… Well, you know how it goes."

In that moment I'm fully aware why I'm drawn to T. Xanthus Flough.

"What's the matter?" Trigger playfully nudges my shoulder. "Gone radio silent?"

I pretend to turn an invisible volume knob on my headset to full.

"I'm not a chicken." Is what comes out of my mouth. What I really want to say, though, is "I'm sorry."

So incredibly embarrassed. As usual, I hold back. Bury the truth deep inside. A habit I've had for as long as I can remember. How I was raised to be.

I drag my wrist across my face and dry my eyes.

Breathe in twice and stammer, "I— I don't know what came over me."

Apparently, two breaths aren't enough, because before I can say anything else, I run out of air. I'm about to inhale for a third time when a flaming red light flashes on the moving map.

Trigger sees it too. He reaches across my lap, twists the tuner dial to get a blown up view of the alert. An explosive cell of weather building ahead paints over the radar. Trigger grips the dash, levers forward, and squints. Squiggly bands of green iridescent ribbons illuminate the windshield.

"Look at that." I point straight off the nose. The fluorescent glow weaves and bends, wafting like a curtain blown by a giant fan. Billowing, the shear shimmers, reflecting neon-green effervescent lights.

"The aurora borealis," Trigger refreshes the radar picture.

"It's amazing."

Streams of cloud-like beams sway as if moving to an intergalactic concert.

The ribbon weaves. Bends and knits itself into a solid blanket of light. The opaque curtain grows. Its veil erases the stars as our airplane coasts into a faceted spectrum of magnificent colored lights.

A wind gust rips.

The slick plane rocks from side to side.

A second thrashing whip follows, knocking the steady frame off-kilter.

The flight controls dance.

Our plane rolls like a dinghy in rough waters. Then, it suddenly drops.

Trigger chases the stick and just as he collars the yoke, a loud squelchy sound buzzes and the instrument lights flash.

The panel goes black.

"Trigger," I call out, even though he is already clawing for a flashlight. He digs around in the side pocket until he finds the mini-emergency light.

"Reverse course," I shout.

Trigger aggressively banks 180 degrees.

He wedges the flashlight between his teeth, shining the beam at the GPS screen. Fortunately, the Riverside Airport ID—RVS—is still set, and when he presses the "direct-to" button, a straight track back to the airfield appears.

With his finger over the confirm prompt, an intense wind shear lifts the light plane 300 feet, and before I know what has happened, a hearty downdraft thrusts us back toward the ground.

The g-force from the fall sends Trigger's flashlight plummeting to the floor. And when the tiny beam disappears under the seat, the cockpit is black again.

Flying in the blind, the airplane continues to shake. Front, back, side to side. Wavering like a sail torn from its mast.

Any attempt to grab the stick fails.

Even if I catch it for a second, the turbulence lashes so intensely that the yoke slips from my hands. Trigger does the same. Without success. So I do the only thing I can. Plead for the winds to subside.

"Please," I beg the universe, aware that given my last stunt, this request must sound ridiculous. "One still moment. Or even a glimmer of cockpit light." I stare into the darkness, clearly not quite ready to die.

A massive air pocket answers and thrusts the fuselage further down. Karma has come around quickly, and the cosmos are here to collect.

When I suspect the wings can take no more force and are about to rip from their struts, a thick bolt of lightning flashes and brightens the windscreen.

A glint of hope?

I release a short sigh of relief. But it's premature. A thunderous wave strikes and flips our plane upside down.

During the flash, I notice Trigger locate a few pertinent controls—yoke, throttle, and the magnetic compass.

Inverted, Trigger flicks a burst of forward pressure on the stick, and the airplane rolls back to level flight. Another clap of lightning flashes. He looks outside and tries to steady the wings.

"Help me hold the controls!"

I nearly catch the dancing stick, but one final thrash of wind shear removes me from my seat. Driving my head against ceiling. Jettisoning my headset.

Stretched to the limit, the thick canvas shoulder safety straps retract, and my body recoils against the seat.

Locked in tight, I watch as Trigger's head slaps the side window, bounces from the ceiling, and smacks the dash. His chin falls to his chest.

My vision blurs. Eyelids weigh heavy.

Everything goes dark.

CHAPTER 13

Through closed lids, I see a flicker of light.

The power's back on? But how?

Blinking, I knuckle the crust from my eyes to confirm that what I'm seeing is real. Again, a white light pulses from the navigation screen.

"Turn left," the cursor reads, and continues to flash as if caught in a perpetual loop. "Accept heading okay?" The message prompt waits for acknowledgment.

My eyelashes flutter and squint at the digital glow.

The power *is* on. I scan the battery indicator for confirmation.

Yes. I exhale. A positive charge.

The airplane sails straight ahead, flown by the autopilot.

Where are we?

My eyes shift to the moving map.

Rows of jagged green lines cover the notebook-sized screen.

Fried.

No airports, no cities, no digital point of reference.

"Stay calm, Lyre," I mutter. "Fall back on your training." I massage the shrapnel scar on my neck. "What did we practice for getting un-lost?"

Back to the basics. I eye the antique compass. Navigate old-school.

Lifting my sight slightly above the dash, I notice a fuzzy glow radiating from the backup compass.

"West." I sit tall in my seat, look out the windscreen and search the sky. No remnants of the rainbow ribbon, no pothole turbulence. Flying conditions are smooth and clear. So clear, in fact, the stars shine, their twinkling glow speckling the dim cockpit.

"Hey." I turn and nudge Trigger. He doesn't move. His chin sticks to his chest, his tanned skin as white as the racing stripes painted on the propeller.

"As long as I'm around, you'll never be alone." I shudder, remembering Trigger's promise.

Anxious, I nudge him one more time.

No answer.

No movement.

Not a single sign of life.

"You're okay," I chant. "You've got this." I burst into a belly laugh. Not because the situation is particularly funny. At the irony. The crux of the matter—that every time someone says "You can count on me," they vanish. Sometimes even disintegrate into thin air.

"I'm so not okay." Tears drip from my eyes.

How long did the stick-by-you promise last this time? I consult my watch. Ten minutes.

Wait...

I check again.

We've only been flying for ten minutes?

I touch my head. It throbs as if I've been knocked out for hours.

How in the world?

My lip quivers.

I never soloed, and now I'm in charge of a plane I've never flown before. On my own. Motoring over who-knows-where. At night. Without the slightest idea where to land.

The engine hums softly. Miles of land whizz by with every second that passes.

"This can't be happening." I claw my neck scar.

Clenching the dash, I jolt the GPS screen with the heel of my hand. I pound the flashing "Acknowledge" button a dozen times, and although the message vanishes, there's still no digital map.

What now?

Slumping back against the seat, I breathe deep, having taken enough flying lessons to realize one thing. I have to come up with a game plan soon. Before we run out of gas.

Aviate, navigate, then communicate. I chant a pilot's priority list and revert to my training lessons with Eddie. "Don't just rely on the fancy high-tech gadgets, T. Learn the basics. Practice fundamentals, because you know how it goes: the more electronics in the cockpit, the better the chance something will go bad."

Not just bad. In this case, dire.

Dead reckoning. The phrase pops in my head. The Hail Mary way of figuring location—estimating a last known position and then calculating how much time and speed have elapsed.

Twisting around, I look through the rear windows and search for any familiar landmarks: clusters of city lights, airport beacons, or long winding river fingers that might feed into a notable lake. In every direction, all I see is rocky terrain with no roads or water.

Certain of where we started, I'm equally certain that traveling a dozen minutes in any direction from Tulsa wouldn't resemble what I see below.

Terror rips through me. My second-worst nightmare becomes a reality.

I have absolutely no idea where we are.

"Trigger," I shout and shove him harder. "Wake up."

He doesn't budge. His face grays, the color of the waxing moon.

Options.

My body shudders as two strategies play out in my head. Fly until I run out of fuel. Or take my chances and land now amongst knife-edge rocks and narrow stretches of uncertain earth.

Urgently, I check the fuel gauges. Both needles read put-your-head-between-your-knees-and-kiss-your-kiester-goodbye zero.

"Can I get a little help here?" I cry out to no one in particular, suspecting that my earlier attempt to take our two lives negates any credibility I have with the Universe. I reach for the scar on my neck. *Think rationally.*

It's likely Trigger only planned for a quick sightseeing trip. One hour of fuel plus forty-five minutes of night reserve.

Hold up.

I rub over the raised skin. If my estimate of the flying time is right, we should have at least half-full tanks. I recheck both needles; they haven't moved a bit. So why are we running on fumes? With no time to figure the how and why, I grab the flight controls, turn off the autopilot and guess at the best landing spot.

Then, as if by some divine intervention by the patron saint of flight, Trigger's eyes pop open.

"Are we dead?" His pupils spread, and his gaze traces every curve on my face. A warm tingle follows in its wake.

Thank you. I glance up at the sky and sigh.

"Not yet," I answer. "That's the good news. Bad news is, it's dark, there are no noticeable clearings, and we're about to run out of gas."

Trigger shakes like he's been splashed with a bucket of cold water.

Snapping upright, he clenches the controls. "Speed: normal cruise. Altitude: three thousand feet. Heading: due west," he reads from the instruments. Once he appears confident the plane is at a safe elevation, he asks the billion-dollar question. "Where are we?"

He initiates a shallow dive.

Leaning forward, I let him take over. I release the stick and bend my neck until I can see around the backup compass and over the nose. Remind myself that sense of direction has always been one of my strengths. Admitting that I have no idea where I am is not an option.

Cocking my head further, I hold my arm straight out, cheek to bicep, allowing my eyes to track along my stretched limb. Form the longhorn sign, and then turn my hand on its side until my pinky finger aligns with the horizon. Four fingers' width up should lead right to the North Star. That is if we're still in Oklahoma. But since the forever-visible light is a hair below my little finger, half-an-inch lower than expected, I figure we are not just west, but far west. Most likely, somewhere in the desert.

While this fact is important—crucial, actually—I decide to wait. Conceal the unbelievable estimation until I can make sense of it myself. I watch as Trigger sets the Riverside Airport ID in the GPS for the third time.

"RVS," he says as he types. He hits enter, and the destination box defaults to 37 degrees 14'06" N, 115 degrees 48'40" W—radically different from the coordinates of our home base.

"We're not in Oklahoma anymore," I blurt to break Trigger's tunnel vision. After all, it didn't take a pro to recognize a pilot caught in a death spiral of denial.

He acknowledges my comment with a glance, then twists RVS in the cursor one last time.

"What's wrong with this thing?" Trigger leans across me and resets the navigation circuit breaker. A gallant effort, but the only significant change from the hard reset is that the map screen, formerly filled with ragged lines, is now completely blank.

"Hardly progress." I wince.

"Search the sectional chart," he barks, as he unclips the map from his kneeboard and passes it over.

I unfold the chart that covers the western part of the nation over my thighs. Tracing with a fingertip, I graze over the flat elevations in Oklahoma and skip to the brown contoured shading on the foldout. Colorado, Nevada and New Mexico all have hills and mountains. Matching the layered peaks on the chart to the ground below, I conclude we must be in Nevada.

"Makes sense," I say aloud. Better understanding the results of my star experiment. "The North Star is lower in the sky."

And Polaris never lies.

"We're definitely in the southern part of Nevada." My finger circles a twenty mile area in the middle of the heavy shading.

Trigger's brow wrinkles. "Are you some kind of astronomy expert?"

My lips curl like I have a secret. I keep it trapped and gnaw the inside of my cheek.

Go ahead.

Considering his compassion after my performance earlier and his you-can-count-on-me speech, it might be okay to let him in. A little.

Gradually my jaw relaxes, my lips part and I smile. "Celestial phone app."

Trigger hoots. "Resourceful. Surprisingly resourceful."

He playfully bumps my shoulder; a surge zaps through my extremities. Uncomfortable and easy. Awkward and sensational. Similar to a hit on the funny bone.

Immediately, our attention is drawn to a red light blazing on the dash. The flashing low fuel warning shifts Trigger's easy expression.

"Fifteen minutes," I set the stop clock. The short time we have before our sleek rocket morphs into an unpowered lawn dart.

Trigger slows the engine to conserve the remaining fuel. "Okay, Sacajawea, find us a place to land."

After scouring the surrounding landscape once more, I see no viable place to safely let down. "There has to be a dirt road, dry river, or open mesa." Holding the map against the dash, I take a final glance.

Pointed peaks and steep slopes.

Nothing smooth or graded for an emergency landing.

Forever determined, I adjust the chart, aligning the symbols to our ground track. And just when I've vetoed every option, a series of dull lights spark from below.

Please, don't let this be a dream.

I shut my eyes. Then peek through a cracked lid to see red and green bulbs glowing like a holiday yard display.

It's not a dream. Not an oasis or a figment concocted by my desperation. I squeal with delight.

The strategically placed bulbs outline the shape of a Christmas tree flipped flat on its back.

Another spark. I blink. A runway appears.

"Airport, ten o'clock," I yell, pointing to the white flashing lights. Christmas in September. Fortunately, our gift came early this year.

Trigger's big blues bulge, and his neck pulls back. "The rabbits are, ah, in sight," he says, banking steeply towards the beginning of the lighted area.

Among the sounds of the engine and Trigger's voice calling out the landing checks, I hear something staticky and muffled in the cockpit.

"What's that?" I root around my feet searching for the source. I listen closely for a moment and hear a man's voice crackle from the floor.

"Who was…" Trigger's words trail off when he notices I'm tugging on the rubber cord attached to my loose headset. Once the gel muffs cover my ears, I reach around the center console and do the same for him.

Over the intercom, an air traffic controller transmits, "N111X, the airport is ten-thirty and three miles, call the field in sight."

With the white edge lights on high intensity, the rectangular layout of a runway fills the windscreen. The letter "P" is blocked in reflective paint, indicating that the airport is private. A huge dry lake sits at the opposite end of the airport. Designated overrun, I suspect for planes in distress.

Like us.

"N111X has the field in sight," Trigger replies. He releases the mike and aims the spinner toward a runway built long enough to handle a reentering space shuttle.

"11X is cleared to land Runway 32," ATC confirms.

After lowering the landing gear, Trigger adjusts the flaps. Once the airplane slows to approach speed, he descends, following the glide path lights.

"Red over white, we're all right," Trigger reassures.

I stare at the Hershey-bar path lights on the left side of the threshold. Although the color combination shows us descending on target, a sinking feeling settles in the pit of my stomach.

It's too perfect.

Just as it was moments before the blast.

I trip over untied laces. On all fours, settle back on my heels, drying the oily liquid from my palms. In one arcing pass I manage to corral the contents of my flight bag; crawling forward, I gather my stray medical certificate. I hear a tick. A time clock? No, it's more like a click, click, click. Raise my eyes to see Eddie still standing at the terminal door, head down, typing on his phone. Why is he so far from me? An alarm rings in my head.

Horror-stricken, I gnaw a thumbnail. When I woke in the hospital, Mom told me Eddie disappeared. Out of shame, I assumed at first. For botching his assignment. Forever at my side, then at the most dire moment he wasn't there. But then I learned more.

I miss you. I trusted you. I hate you, Eddie. A sting stabs my heart.

"No worries, Tana," Trigger says as if he heard my thoughts. "Sounds like they're expecting us."

"How can that be?" I bury the pain. "We didn't even know we were coming."

"Listen." Multitasking, Trigger adjusts the throttle another inch. "I'm not comfortable, either. But this is the only landing strip for miles." His voice cracks. For the first time, I consider the possibility he may have similar concerns.

He's right, though, as much as I hate to admit it. At any second, our fuel tanks will run dry, and the engine-heavy airframe will plummet back to earth.

Trigger lays out a plan, "We'll land, refuel, and find someone who can help us figure out where the heck we are."

Simple enough. A plan I think we both know won't keep.

"You good?" Trigger asks.

Even though I nod "yes," my instincts scream "no."

"Agreed," Trigger continues to split his attention between the instruments and the runway. "Call out my altitudes."

I make standard reports. "Fifty feet… Forty," I read from the altimeter. "Twenty feet above the ground..."

Thousands of practice hours have served Trigger. Despite my kamikaze maneuver and a tumultuous geomagnetic storm, he remains a steady stick.

That is, until the wheels hit ground.

CHAPTER 14

The nose wheel touches pavement. The windscreen fills with a blur of camouflage paint schemes. Four all-terrain vehicles blaze in our direction. High beams burning bright.

I shrink in my seat, bracing boots against the dash. Chest heavy with the feeling that I've let my guard down. What are the chances an airport miraculously appears at the very moment we are nearly out of fuel and about to be forced to land? Slim. If I had been born a cat, my ears would be perked, tail bristled.

"Be vigilant, Tana." Mom's warnings bubble in my brain.

The plane, a compass, the offer of a joyride from a practical stranger. When linked together, the coincidences don't seem so random. I squint at Trigger and then look outside, counting four uniformed men per vehicle.

Could they be... My heart seizes. *...here to tie up lose ends?*

Both of my sides tighten, my neck stiffens, and my jaw locks. I've gone ahead and done the very thing Mom warned me of and played right into their hands. *Add it to the list of ways I have disappointed my mother.*

"Who are these guys?" Trigger asks, focused on the off-road Jeeps crossing center field. A dense dust funnel swirls behind them. If he's part of all this, he's a very good actor.

"Welcome wagon?" I gulp, mind-swapping the image of the aggressive caravan for the endless parade of compassionate neighbors that visited our house a few days after we moved to Tulsa.

Deny, deny, deny. My eyes edge above the dash.

Despite my efforts, these men don't appear to be carrying covered cake plates or loaves of homemade banana bread.

Trigger stomps the rudder pedals. I jerk forward. The brakes squeal.

"More like neighborhood watch. I count sixteen men, including the guy with the megaphone," he says, gesturing at the mountainous, muscular man towering over the roll bar of one Jeep. "I don't remember ATC saying anything about an escort. Do you?"

I shake my head and watch Trigger's body language. His legs are still, his hands steady, and he maintains solid eye contact. He appears to be telling the truth. *Maybe he isn't involved.*

Outside, the caravan's single-file formation splits and the lead vehicle parallels the runway to match our plane's dissipating speed. The three remaining Jeeps accelerate and take the lead.

When our plane finally slows to a crawl, Trigger turns right onto a double wide taxiway. As if on cue, the Jeeps shift formation, fluid yet precise, reminding me of a marching band. Two by two, the pairs drive onto the asphalt, circle around, and settle into a straight line opposite our idling propeller.

The metal barricade edges forward, headlights shining on our propeller.

I sit up to see who will flinch first—the Jeep or the plane? Before I have a chance to guess, Trigger jams the toe brakes and screeches to a stop. Without a doubt, the team dressed in head-to-toe black is not here to pay a social visit.

"Pull over," I shout. "Open the door."

"Huh?" Trigger's head snaps around.

"They want me, not you." An earsplitting tone rings out in my head, and I relive the fiery orange flame mushrooming in the air. "No." I bite my lip. "I already tried to take you down with me once. I'm not going to let that happen again."

"Tana, what are you talking about?" Fear eclipses his steady eyes. "No way these guys knew we were coming; I practically bullied you into flying tonight." His mouth curls like a rip current, chased by a hang-ten smile. "The storm was a fluke; no one controls the weather."

A trickle of Trigger's logic begins to break through. Inside my head, an iron door slams and a deadbolt latches. "Please, you seem nice, but I can't lose another…"

"Leave you here alone?" He balks. "Not a chance. Double or nothing. We're in this together. If you're uncomfortable, I'm uncomfortable." Trigger's eyes drift to the airport diagram.

I peer over his shoulder, careful not to make any sudden moves. "You're not considering…" *Running.*

One runway and four taxiways. After analyzing the ground sketch, it seems the quickest escape route includes a sharp 180-degree turn followed by a full-throttled dash back to Runway 32. The only other viable option is to continue straight ahead and bust through the blockade of tricked-out, rock-climbing, ditch-jumping four wheelers.

What are the odds we beat the caravan to the runway?

I examine our dented wings, lawn-mower-sized tires, and my partner's jittery wrist resting on the throttle.

Fifty-fifty?

My gut cinches. Then there's the fuel situation.

Bear in mind, we landed with the warning light on. Although not legally old enough to drive, I recall the countless times Eddie let me get behind the wheel and practice within the bounds of the compound fence.

"Don't ever let the tank go below a quarter, Tana," he drilled.

Never mind pressing on with the forbidden, you-better-find-a-shoulder-to-pull-off-on idiot light flashing.

Eddie, why did you pretend to be my friend? My heart cries, but my conscious mind counters with a weighted reality blast. Every word Eddie said was a lie. Every act, part of an intricate plot. Feeling my chest about to burst, I breathe in. And when I exhale, the anger resurfaces four-fold.

Wait until I get my hands on that poser.

After a quick recalculation, I estimate our chances. Twenty percent, at best. All I can do is hope Trigger is good at math.

A half-second passes before my partner handles the throttle and then glances over his left shoulder. The muscles in his thighs tighten. His boots slide from the foot brakes to the rudder pedals near the floor. "Time to get the hell out of dodge," Trigger says.

I hold my breath as his throttle hand creeps forward. The engine revs and I clench my shoulder straps. Perhaps he's better at science.

Just as Trigger smashes the left rudder, a gravely voice echoes over a megaphone. "You're a little late." A screeching, high-pitched tone follows. The man shakes the handheld and then continues, "Fly-in hours ended at six."

As fast as he advanced it, Trigger slides the power back to idle and realigns the nose wheel with the Jeep's high beams.

"But as you can see, we're in the middle of the desert with a ton of time on our hands." The man's words vibrate like he's speaking through a tin can. Hollow and ample, but not necessarily unfriendly.

My nerves ease. Slightly.

"Follow us to parking," our guide orders, like we have no other option. He swings down into the passenger seat and the driver flashes the headlights twice. Reverses, flips the Jeep around, and retreats down the runway.

"See." Trigger follows. "Nothing to worry about." His assurance seems more for his own benefit than mine. "Friendly."

He gooses the power and tracks behind the lead vehicle. The remainder of the commando convoy trails behind.

"Yes," I say. "Awfully friendly for complete strangers."

CHAPTER 15

Jeep, plane, Jeep, Jeep, Jeep. The caravan holds tight formation, corralling us toward a massive hangar complex. Three identical steel doors stand in a row, stark and unmarked, painted to look old. As we round the corner, our lead peels off and aims for the ramp in the middle.

The thick-bodied greeter jumps from the rolling vehicle, jogs a few steps and then plants his huge boots flat on the ground. He faces us, glances back to the four-story hangar entrance, and then raises a pair of lighted marshaling-wands above his head. I notice he wears an eye patch.

Trigger follows the glow sticks' forward motion until the pointy tip of our chrome propeller is inches from the greeter's broad chest. When the man crosses the wands into an "X," Trigger stops.

"Gutsy," he adds when the marshaller doesn't waver.

Through the rotating prop blades, I see the lighted wand slice lengthwise across the greeter's throat. "Brave or a dare?"

Trigger interprets the gesture and kills the fuel supply. Starving, the engine coughs, sputters, and then quits. The twisting blades freeze. Trigger sets the parking brake to make sure the plane doesn't creep forward.

"Lights and master switch to go," he says, but instead of completing the final checklist items, he grabs a pocket-sized notepad from his kneeboard and scribbles down the mystery airport's GPS coordinates.

"What are you—"

"Shush," Trigger hushes and verifies the written number against the one on-screen. I'm not sure why, since we're leaving ASAP and as far as I know, we have no intention of ever coming back. "Shut off any powered switches," he murmurs and I run my fingers along the sub panel and toggle off any live electrical breakers.

Meanwhile, Trigger reaches over his shoulder and pops the door's pressure seal. He climbs out onto the wing and then ducks back into the cockpit to offer a hand.

"Don't rely on others, Tana. Do things for yourself." I rub my temples. Even a thousand miles away, Mom's words still ring in my head. I look at Trigger's outstretched hand. *Why is everything so complicated?*

I'm already straddling the center console, one half-moon occupying real estate in the left seat. I lean over, curl my fingers around the doorframe and hoist myself up onto the cramped wing walk.

As I rise up to stand face-to-chin, I tilt my head and notice something strange stirring in Trigger's sea blues. A misty gaze I've seen once before. At orientation, as he spoke to Brooklyn Dehavilland.

Does he have a concussion? I search deeper into his pupils. Then I sense that invisible force tugging me toward him. *Is he...interested?* I remind myself that I'm hyper-allergic to drama and smack away the 'ping-pong starting to volley in my head. *Fuel and find a way out of here. Stick to the plan.*

Anyway, he has a girlfriend.

I turn away from Trigger's gooey gaze. My cheek grazes his stubbly chin and sends the normally-steady aviator off balance. He rocks back on his heels, his arms swim, and he stutter-steps, leaps from the slick wing and lands on the tarmac. Once balanced, his lips seal. Bug-eyed, he shakes his head.

"What?" I murmur, considering I may have misread his intent. "Did I leave the power on?" I bend and recheck the cockpit switches. After a quick scan of the lower panel I realize I did everything he asked. Confused, I nibble a nail and stretch a leg for the foot peg.

Trigger shoves his hands deep into his pockets as I spin and step backward off the wing.

"Is the parking brake off?" The greeter stomps around the propeller to the front side of the wing. He starts to crane his neck to get a look inside the open gull door when Trigger lunges forward, shouldering his way past the mountain of a man.

He snatches the small notepad, tears the handwritten airport coordinates from the miniature ring binder, and before the greeter has a chance to see, quickly crumples the notepaper in his palm.

"Sorry," Trigger apologizes. "Thought I left a switch on." Lock-jawed, Trigger hangs a thumb on his belt loop, and the greeter follows suit.

After a second stiff thumb hook from the sky surfer, our host widens his stance, using his remaining digit to frame his pants zipper.

Terrific, thumb jousting.

Recognizing that they're posturing, I call out, "Draw."

Both pocket-slingers flinch.

Trigger breaks the bravado. Easing back, he allows our host an unrestricted view of the instrument panel.

Eager, the greeter leans into the cockpit, far more focused, I think, than just a curious glance. His eyes bounce from right to left, windscreen to floor mats, as if he's searching for something. Then his gaze holds for a long second on the center of the dash.

Really? Ogling over the airplane's equipment?

And people say girls are competitive.

Trigger flexes his chest and leans against the flaps. "Brake is off," he says and points to the handle near the floor. "In case you're interested."

"She's loaded," the greeter pulls his green gaze from the antique compass. He lifts the rope slung around his neck and wedges two triangle shaped blocks on either side of the nose wheel.

"Yep," Trigger agrees. "The mag compass is vintage."

As Trigger ramp-chats with the man, a wisp of air lifts my bangs and I get a clear view of the remaining field. The airport is basically abandoned. Unless, of course, you count us and the greeter's remaining crew.

Expanding my visual field, I search the entire square mile of airstrip. Much of the same. A dry, dusty, abandoned wasteland. The perfect place to make liabilities vanish.

Out the corner of my eye, I catch the remainder of the caravan lurching forward, surrounding our bird like a pack of hunting wolves. With a subtle nod from their commander, the team exits their vehicles and falls in line. Balled fists on their hips, they stand elbow to beefy elbow. The outlines of concealed weapons become visible.

The greeter pinches his thumb and index finger around his upper ear. A blue light glows, and he reads our plane's tail number aloud. "N111X." Then releases his helix. When the blue halo fades, his faux-friendly expression disappears. He squints at Trigger. "Don't have you on our roster for this semester, but the tail number is on the running list, so you've been cleared to enroll."

Enroll?

My stomach caves as if I've been sucker-punched.

This has to be a setup.

I pull my collar tightly around my neck and prepare to run. Trigger is at arm's length, opposite a man who stands head and shoulders taller than him.

I need to warn him.

"Welcome, candidate," the greeter offers a hand. "I'm McDunney, chief of security for the Pioneer Academy."

Academy?

My insides spasm.

Don't you mean more like prison?

Trigger, however, acts unaffected. Normal. Like the evening is going exactly as planned. "T. Xanthus Flough." He accepts, with a hearty shake.

"You mean the son of the dog-fightin', bunker-busting, never-miss-a-target, Colonel Lamar Flough?" one of the guards says from the perimeter, probably knowing the answer.

A sparkle of Hollywood stars dances in the security specialist's eyes.

McDunney's dumbfounded gaze tracks Trigger as he moves back to my side.

Wait a second.

I, too, watch the sky surfer.

Is it possible they're not after me, that they want Trigger instead?

"Great," Trigger mumbles, so only I can hear. "Here we are in the middle of who-knows-where and I still can't get away from my dad's reputation." He kicks the ground and launches a loose stone.

McDunney's second-in-command joins him, and both men's mouths remain open wide enough to hold an airliner.

"Such a honor to meet you." The uniformed man moves and hunkers down on Trigger's hand.

The prodigal son of the legend grits his bright white teeth and grins.

I sigh heavily. My pulse levels.

Caught up in the celebrity moment, I don't notice right away that one of the chief's guards has slipped away from the group. The sound of a winding motor, however, catches my attention. An engine spools, and the door on the new-old hangar cracks, giving me the impression that what comes next won't get us any closer to leaving here.

A tractor-like tug grinds across the pavement, then arcs around the front of our plane and edges forward until the tow bar hooks on the nose wheel. The missing guard slides from the driver's seat, releases the parking brake, and confirms the bar's locking pins clip taut.

Satisfied, he hops back on the tug, reverses, and drags our bird toward the center apron. The heavy bi-fold door opens wide enough to clear both wings. But before the plane disappears in the arched metal cavern, I notice tiny streams of fuel dripping from both wing tanks.

"Trigger." I clear my throat. The pocket door stops briefly to allow the electric motor to reverse direction. A loud bell cycles as the waffled doors rumble. The nested panels extend and then seal shut.

"Ahem, um..." I groan, much louder this time, pretending to clear a giant tickle. Without as much as a glance in my direction, Trigger slaps the center of my back.

So much for being subtle.

I pinch his arm.

"What was that for?" he complains, massaging his reddened skin.

I throw a look to the secure hangar. "Your fans on the welcome committee just jacked our ride. And…" I lower my voice, "fuel is leaking from both wings."

Before Trigger has a chance to inquire, Chief McDunney offers an explanation. "All the student aircraft are stored in transient Hangar B. Surely you wouldn't want that fine machine outside baking in the high desert sun." He either doesn't notice our fuel problem or chooses not to mention it.

Students? How are we students?

Desperate, my eyes search for an anchor in Trigger's sea blues. The chief wedges his way between us, craggy mug facing me. Wide as he is tall, his solid midsection cuts off all lines of communication between me and Trigger.

Lowering his chin, McDunney frowns and presses a firm finger into the raised scar on my collar bone. "And you are?"

The scent of rotten egg salad and burnt toast leaks from his mouth. I turn away. A sharp pain shoots from my molars to my toes. "Ouch," I squeak.

"Tana… Tana," McDunney's slate eye narrows. His neck ticks side to side as if hacking items off a memorized list. After rolling his chapped lips over one another, his black leather eye patch wrinkles. "There's no Tana on the candidate list."

He clenches my arm and drags me towards the all-terrain vehicles. "Pioneer has a strict zero-tolerance policy for academic crashers," he grumbles. "There are always a few of you alphas who think you can coast in on the wings of other students."

"You're hurting me," I cover his fingers with my free hand. Squeeze tight, twist, and kneel to gain some reverse leverage.

"Sorry, Miss Wannabe." He easily thwarts my move by sliding an arm around my waist. Folds my torso over a hair covered forearm in the way he might carry a jacket. "First lesson at Pioneer—there are no second chances for first-time rule breakers."

I raise my chin, trying to keep eight pints of blood from pounding against my forehead, and see Trigger aggressively criss-crossing McDunney's track. "Whoa, hold up, Chief. She's not on the list because…" he stretches his words, looks at the chief, scans the guards and clasps the back of his neck. "Tana's my… sister."

McDunney halts. "Sister?" He spouts incredulously, lowering my feet to the ground.

"In fact, we're twins."

"Twins," I repeat, as uncertain as the chief.

Trigger nods, and throws an awkward arm over my shoulder. "Fraternal."

I bite my tongue to stop from screaming, *"Are you out of your mind?"* Silently, I consider that perhaps Trigger's the one with the death wish.

The chief looks skeptical. He reaches for his ear halo, likely to verify our claim. Trigger adds, "You won't find any record in Pioneer's database, sir. When my parents split, Tana went with my mother."

McDunney snorts. He drags a questioning eye over me, scowling. "Everyone knew Lamar Flough had a son, but I never heard any rumors of a daughter."

"That was by design," Trigger carries on with the charade. "My mom was never into what came with being a wife of a national hero. So she moved away, some remote part of Texas, cut all ties, and took Tana with her."

Unbelievably, I feel McDunney's grip loosen from my bicep, and if I'm not mistaken, a glint of sympathy overpowers his accusing disposition.

This has gone too far.

I shake my arm loose. It's one thing to be serious about security, but another to manhandle a student.

Before the situation gets completely out of hand, I dig in a cargo pocket and palm my cell phone. As much as I hate to admit it, I need to call home.

Disgusted, I press the power button.

Huh?

I try again, and after a couple more failed attempts, I guess my phone is fried. *The storm.* I shiver. *Lightning.* My pulse quickens. I'll bet the same thrashing bolt that knocked out the instrument panel toasted our electronics.

Now what?

Battling the instinct to sprint as fast as I can towards the hangar holding our bird, I stand steady, angling the dark handheld screen so Trigger can see.

"Dead battery?"

I shake my head. "Before we left, it was fully charged."

The chief snatches a satellite phone from his belt, and for a minute I think he's going to offer to make a call for us. But he makes no such offer. He dials a memorized number, and from the exchange, I assume it's his superior.

After a few positive nods he clips the phone back on his waist. "Orientation for transfer students starts first thing in the morning."

"We'll take you to the dorms where all the candidates stay," he says. "Flough, you ride with Number One." His stern voice shifts playful. "Your resurrected twin, with me." He motions his team back to the Jeeps.

"Chief," Trigger touches his broad shoulder. McDunney whirls around. "My dad would kill me if I let her out of my sight, it being her first time away from home and all."

Together, they turn to look and, on demand, I produce a streaming tear.

"Ugh, alright," the chief grunts, disgusted. His eyes, however, remain trained on me. He licks his lips and swallows. "Candidates with me—together."

Quivering, I glare at Trigger. "Land, fuel, and be on our way," I remind him. "Now we're twin student candidates?"

He presses his index finger against his lips and pulls me protectively to his side. As we walk hip to hip, Trigger flashes his blank cell screen. Just like mine, no lights, no juice, no way to contact home.

"Don't worry, I'll think of something," he whispers flatly and steers toward the roll bar protecting the Jeep's rear seat. I grab the round steel with both hands and position a boot against the rugged tire.

"That is, if we last that long," I mutter, and Trigger boosts me up.

From the front seat, I notice Chief McDunney examining us in the rearview mirror. His bushy eyebrows furrow. "Are your parents on the way?"

"No," Trigger leads. "I mean my dad is on a training mission. Some hush-hush, need-to-know kind of assignment," he stammers. "I'm sure you can relate."

The chief gives the impression that he believes Trigger's big fat lie. For now. McDunney shifts his attention to me, straightening his bunched unibrow. "What about your mother? At one time, I remember hearing she went a little cuckoo."

Trigger's skin flushes. Well on his way to becoming amped, his words still come across calm. "Actually, after a fierce fight, she died of cancer."

For the second time, McDunney's tight jaw softens. His good eye shows what appears to be a hint of regret, albeit awkward and unnatural. "Sorry—tabloid gossip. I should have known better."

I turn to Trigger, desperate to know if any bit of this wild tale is true. When his face resembles what I see in the mirror every day, I know, at the very least, that his story holds something painful.

"You're not the only one who's lost a parent." Blinking, Trigger's gaze falls to the floorboard.

I reach across and touch his hand. Pins and needles tingle against my palm.

The Jeep slides from side to side as it motors over the dirt road. A desolate mile of sand, cacti and tumbleweed pass; coyotes wail in the distance.

Out on the horizon, I see what must be our destination: the sole lighted compound, situated high up on the mesa. As we get closer, I can make out a series of buildings completely enclosed by a ten-foot fence. From this point of view, the adobe-style structures appear to float. No roads or bridges extend in or out. Similar to a medieval castle protected by a deep, winding moat. But we're in the desert, and the jagged cliffs aren't protected by water. Instead, they are topped with rows of spiraling razor wire, steeply cascading down into a dry trough of impassable earth.

When the Jeep swings around the backside of the complex, a narrow access road materializes.

The driver pauses at a heavily guarded security gate to flash an ID badge. "Two stragglers," he explains.

The gatekeeper shines his flashlight in the backseat and around the frame of the vehicle and then checks behind each of the tires. "Clear," he reports.

A second man in the command center opens the fence.

As the gate seals behind us, the chief points to two sandstone buildings near the front of the campus. "Girls' and boys' dorms. Your temporary accommodations while you check out the school."

You mean while we figure a way out of here.

I release Trigger's hand and skim my palms over my pants.

The Jeep rattles, climbing the hill to the dorm entrance.

"Ladies first." McDunney steps out, grabs my waist, and lifts me over the massive treaded tire. As my feet touch ground, his hands inch up my ribcage. His fingers shimmy until they catch on my bra strap, where they linger. Startled, I look up to see a surly smirk slide over his lips. Then, from behind, my black duffle jolts his shoulder. It loosens his grip, allowing me to break free from his old-man strong hands.

"Incoming," Trigger says after the fact, shrugging at McDunney.

The chief sneers, winking his uncovered eye at me, and skulks away.

Trigger leans over the open frame. "Find you first thing in the morning."

I make my face blank. Think of absolutely nothing. So he can't see I'm afraid.

Trigger stretches further, reaches for my wrist and squeezes. "Promise."

CHAPTER 16

Lost in the smoke, I stumble in darkness. Waving my arms, struggling to feel my way. "Tana." I hear my name. Cough and run further into the soot fog.

Dad, is that you?

Startled from a deep sleep, I wake to a pounding sound. From the lack of light in the dorm room, I assume it's not quite morning. In fact, the intensity of the darkness leads me to believe it's still the middle of the night.

Boom, boom, boom.

I twitch at the weighted thuds. Whoever's at the door is committed to getting in.

"Medical," a raspy voice announces, a moment before barging into the room.

Light leaks in from the opening at the doorframe, and I see a short, squatty shadow crossing the bare floor. Dressed in white, the stocky woman kneels next to my bed. Without any forewarning, a sharp prick punctures the top of my hand.

"Hey." I try to jerk away.

The chubby fingers wrapped around my forearm squeeze tighter, and I feel an uncomfortable pinch as something stiff slides under my skin.

"What's going on?" I protest.

The nurse with the winch-like grip ignores the question and tears a piece of white tape from a roll and secures an IV tube. I breathe through my nose and curl my fingers into fists.

"Fluids," she says with a thick accent, while massaging the soft gushy bag dangling from her wrist. "All candidates who visit the desert become dehydrated."

I'm not a candidate.

My arms swing fiercely, unnerved by not knowing what's dripping into my veins. I've taken a few swats when a cool sensation climbs my arms. I shiver for a moment and then suddenly feel very calm. My balled hands unravel as I lose control of my muscles. A fuzzy haze clouds my thoughts. Drowsy, my mind catches up with Nurse Unsociable's vague explanation. *"The desert dehydrates."*

Funny thing though, I don't feel thirsty. Levitating out of my body, perhaps, but not the slightest bit parched.

"Get up." The nurse says. Conveying a lack of tolerance for any kind of insubordination. "It's time for your physical."

"Wa—wa—wait," I say through rubbery lips and sigh with relief, now understanding the mix-up. I have already had my high school physical. The one required for admission at National back home. *I'm sure if I explain, tell her my records are on file there…* My brain sloshes over the last few hours. *Then she'll know I'm not Trigger's sister.* "I, I—"

The nurse interrupts. "Tell it to Dr. Freed."

A doctor. Perfect. I can tell the truth and Dr. Freed will be required to keep my secret. Doctor-patient confidentiality. I'll get a pass on this unnecessary physical.

"Take me to the doctor."

I kick off the sheets and wobble to my feet. The room spins. One thing is for sure: there's more than electrolytes in the hydrating IV elixir. The nurse steadies my arm and guides me to the door.

Lucky for me, I still sleep in my clothes.

In the hallway, she helps me into a wheelchair. Lifts my feet into the rests and then steers down a stark corridor. For as long as I can see, the floors and walls are a puke-gray color. Pukey to me, I suspect, because of the nausea gurgling in my stomach.

Seconds pass. Maybe even minutes. I stare up at the ceiling and try to keep track of the incandescent light fixtures. A habit Eddie nagged into me, so I'd always be aware of my surroundings.

One, two, three

My mind spirals. To Trigger. To Tulsa, the first day of flight class. Outside, when he stood opposite me on the hangar ramp. We had barely met, but that didn't stop him from lending an attentive ear. Or using his hang-loose smile and his big-sky eyes to coerce me back in the air.

Why was he being so nice?

I can't help but wonder why the sky surfer, who seems to have the world at his feet, would bother to extend such a gesture.

But is he really a friend?

The picture swirls, and now I see his face beside me in the home-built's cockpit. Frames flip as I relive how I tried to crash his plane. Still, he claimed he was willing to stick by my side.

Doesn't make sense.

I float weightless, as if suspended in deep water. Questions continue to surface, floating through the liquid-induced fog.

Is he some sort of adrenaline junkie? Mental case? Or a do-gooder who takes on friends who are fixer-uppers? And then, going out on a limb, he calls me his sister? Which begs the question: If lying comes so easily, is he really good for his word?

Anyway, who really cares?

I visualize my arms lifting over my head, like I'm doing a dead man's float, allowing me to sink further into the haze.

In my experience, all promises wind up broken.

As if a drain is opened, the fluid swirls and disappears. Trigger's face smears into the dingy drug mist, and again I notice the green-blue lights passing overhead.

I continue counting, "Four, five…"

When I wake again, everything's different. For starters, I'm warm. Dry and toasty. Snuggling in a quilted blanket. The sunny yellow walls of the corner room remind me of Gran's house. Bright and soothing. Opposite from the institutional, bile-color halls. White umbrellas like the ones photographers use are arranged over my bed, shading my eyes from the harsh incandescent lights. An opaque curtain serves as a divider.

Under the covers, I feel for the IV. Shocked to discover it still taped to my hand. Rolling onto my side, I trace the clear flexible tube to an empty plastic bag. Proof that I'm rehydrated. Even though I don't feel any better.

Frankly, I feel worse.

Thinking of liquids, I search the room for Nurse H2O. But as far as I can tell, she's nowhere to be found.

Additional minutes pass, and the curtain sectioning my area swings open.

"Good morning." A cheery woman with a nurturing smile walks to my bedside. She reaches across my covered legs and grabs an electronic template. "Sorry about the four o'clock wake-up." She tucks the soft blanket securely around my waist. "But I understand you arrived at the last minute." She reads as she speaks, extending a slender hand. "I'm Dr. Belinda Freed. Lindy."

My vision remains blurry, so when I reach for her I miss.

"A little groggy, I see." Dr. Freed types on the template. "Ursula can be a little heavy handed with the antihistamine."

"Antihistamine?" I cough.

"We give it as a precaution," Dr. Freed says. "Would hate for you to have an allergic reaction."

Reaction to what? I'm about to say, when my tongue swells.

Freed begins the pre-exam questions. "Okay, Miss— is it Flough?"

"Lyre..." I gurgle.

"Lyre. Hmm, why does that name sound familiar?" She pauses for a second and then goes on. "Anyway, I don't see any medical history listed."

"Well," I slur.

Dr. Lindy rests a reassuring hand on my arm. "Don't try to talk, dear," she says. "Didn't you receive our standard entry form?"

Seriously? You're the one who keeps asking questions.

Officially confused, I shake my head and cluck my bulging tongue.

"No worries," Freed takes my pulse. "We have everything right here to perform a freshman physical." She slides on a pair of surgical gloves and then organizes instruments on a rolling tray. "Were you waitlisted?"

Helpless, I respond with a second cluck.

"No? Hmm." Freed checks my pupils. "Guess I just assumed, since you came in after hours." She examines my ears before sticking a wooden Popsicle stick in my mouth. Simultaneously, the blood pressure cuff attached to my upper arm inflates. "You must be thrilled," Dr. Lindy makes a few more notes on her pad. "This semester, Pioneer had thousands of applicants."

Thousands? I only applied at one high school. National, in Tulsa.

"Slots here are prestigious," she says pretty comfortable with the one-sided conversation. "Highly coveted, in fact. Many influential people pull strings and offer to donate all sorts of things in hopes of buying their children an opportunity to be part of our custom program. What they don't know is that Pioneer has a code." Her blue-green eyes sparkle. "A legacy. Bloodlines that trace back as far as the Second World War."

Lindy touches a watch on her wrist, spinning the chunky band, centering its face. From where I lie, the piece looks far too big for her. Uniquely, the steel face is hashed to resemble directional lines on a compass.

"Regardless of financial resources," she confides, "only students with birthrights are considered for admission."

Birthrights?

My chapped lips pucker. Although I come from accomplished roots, I'm not aware of any Lyre endowments bestowed at birth. But the Flough legacy—well, that's something else altogether. Military pilots, war heroes, advisors on every top-secret mission ever to take to the air. Good thing the son of the living legend vouched for his twin sister.

With the remnants of the antihistamine drip wearing off, I come to the simplest conclusion. Is it possible that McDunney was right? I rode into Pioneer, wing-walking on Trigger's credentials?

Brain fog alert.

My forehead throbs. First, Trigger never mentioned Pioneer, never mind the fact that he seemed to have no idea how to get here. And second… My swishy line of thought rewinds to last night. How McDunney seemed unfazed by Trigger's unscheduled arrival. Almost as if he was waiting for it. Even went as far as to admit that the Flough name remains on some running list. Trigger is accepted as a "candidate," no questions asked. Without even lifting an academic finger.

Or did he?

My mind runs possible scenarios. Maybe the Floughs have been keeping a very important secret.

"Well, congratulations," the doctor says, completing the typical poking and prodding of a physical exam. I'm not really sure if she's referring to my health or to the fact I've been invited to attend Pioneer. When I think the probing is over, she lifts a long needle from her tray.

No way.

My eyes bulge. I yank both arms back and bury them beneath the blanket.

"No need to worry, dear." She gently caresses my arm with a reassuring hand. "It's just a shot every candidate is required to get before orientation."

To say I'm skeptical is an understatement. I know better than to trust anyone who uses the phrase "just a 'shot.'"

"The injection is the first of a two-step process that will help you get connected to our student network."

Two steps? Network?

Dr. Lindy taps the capped syringe against her forearm to mix two chambers of sapphire-colored fluid. "Once combined, the chemical and saline will heighten your brain's neurotransmitters, opening a pathway for frequencies to wirelessly stream through your brain."

As she rubs an alcohol ball against my neck, I start to shake. As I did as a kid waiting for allergy shots.

Undeterred by my quivering, Dr. Lindy steadies a patch of skin and forces the needle in.

A prick. Then a sting. Chased by a slow, easy burn. She edges the needle out and covers the pinhole with gauze and a bandage

That's it? Not so bad.

I assume the painful part is behind me.

"Halfway there." Lindy says.

Bolt.

I attempt to squeeze my quads to test muscle control. Unfortunately, my weighted legs are pools of fleshy mush.

Freed picks up a device that resembles an ear-piercing gun.

"*Ow…*" I wave no thanks and cluck like a mad chicken. I shield my ears that are already punctured with two sets of holes.

Lindy brushes her cropped hair back to show me a flat disk attached to the cartilage just below the top of her ear.

"Everyone on campus has one." She balances a tiny stud on the tip of her finger. Like a badge of honor, the stud bears Pioneer colors, perhaps as a symbol of school spirit. But the pronged stud and piercing gun are a far greater commitment then a ball cap and face paint.

The metal disc clicks as she loads it into the cartridge and cocks the plastic pistol.

"This is the receiver. Think of it as a cyber-doorbell." Freed matches the gun's sharp tip to the curve near the top of my ear. With no countdown, no warning, the chamber snaps and something pointy breaks my skin. A warm drop of blood trickles down my lobe as the sharp post drills through. I reach for the stud and rub its rough texture. On the back, three short prongs latch onto my cartilage.

"Earth magnet," Dr. Lindy says. "Indestructible."

Although I didn't fight being torn from bed in the middle of the night or argue against the strange blue shot, Freed has stepped over the line.

A piercing for potential students? Is this some sort of twisted initiation tactic? What if I have no intention of attending Pioneer? Do I have to walk around for the rest of my life with a heavy-duty magnet stuck in my ear? How do I know Pioneer is really so highly coveted? *What—I should take your word for it? We've barely met, Doctor, and now I'm wearing a bulletproof magnet.* Even for an academy hidden in the desert, this form of initiation seems extreme.

I suck in a deep breath and opt for the lesser of two threats. Force every bit of air from my lungs and scream, "Chief McDunney."

The name has barely left my lips when Pioneer's security chief storms into the room. Dr. Lindy snaps up, and the ear gun tumbles from her fingers. She ignores the sound of metal crashing on tile, leans against the bed, wide-eyed, and grips the sheets.

"Oh, no," she mumbles. "Not him."

"Everything okay in here, Lindy?" McDunney snarls. His heavy brow lifts his snakeskin eye cover.

I raise to sit up, but Dr. Lindy holds me flat.

No. She shakes her head ever so slightly. "All good," she replies, edges of her mouth twitching. "Ms. Lyre is terrified of needles, is all."

His brow hikes another notch. "Good to know."

After the chief's face disappears into the puke hall, I face Lindy and notice wads of crinkled sheets balled in her fists. "If you're ever in trouble, hold the stud and blink. Someone will come to help you."

About to ask what sort of trouble, a screeching sound rings like a siren in my head. My earlobe burns, and I hear distant voices. Hundreds of conversations, even though Dr. Lindy and I are the only ones in the room.

I reach up and touch the fiery magnet.

"You're connecting to our intranet," Freed releases the bedding and swipes a mirror from her cart. Shifts the reflection to show a turquoise halo of light glowing beneath the new stud. Seeming to brush off the exchange with the chief, she is once again the bubbly professional.

"Anytime anyone on the campus speaks," she points to the glow, "you'll be able to hear."

Slowly, my brain buffers the flood of voices until I can separate individual conversations. Orientation times. Homework assignments. A collaboration of video gaming strategies.

"How can it be?"

An additional influx of small talk streams into the mix.

"If you touch here," the doctor says, holding the rock's center, "the volume adjusts from loud to soft."

The amazing sensation of hundreds of voices streaming in my head curbs my desire to plead for reinforcements. Instead, piques my curiosity. Even eases my nerves. I begin to weigh the benefits. The incredible fact I'm able to virtually connect to every student without a handheld or laptop. No plug, no charger; everything required is conveniently in my skull.

"Epic."

"Yes," Lindy says.

I lift my hands, twist them front to back, confirming there is no actual handset. Understanding why thousands of parents were so willing to do anything to send their children to Pioneer.

"Final, final step," Freed opens a small contact case. "This part is easy. I designed these little beauties myself." She blushes, revealing two paper-thin lenses floating in topaz fluid. "Not only will you be able to hear every conversation," she adds, "but with the assistance of the lenses you'll be able to see through the eyes of anyone connected."

Even though I don't completely understand, I hold still when she reaches toward my naked eye. With the assistance of the hand mirror, I see that the soft lenses are tinted to match my green-gray irises. The smooth plastic wraps around my eyeball. Such a perfect fit, in fact, they're nearly impossible to detect.

Overwhelmed by the heightened senses, I blink and try to focus on the collage of three-dimensional images.

"Way too many things to look at." My eyes flutter as if I'm having a seizure.

"Relax, don't worry," Dr. Lindy assures. "Right now you are processing the entire bandwidth. Three separate data streams. Student, administration, and security. By morning, the student frequency will be the only one you'll hear."

I touch my receiver earring and gently lower the volume. Some of the chatter fades, but I struggle to hear her over the rounds of white noise.

"I realize this is a lot to take in, Tana. Tomorrow, your orientation mentor will teach you how to accept and deny the constant stream of messaging." Freed shoves the triage tray aside and helps me back to the wheelchair. "There is one other thing," she says, rolling past the curtain to the door. "Never try to take them out." She retrieves a pen light from her lab coat and shines it on her own lenses. "They're meant to be worn 24/7." Her spindly fingers move my hand from the stud. "Both the contacts and the audio receiver have to be surgically removed."

At once, the nausea returns. The shakes. Chills. Sweat coats my neck. Reality crashes. Regardless of the flowery rhetoric, I'm acutely aware of the monumental effort it will now take for Trigger and me to leave. Surgery, at the very least.

And at the most?

I don't want to figure.

When the clinic door motors open, we turn a sharp corner and wheel along the throw-up corridor. Halfway down the hall, I think I see Trigger slumped in a matching wheelchair, a curly headed man in a lab coat hovering over him. Passing by, I see an IV in his hand, but no piercing in his left ear. He must be next, I assume, and I reach to warn him. But my chair swerves wide, keeping me well clear.

The lights overhead smear. My eyes are heavy. Hundreds of voices stream through my head, layering over one another, and then fading until I can barely hear. *"Stay away from Chief McDunney"—"McDunney was a soldier"—"The chief did time in prison"—"Never get caught alone with McDunney"—"How did an ex-con become head of security?"— "McDunney is a perv."*

My chair jerks and my eyes flick open. Ahead, I see a narrow hallway that appears endless. My head tilts back again, and the lights pass by like road stripes on pavement. A new voice joins Pioneer's in-skull network. Stronger and louder than the others, so it's clear.

"Our guests are in medical?" A man's voice vibrates across my eardrum.

I recognize the speech pattern, certain I've heard it before. "Whose voice is that?"

My head rolls over to my shoulder. My eyes pop open to see a virtual sheet of thumbnails projected ahead. Images of students engaged in conversation appear and flash across my view.

The clips shuffle like a deck of cards and as I try to figure out who is talking the loudest, the voice disappears. Its void is filled by the rush of softer voices.

"McDunney isn't who he appears"—"Don't turn your back around McDunney"—"The chief has secrets."

Desperate to narrow the field, I concentrate harder. Listen for a distinctive tone amongst the constant chatter.

"Affirmative, sir," the utterance returns. Providing me another opportunity to match a thumbnail to the voice.

The flipping frames halt, and I see a scholarly looking man sitting at a grand desk stacked with files.

"So our contact in Oklahoma was able to tweak the experimental plane?"

"A slow fuel leak in both tanks was the perfect solution."

"You verified the compass?" He adjusts his bifocals.

"Lamar Flough's son, without a doubt."

"Good. Very good." He steeples his fingers. "We couldn't wait any longer; we need him here now."

"The boy wasn't alone, you know." A lit cell screen comes into frame and I see a snapshot of Trigger and me on the ramp.

"That was unexpected. The mother resisted, and she wore the pants in that family. I think today's our lucky day." He lifts his head, and in doing so reveals who he's speaking with. "A twofer."

I clench my throat as a man with an eye patch enters my view. Chief McDunney stands stiff at attention. "Turn me loose," he says, "and I'll even the score."

"Patience," the scholar replies. He reaches to the edge of his desk and straightens his etched nameplate: Otto Funkhouser, Academy Director.

I reach for my stomach and retch.

CHAPTER 17

Waking, I breathe easy, the sun's rays warming my forehead.

What a nightmare.

I rub my eyes, knowing there's no such thing as cranial streaming, virtual contact lenses and schools so elite they purposely omit their location from maps. Enough.

No more case files, police interviews, or interrogation videos before bed, I resolve, and then immediately backtrack. Understanding that catching a killer requires total commitment to research. *Okay, maybe just scale back on interrogation footage.*

Positive last night's wild adventure was no more than another anxiety dream about death and flying, I clear my mind and listen for voices just to be sure. As suspected, it's perfectly silent.

Cracking an eyelid, I anticipate seeing fractured sun streams burning through my hundred-year-old bedroom window. Instead, once focused, I see barred glass.

Faster than you can say barrel roll, I flip on my back.

Where's the antique ceiling fan? And thin shears dangling around my canopy bed?

Tossing off the covers, I inventory the surroundings. Four stark walls, twin bed, basic desk, closet and laptop computer.

I reach for my ear and a pronged stud pricks my fingertip. *It wasn't a dream.* Fists fly to my forehead. *We are stranded in the desert.*

Where are the voices? I lift my chin. *The network?* I twist my head and see a trail of dried blood on the pillow. Dr. Freed said that by morning I'd be tapped into the students' frequency.

Lying flat again, I stare at the ceiling, studying countless pen marks poked into the popcorn textured tiles. *Did every dot represent a candidate who had occupied this room?*

From beneath the crack in the door, smoke enters. I suck a huge breath, thrust the covers over my head and ball into a cocoon. An unexpected scent spreads. Mummified, I sniff the air.

Eggs and bacon?

A sticky-sweet smell chases, mingling with the aroma. Maple syrup. My favorite.

I think of my mother.

Forever a slave to the instant and the boxed when it came to cooking, not many professional chefs can rival her frozen toaster waffles. As fast as it comes, the happy memory sours when I consider the last words I didn't say to my mom. The truth. The fact that Trigger and I weren't really doing homework and went on a joyride instead. I also kind of wish I had skipped the disgusted face and eased back on the sarcasm. Aware that I was short, rude and disrespectful. Throw in the overnight disappearing act and...

Sensing the onset of an emotional tsunami, I suck in and squeeze my stomach muscles tight. The core tension keeps the tidal wave of tears at bay, until I'm confronted with the reality that Mom's worst fear might have just been realized. First, she lost my dad. Now, despite the move, paranoia, security systems, surveillance, and barely leaving my side, she still may have lost her daughter.

Deny, deny, deny.

If it's not said, then it's not real.

Uncertain of the why or how of going forward, I do know one thing for sure. If and when I get home, a whole world of trouble will greet me at the front door.

But as I sit alone, staring at four dismal walls, the threat of perpetual house arrest lingering, I'd give just about anything to have my mom walk into my dorm with a plate of infamous waffles in hand.

That version of her doesn't exist anymore.

Fists return to my forehead. The fantasy shifts; I know that if she were here, all I'd get is one hysterical, marathon lecture.

Never mind.

I hug the bed's comforter to my chest.

I'm better off on my own.

I jump at the thud of someone barging through the doorway. *No, not Ursula again.*

I pull the sheets up to my chin and pretend to be asleep.

Feather-light footsteps tap across the tile floor. Through a slit eyelid, I spy an obnoxiously upbeat brunette with impossibly great hair. She flips the overhead light, tosses her kinky locks, and coos like a mourning dove.

"Time to rise and glow." Her lips pucker and she hums a perky get-up tune.

Desperate to be invisible, I squeeze my lids tighter.

"Oh, no, you don't." The human alarm clock skips over and shakes her bushy head. "I see the whites of those tormented hazel eyes."

Caught in the act, I stir. "What time is it?"

The girl, who looks to be about my age, peers at her watch. "Six. Orientation is in an hour."

"And you are?"

"Your student liaison." She plops on the foot of the bed and bounces. "Soraya Harb." She seat-drops again and propels herself in the air. "Second-year student at Pioneer." Her words jolt from her lungs.

My mentor's assessment is right on target. Compared to Soraya's sparkling emerald irises, mine must appear dull and murky. Vexing. But little does she know, I'm extensively schooled in the art of social graces. The next logical question comes compliments of a two-year cotillion experience. Although I'd adamantly deny it if asked, my parents made sure I completed the entire social etiquette program start to finish.

Soraya's ethnic features make me believe she's not from the States. "Where did you grow up," I ask.

"Born in Lebanon and then lived briefly in London." She continues to bounce.

"I lived in the UK, too," I find myself saying without filtering. Surprisingly, with a tiny bit of enthusiasm.

Soraya grins. Warm and sincere. Simple in a way that makes me feel like everything about this mixed-up school is somehow okay.

"But now I live here," she says. "On the Pioneer campus. My parents work in research and development for the school."

Where is here? I want to shout. Remembering I couldn't pinpoint the school's airport on the map. But one of the many things I learned as the daughter of two diplomats was to pause before speaking. Scrutinize every word, in order to avoid leaking information that gives away the upper hand. For example, *"I don't have any idea where we are because I got knocked out while flying through a geomagnetic storm, woke up a thousand miles away from home and then landed at a secret airport only to be woke in the middle of the night to get contacts and an ear piercing. Oh, by the way, I have no intention of attending Pioneer."*

Yes, this is definitely the time to use my filter.

All things considered, self-survival in particular, I decide that official candidates for enrollment should know, at the very least, where the campus is located.

There is one question, however, I figure won't raise suspicion. "What about the network?" I sit up and rub my freshly pierced lobe. "I don't hear anything; Dr. Freed said you would show me how it works."

Soraya's lips pucker like she tasted something sour. "We're teenagers, right?"

I nod, entertaining how infrequently I consider myself part of that demographic.

"Everyone's probably still asleep."

For some reason I crack up. Strange. Like something I used to know how to do, but haven't tried for a long time. After a round of gut busters, the tension in my body unravels. I relax. It feels good.

"I guess you're right."

"As far as the Intranet..." She hooks a chunk of curls behind her ear and demonstrates. "The common chat stream is live from seven until midnight."

Was it the spiked IV elixir? Because I heard voices outside the operating parameters. At 4:00 a.m. One in particular, I wish I hadn't heard.

"At least those are the school's sanctioned hours." Soraya's faceted eyes darken. "There are other ways though." Her sugar-sweet expression shifts. "Means to communicate privately, outside the main network."

Hang on—are those horns growing from her head?

Curious, I meet her defiant gaze. "Teach me?"

Soraya sits cross-legged and presses her fingers against her ear "Tana Lyre," she says, pinching the metal. A blue glow illuminates the tips of her fingers. Reacting faster than any wireless I've experienced, an overwhelming buzz warms my inner ear.

"Do you feel it?" My liaison asks, then pulls a compact from her shoulder bag and positions the mirror so I can see my own reflection. Soraya points to the turquoise halo highlighting my receiver. "Touch it," she instructs.

I do as I'm told. Hit the smoldering metal surface once, and in front of my corrected eyes, up pops Soraya's picture in the right corner.

"You can accept or deny my chat request," she says. "Two taps for yes. Three for no."

"Wild," I touch the receiver twice. My virtual screen twitches. Soraya's thumbnail shrinks to a small cube, and then two separate vantage points split the remaining field, butted against one another.

On top is what I'm actually seeing, Soraya, the floor and the walls behind her. But what appears on the bottom is something else all together. I see my own face and a small dresser over my shoulder, as if I can also view from Soraya's vantage.

"But how?" I stammer.

My orientation mentor twists her head and pans around the rest of the room.

Desk, chair, computer, duffle bag.

Everything she focuses on crosses my visual. "While we're connected," she says, "you can see everything I do and vice versa."

"And when I speak?"

"I hear you just as if you're standing next to me."

"Only if we're in the same room, right?"

Soraya bunches her face and giggles. "No, silly, what would be the point of that? As long as the network is up and running you can connect, see, and speak to anyone, anywhere on campus."

I shut one eye, trying to process the science behind my enhanced vision. Alternating the lid open and shut, I say, "It's like looking in a mirror."

"You can thank Dr. Freed for that benefit. One looks out, and the other reflects back."

"When I'm connected to another student?" I continue to squint and Soraya grabs my arm and shakes her head. "Relax, try to glance around naturally, you'll get used to the lenses before too long. Oh," she says. "Even if you're not connected to anyone else, the reflective contact still works. Only, the feed displayed will be of you head-on."

"A reflection."

"Keep in mind, though, mirrors have blind spots." In an instant, Soraya's picture vanishes from my screen and I'm left with my own forward perspective plus what I might see if filming behind a camera lens.

"Awesome," trickles from my lips, even though I should probably be acting like this tech is no big deal.

I recollect the pact I made with Trigger. The promise to stick together. If Soraya sent a message to me, then I must be able to contact him.

Think before you act, Tana.

If I can hear others, then they must be able to hear me. I pause to make sure I'm not about to do something that will draw unwanted attention.

We're teenagers. Soraya's reminder repeats in my head. And what is one of the top priorities for girls our age? Connecting with smoking-hot boys.

"I came with someone."

Soraya's full eyebrows arch as if she craves more information.

"My, ah, brother. Trigger." Lying comes easier than I expected. "We're twins."

Soraya sits perfectly still, making it difficult for me to read her.

I go on, attempting to sound casual. "Do you think I can try messaging him?"

Although clearly interested, my mentor forgoes asking follow-up questions. She watches me in the way a detective might observe a suspected criminal.

"Sure," she shrugs. "Send a request. If his implant is up and running he'll be easy to locate." Her gem-colored eyes linger.

"T. Xanthus Flough," I speak like a robot, pressing hard on my disc. When I let go, a flush of heat toasts my helix.

"Brother, huh?" Soraya's lips curl. "I thought your last name was Lyre?"

"Long story." I whisper, unsure who is listening.

"A juicy one, I hope, but it will have to save until later." Soraya rechecks her watch. "Group welcome begins in thirty minutes. The assembly is in the main hall."

Kicking off the comforter, I stand, fully dressed, opposite my mentor.

"Do you always sleep in your clothes?"

Fair enough question. Fortunately, my filter engages before my mouth gives up another piece of keep-to-yourself-information.

"Just a little out of sorts," I say. "Being away from home." Not a word of it true.

Reaching in my duffle, I pull out my National School uniform. Shake out a pair of wrinkled black cargo pants and a creased white blouse.

Mom strikes again. This time, her hyper-preparedness works in my favor.

Soraya wrinkles her nose and climbs to her feet. "I'll let you change." She examines my outfit and raises a manicured brow. "Meet you in the dining hall in ten."

I have just buttoned my blouse when a tingle tickles my lobe. Two taps later, Trigger's irresistible surfer smile appears in my panoramic view.

"Neat trick," he says. Our eyes match and his cheesy grin stretches further. "By your side, just like I promised, T." Even virtually, I feel the effects of his intense stare. "Some people keep their word."

CHAPTER 18

Even though Trigger and I are in separate dorms, the high resolution of Pioneer's virtual connection makes it seem like I'm walking next to him into the boys dining hall.

Incredible.

Part of me, however, is still not convinced it's real.

"What a night," he sighs.

"Understatement," I reply. In the short time we've known each other, I've discovered Trigger possesses an innate ability, a survival skill of sorts. A way of shrinking mountainous situations into nothing more than manageable anthills.

"For a moment there, I was sure we were abducted into some covert government experiment." The sound quality is so crisp I swear Trigger's lips are up against my ear. "I guess growing up military has made me a little paranoid."

"Paranoid, prepared, crazy." I tease, thinking that these words are often synonymous.

As I follow Trigger via Pioneer's in-skull network down another bile-colored hall, somehow it feels reasonable to be suspicious.

"Check this out," Trigger turns as if I'm really there. Laughs, then says, "This whole talking to an invisible friend thing is going to take some getting used to."

Forging ahead, he rounds the corner into the cafeteria. In lieu of picnic-style tables the floor is sectioned with clusters of custom gaming chairs. Attached to each contoured racing-style seat is a foldout table, laptop, multiple hand controllers and an HD screen. Whizzing around, an army of harried servers moves between the squared sections delivering breakfast like carry-out pizzas.

"For real?" Trigger marvels and must be rubbing his eyes because, for a minute, the lower part of my screen blurs. Although in the blind, I can tell from the weight of his sigh he probably thinks he did die in the storm last night and woke in high school heaven. Video games and breakfast pizza. What else could we ask for?

In short order, the digital fuzz disappears and Trigger's visual returns.

Sharing his view, I see students sitting in small groups, gazing off in space, speaking, but not making eye contact with anyone in particular. Scarily reminding of the time I volunteered with patients in a mental institution.

Speaking of crazy people, I see Trigger weave through the workstations and swipe a loaded omelet slice from a server's spinning pie pan.

"Do you think Pioneer has an upgrade that delivers virtual to-go orders?" I ask.

"Why not, they've thought of everything else."

I watch as Trigger wolfs down the breakfast slice. It oozes with sizzling cheese, making my stomach rumble. "Although this place is impressive."

Awesome, actually.

"I'm going to try to get a computer or phone. Stick to the plan and find a way out of here."

Land, fuel and go back to what? I go over our pact, suddenly feeling very tired. Dead-end research, mom's hawking, Professor Flough's stick-to-the-rules flight class.

I look away from the sky surfer's view and smile at my orientation mentor.

Maybe it's not such a bad idea to see what Pioneer has to offer.

Trigger struts forward, checking each quad for an open seat. Through his point of view, I see students researching assignments online, while splitting screen time with what looks like some sort of special forces video game.

Nearly at the end of the room, an open chair appears, remote and isolated in the furthest corner. "Golden," Trigger strides. Unlike the rest of the groupings, this area is set up for two rather than four. "Anyone sitting here?" he asks the other student who is dressed in a chalk-white jumpsuit covered in patches, resembling a heavily sponsored NASCAR driver. The occupant shakes his head, his eyes covered with chunky, blue-green bug goggles. Hideously large, they have headlamps and miniature windshield wipers.

"What are you playing?" Trigger doesn't seem to notice the aftermarket eyewear and shifts his sightline to the nimble hands gliding across three keyboards at once. In the upper left corner of my visual, thumbnails flash as Pioneer's database searches for a match to the candidate opposite Trigger.

"It's not a game," the young man defends as a bolt of lightning flashes across the screen. Trigger and I duck, though we're aware that the three-dimensional rendition of the supercell was only generated by a computer.

"It's my Earth Science homework." The techno gamer hits the pause key, forcing his building thunderhead into a digital holding pattern. He nudges the swivel table off to the side and removes his custom eyewear. On screen, Pioneer's facial recognition task bar presses on, narrowing the field to three potential students.

"Henry," he introduces, as his profile and a chat request automatically appear on my visual. I double-tap my receiver and add the benefit of Henry's view. Trigger's hand flies to his ear as if observing more than two conversations is more challenging than it appears.

"Henry Aska Gu," the boy adds, glancing at the chair next to him. "That seat is yours, I mean, if you want it."

"Aska Gu." Trigger accepts the invitation and maneuvers into the racecar-style seat, adjusts the harnesses and straps himself in. Appearing right at home, as I imagine he is in the cockpit of a fighter jet.

"Chinese and, possibly, from somewhere in the Caribbean?" Trigger asks.

"Barbados," Henry touches his wiry curls. "My mom's side. Long, sad story. My dad is, well, he's Chinese-American. Impressive, how did you know?"

"Military."

"Oh," he salutes. "So you're a transfer student?"

"Yep, here for orientation," Trigger ignores the gesture, answering like he has spent the whole summer, not the last twelve hours, planning for the school visit.

"Liar, liar..." I whisper.

Again, he swats his ear.

"This is my third year at Pioneer," Henry's sightline drifts, distracted, I assume by the intense anvil cloud growing on his monitor.

"He's a junior?" I say, only connected to Trigger.

Even seated, the way the baggy suit hangs on Henry makes him appear much younger. His skin is spotted and shiny, and under the retro wrap goggles he wears thick black glasses. Not the trendy, smart-looking frames favored by celebrities, but the plastic, horn-rimmed, pop-bottle kind that are required to correct terrible vision.

If I had to guess, I'd say he's younger than us; compared to Trigger, Henry measures head and shoulders shorter.

"So what do you think about Pioneer?" Trigger watches Henry tap a joystick, shuffling numbers around what appears to be some sort of page-long equation.

Lost in the complicated calculation, the whiz doesn't answer.

Levering forward, Trigger peers outside the bucket seat and scans the cafeteria. "Nothing special here," he laughs. "From what I can tell, Pioneer is just like every other high school."

Something Trigger said must have struck a nerve, because Henry's flying fingers freeze, his back arches like an angry tiger. "There's nothing typical about this school," he says, gritting his teeth.

Trigger throws an arm around Henry's neck and draws him closer. "Nerds." He points to a foursome in the far corner who have even less fashion sense—but more friends—than Henry Gu.

"Techies." Henry corrects.

Trigger proceeds clockwise around the room.

The next group looks to be playing a heated game of charades.

"Artsy crowd?" Trigger stabs.

Henry scratches his wide fro. "Innovators and politicians."

"And finally…" Trigger names the last quad to the right. "Let me guess," he says staring at a huddle of clean-shaven boys dressed in suits. "The cool kids."

Henry coughs and refocuses on his computer. "More like the future of Wall Street."

None of which, I notice, are groups where Henry Aska Gu belongs.

"Like I said, typical."

Disgusted, Henry tsks, drawing Trigger's attention back to the bright screen. With light speed, the whiz toggles over the complex formula and flips a mixed fraction. "I'm not sure where you're from, but this school is really the only option for me. For kids like us."

Us?

"What do you mean?" Trigger has barely spoken when something jolts the back of Henry's chair.

With Trigger's view trained on Henry, I can't see behind the gamer's seat. Another blind spot, just like Soraya had warned.

"Got something to aska you, Gu."

A kid wearing an athletic-cut, pinstriped business suit ducks around the molded foam and appears front and center. He stands, smooths his slicked comb-over and bumps the chair again. This time, much harder.

Startled, Henry juggles the joystick, striking his head against the shoulder bolster.

Trigger launches to his feet, and in no time, he's breast to breast with the shortest of the Wall-Streeters. My receiver echoes with two separate, thumping heartbeats. Pounding like a pair of pistons.

"Land, refuel, call home, and get out of here," I say. "That's the plan, remember?"

Undeterred, Trigger's heart thumps faster.

"Who's your new friend, freq. geek?" The rest of the suit's quad files around him.

"Four to one-and-a-half." I say. "Tough odds, if you ask me. Did you happen to notice your nemesis is the smallest in the group?"

Despite my warning, Trigger holds steady. The head Streeter matches his posture. The three remaining suits close the circle. Trigger's clenched fists raise to his chin. The suits step in. Elbows cock. Knuckles flatten.

As the future of Wall Street wind up, Henry hollers, "Guess you don't need what I have."

Startled by the shrill, all heads spin around.

"What we agreed to," he continues, his voice calming, "shook hands on." Henry lowers his goggles. "Or does the future of Wall Street have no code?" After a long, wide-eyed stare, the whiz retrieves his controller from the floor and goes back to work on his pending equation. "Anything happens to my new friend," Henry's fingers dance over the keys, "if he as much as trips on an untied shoe lace, our deal is terminated." He shrugs. "You choose."

Unquestionably poised to fight, Trigger's chest remains glued to the loud mouthed Streeter.

One of the suit's tailored friends touches his bristled shoulders. "Don't worry, man, we're close to figuring it out," he winks at his partner. "Then you'll have the chance to deliver what freaks like him deserve."

He steps around, splitting Trigger and the Streeter.

The aggressor lowers his hands and takes a slight step backwards. "It's all right, Top." He dusts lint from his buddy's padded shoulder. "Before long, we'll have no use for that butt kisser."

"*Click, click.*" The leader signals from the side of his mouth. "See you on my shoe, Gu."

Gritting their teeth, the financial quad button their matching jackets and disappear into the hall.

"Reckless," I say, referring to the sky surfer's "fight first, ask questions" later reaction.

"More like suicidal—we are twins, after all, Sis," Trigger empties his lungs. "Backing down is not in my blood." Collapsing into his seat, he looks at Henry. "What's that all about?"

Henry squeezes his controller. "Usual stuff, just the future of the U. S. of A."

Beg your pardon?

"Huh?"

"Like I was saying, Pioneer is the only place for *us*."

I'm beginning to understand why Henry sits by himself.

"Help me out here, Henry. This school, with those jerks, is for you? How do you figure?"

"We're the same. You, me, the techies, the Streeters."

"Don't know, man, after witnessing the events of the last five minutes, I'm struggling to make a connection."

"We are the offspring of the most powerful and influential families in the nation. Lawyers, bankers, scientists, athletes, entrepreneurs. A network of national heroes, who strive to keep our country one of the strongest in the world."

"Hold up," Trigger interrupts. "A country is only as strong as its foundation. Firefighters, policeman, road workers, electricians and war veterans are equally important parts of the equation." With every sentence, I imagine his spine straightening.

As Trigger and Henry banter, I begin to wonder about the curriculum at Pioneer. Is a shop class offered? Arts or music? Or is this specialized academy simply the fast track to a high-profile, high-paying, influential career?

Henry toggles his thumbs over a sequence of keys, and the building storm onscreen freezes. "Pioneer prepares us to accept our legacy, to be ready for the future. Wait," Henry's assured expression appears confused. "You do have a compass, right?"

"What does the compass have to do with all this?" I ask, guessing Trigger's thoughts.

Not acknowledging my question, he answers with a simple, "Sure."

"Then you're with us." Henry straightens. "Pioneer prepares candidates to accept their legacy, to be ready for the future. He climbs to his feet and punches his controller in the air. "To be catalysts who'll change the world."

Let me guess, Pioneer's school cheer?

"No one knows the future, my friend." Trigger says.

Henry shoves his heavy glasses up on his nose, and his tall nested hair rocks side to side. He stops and shrugs. "Guess you'll find out anyway."

"Find out what?" Trigger and I ask together.

"Your destiny."

All right, hyper-smart or not, Henry just cannonballed into the deep end without knowing how to swim. Trigger is good at flying. That's a fact. His father groomed him to be a pilot. No real mystery there. But is aviation his destiny? The job he was born to do? Without the help of some mythical magic ball, how can anyone really see the future?

Steadfast in the tangible, the Lyre logic test doesn't support the fortune-teller explanation. How can some unknown school, tucked away in the desert, have all the answers? They can't. Don't. The only reasonable explanation is that their mysterious hydrating elixir is messing with everyone's minds.

Still, something in Henry's conviction, the passion behind his words, makes me curious.

Trigger too, I guess, because he asks a follow-up question. "How exactly does Pioneer claim to know everyone's futures? Hours of aptitude tests, one-on-one interviews?

"Brainwashing." I say.

"Or is it more of a 'go out in the woods and see who survives' kind of program?"

Instead of becoming defensive, Henry appears totally relaxed. He stands up tall. Hands firmly on his hips, he smiles. "They have a pill."

CHAPTER 19

"A pill?" My voice streams through Trigger's ears. Just when I'm starting to get marginally comfortable with the IV, the involuntary piercing, and the voices in my head ...*zing*... another indigestible gets thrown in the mix.

"What kind of—" I begin to ask when Trigger's view disconnects. His picture vanishes, and my visual expands to show what's ahead of me and a way-too-zoomed-in picture of my appalled expression.

Weird.

In no time at all, the clamor of the student frequency returns, thumbnails of faces splatter my visual.

"Come on." Soraya loops her arm around my elbow and guides me from breakfast to Assembly Hall. "Time to learn all of Pioneer's secrets."

Over the weathered wooden doors, a needle splits a metal plaque in the way old-fashioned elevators report servicing floors. This arrowed tip, however, points straight up at the only marking on the curved plate.

"North," my mentor says. "If you haven't caught on, the school is obsessed with sense of direction." The rusty hinges whine as she tugs on the door.

Transom windows, the kind I've seen in churches, allow sunlight to crisscross, brightening the auditorium.

"Let's sit in front." Soraya points and passes rows of seats, which resemble club-style recliners.

As we meander down the center aisle, I take the opportunity to touch my earring and instant-message Trigger. My ear flushes, signaling the request went live. As soon as I let go, I feel a hand on my shoulder.

"Don't worry," Soraya ushers me across the third row. "We'll save a seat for your brother."

Facing the back of the nearly full room, I sidestep until I reach four empty seats. Two for the supposed candidates and two for our orientation mentors. I stop at the second chair, kneel on the thick cushion and watch for Trigger.

Soraya surveys the remaining three before choosing the seat next to me, and despite the noise level in the room, an awkward silence settles. Absent Trigger's voice in my ear, the student stream resonates louder; deafening and chaotic, like a sports stadium full of people talking all at once. Not yet accustomed to the enhanced visual, either, I close my eyes and listen in order to separate the voices.

At first I'm unsuccessful. I hear bits and pieces, but no recognizable words. But after a minute or so it changes. As if my brain synapses fire and isolate each individual conversation. Now I can hear everything. Students rehashing summer trips, organizing study groups, hopelessly weighing the pros and cons of different career paths. I have to admit that I'm enticed by my newfound ability. Being in the know without even uttering a word.

Lost in the sea of virtual chatter, I forget my surroundings. Forget about Soraya and the fact that I'm being incredibly rude. Opening my eyes, I glance at her. She's staring at the chair ahead, looking bored.

I think of my rusty conversation skills. *It's like shooting touch-and-go landings.* A little wobbly at first, but after a few cycles it will feel normal. *Make eye contact. Listen carefully.* I recall the basics. Thinking that if Trigger and I ever want to get out of Pioneer, having an insider like Soraya as an ally might be useful.

With this in mind, and despite not being in the mood to talk, I face my mentor. "What are you studying?"

She perks up. "I'm going to be a risk officer." Her voice is definite, without an ounce of hesitation.

I don't mean to, but I'm sure I wince. For starters, I have no idea what a risk officer is, and beyond that, how is it possible that a sophomore in high school already knows exactly what she wants to do? In her career or otherwise? Most days I feel satisfied just to get through, never mind contemplating the foreseeable future.

All of a sudden, I feel behind the power curve. Honestly, more like a statistic not even charted on the bar graph of success. After all, every spare moment I have is spent not on researching careers or visiting colleges, but on tracking Dad's killer.

Perhaps Soraya has some formula, a plug-and-play shortcut to discovering my professional track. Can't hurt to ask. "How did you know you wanted to be a risk officer?"

"Easy." Her nose crinkles again. An expression, I'm beginning to think, that means she doesn't really get my questions. "It is destined," she clarifies.

My mouth gapes, according to the projection through the reverse view of Dr. Freed's contacts. Wide, like the cargo hatch of a heavy military transport designed to deliver tanks. Still slow on my feet, the obvious response escapes me.

Destined how?

Is what I really want to know.

And what if you're wrong?

I mean, how many things do you actually get right on the first try?

Now locked and loaded with an arsenal of reasonable rebuttals, I'm about to find out what she meant when I'm interrupted by the sight of Trigger at the end of our row.

"T. Xanthus," I call, waving to catch his attention.

His head whips around, skin flushing bright red. "Tana." He makes a playful fist and sidesteps in our direction.

As he shuffles closer, Soraya's chin rests on my shoulder. "Is that the future Mr. Lyre?"

"What?" I spin, butting my forehead on hers. "Ew, gross. Marry my brother?"

My tongue sticks to the roof of my mouth and I suck it loose. Scratch the nape of my neck, picturing Trigger and Brooklyn.

"Umm..." Soraya groans as if she just swallowed a spoonful of creamy milk chocolate. "Lemon lime soda sipped through Red Vine licorice." She flings her arms around my shoulders and squeezes. Despite my upbringing, Mom's family rule sparing use of public affection, I don't even try to wiggle free.

Arriving at the seat next to me, Trigger sits and slugs my shoulder. "T. Xanthus?"

"I was trying to get your attention."

Trigger grins, like he is about to say something and then reconsiders. Instead, he collapses against the plush seat and bounces. "You sleep okay?"

"Like I was super-hydrated." I nudge him and then introduce Soraya.

It is unlike Trigger to be impolite, but he barely says hello before something at the end of the row steals his attention. Henry and the alpha Streeter, engaged in what appears to be civil conversation. We both watch as the suit clasps Henry's shoulder in the same manner he'd greet one of his own quad. After a few nods, Henry and the Streeter shake hands and the suit struts to the front row to join his friends. Alone, Henry searches the room for a place to sit.

"Gu," Trigger yells above the crowd and signals him over to the vacant seat on his left.

"Me?" Henry points to his chest.

When Trigger waves again, Aska Gu wastes no time hurdling his classmates' legs, many of which find their way into the aisle.

Clearing the last trip hazard, he sighs. "Thanks, man," Henry says, happy, I suspect, to be included. He rubs his palms together and stares at the hardwood floor. "I really don't have many friends."

"Now you do," Trigger replies. Once Henry sits, I overhear Trigger ask Henry about the Streeter. "What's up with the suit?"

"Suit?"

"Him." Trigger looks to the Wall Street Quad.

"Oh, those guys."

"I thought you hated each other."

"Technically, they hate me." His hair bounces like a bobblehead. "I could really care less about them."

"But they insult you. Harass you. Push you around."

"They're a means to an end." He massages his ear. "They might despise me, but they can't live without the Gu."

Henry may have explained to Trigger why he considers himself indispensable, but if so, it was after my visual went haywire.

I'm about to get in the know when a tall, lanky man with a scholarly face steps in front of the lectern.

I know him.

Or at least his virtual picture.

So the image I saw after medical was real.

The conversation wasn't a fabrication of my antihistamine-induced out-of-body experience. This man spoke to Chief McDunney. He's the one who inquired about the compass and Professor Flough, and somehow he knows who I am.

I have to tell Trigger.

A hush ripples through the room. Intranet chatter settles as the man rubs the corners of his mouth. "As most of you know, I'm Dr. Otto Funkhouser, Director of Pioneer Academy."

Ever so slowly, I tilt my head. And just when I'm about to whisper, Dr. Funkhouser continues, "We are about to embark on a new adventure, a journey that will set your lives in motion."

A loud roar from the student body echoes through the hall.

"Two days from now, the semester begins, and the fall candidates are mixed among us. Each of you 'newbies,' " the director quotes with stubby fingers, "will shadow your assigned upperclassman."

Henry knocks Trigger's elbow from the armrest. "Guess I'm your student mentor." He snorts.

In a second flat, Dr. Funkhouser scolds him with sharp eyes. "Candidates, after you have experienced a typical day at the Pioneer Academy, we will meet back in this room for a very important part of your orientation."

"Is this guy for real?" Trigger speaks in my ear.

I whisper back. "I have no idea."

A vibration buzzes from Henry's pocket. He retrieves his cell and reads the text message.

"My dad needs me. Pronto."

He nudges Trigger and rereads his father's note.

Sweat beads on his forehead. "Meet me in the weather lab," he says, gathering his pack. "When Funkhouser finishes."

"The lab?"

"Last building at the far end of campus," Henry explains. "With any luck there will be a single, puffy cumulus cloud hovering overhead, otherwise I'll be dead."

Henry stands and giant-steps over a classmate's stretched feet. Balancing on one foot, the leg he just straddled raises, sending Henry tumbling helplessly to the floor.

The tripper snickers and fist-pumps his neighbor.

Trigger's mentor climbs to his feet and skulks out of the room.

"At the end of the day, we will meet back here," Dr. Funkhouser instructs. "Ursula from the health center will hand each of you one of these." He holds an inch-long capsule between his thumb and forefinger, eye-level, so the entire audience can see. "If you choose to join us at Pioneer, take this pill before you go to sleep tonight and your true talent, your career, your future will be revealed."

The already impossibly silent hall becomes eerily still. Funeral-home quiet. As if every Pioneer student collectively holds his or her breath.

"But if you're not quite convinced to seize the grand opportunity in front of you," the director drops the capsule into his palm and stuffs it into his pressed pants pocket, "you mustn't take the pill."

Soft voices murmur as the candidates speak to their mentors. The director waits, and when silence resettles he finishes his speech. "For the undecided who may desire more time to make a decision, we will have an open campus tomorrow to sit in on classes, visit with professors and talk with your parents."

Soraya takes my hand. "Remember, you asked how I knew what I was born to be." She glances at the director with admiration. "The pill showed me."

So that's what destiny looks like?

Shuddering inside, I hold my face muscles taut to disguise skepticism.

"You cold?" Trigger asks as goose bumps prick my arms.

Before I can answer, he shrugs off his bomber jacket and drapes it around my shoulders.

Not cold. Stunned.

Trigger lightly drags a reassuring finger across my wrist. Kind of like he knows the air temperature has nothing to do with my chills.

"By dusk tomorrow, you will have to make a final decision," Funkhouser straightens his bowtie. "Stay and join the fast-track to a certain future or go back home and take whatever card chance deals you."

On cue, the first class bell rings. Summoning the prodigal sons and daughters to step up and seize their destinies.

"You coming?" Soraya pops up, snatches her backpack and moves into the aisle. A wave of students file from their seats and rush to the back of the hall. "Second bell is in five."

I push to my feet and Trigger tugs on my sleeve. Pulling me close, his lips graze my ear. "No matter what, do not take that pill." As I process what he said, my head comes around.

"Have you lost your mind?" I lift my chin and focus squarely in his eyes. "Not a chance."

Trigger sinks his face into my hair. "Even if this place seems perfect."

I turn and glance at Soraya. Confident, direct, with an edgy attitude that makes life seem like a wild adventure.

How does she do it?

I watch her. Focused, centered, comfortable.

Did she learn these skills here at Pioneer?

I don't fight the smile tugging on my lips and entertain the possibility that under different circumstances Soraya and I might be friends.

A sinking feeling settles. The sense of doom that descends anytime I'm about to feel happy.

I shove Trigger away, step backwards and zip my backpack. "There's no such thing as perfect."

Avoiding his face, I let my gaze fall to the compass inlayed in the floor. My eyes skip from the hash mark where we stand, west, arc past north, and stop on east. Locked in on the ninety-degree mark, I reaffirm my path. The course back to Oklahoma. I turn to Trigger. "Let's go home."

"Good." He runs his fingers through his spiked hair and rubs the nape of his neck. "See if you can get Soraya to lend you her cell and I'll find a way to email our parents. "

Even though I know it's the right thing to do, I want to scream "No." Tulsa bound or not, I have no intention of calling my mother.

CHAPTER 20

"Tana Lyre," Trigger buzzes me. Automatically, Henry's visual also joins our chat feed.

I touch my ear twice to accept his request. Soraya and I are already seated in her first hour Information Security class. When Trigger's visual appears, a burst of water splashes his screen.

"Incoming," Henry calls out after the fact. He stands behind a gigantic water cannon dressed in a splash jacket, scuba mask and fisherman waders. "My gust fronts are still a little unpredictable."

"You think?" Trigger sloshes into the weather lab, dripping wet. "Any chance you have a towel?"

As he whisks the water from his face, I snigger.

Soraya doesn't seem to notice. Her attention is captivated by the lecture on firewall breaches and the latest hacker tricks. To me, the professor sounds like he's speaking a foreign language, so I direct my attention to the lower portion of my visual and multitask.

"Yes." Henry kneels, makes a fist, and pumps his arm like a piston. Standing once again, he disappears behind a thick sheet of plastic. Returning, he quickly folds a feather-light square into an airplane and aims it at Trigger. "Finally, my experiment works."

Trigger catches the ultra-light plane, then studies the transparent material. Tinted a desert-camouflage color, tissue thin, we can both see through it as he holds it up to his face. "What am I suppose to do with this?"

How about blow your nose?

Like a magician, Henry shakes a second piece of cloth and demonstrates. He steps on the corner of the napkin-sized fabric and tugs. And just when I think I've seen everything unusual about Pioneer, there is more. He stretches the flexible piece past his waist, around his shoulders and then drapes it like a cape over his head. Trigger wastes no time following his lead and drags the ever-expanding cloth over his back until it measures the size of a picnic blanket.

No longer dripping, Trigger removes his shirt and wrings the moisture from his sleeves, as if the expanding napkin was just some common parlor trick.

Mountain into an anthill. Again.

Trigger looks at Henry. Backed against a cart-mounted turbine engine, Henry's focus is directed to the controls on an adjacent humidifier.

"What exactly are you working on in here?"

"Cloud seeding." Henry tweaks a couple of knobs, then rushes to his laptop and records the results. "Jumpstarting the natural evolution of a thunderstorm."

He returns to the large engine on the cart and tilts the fan blades toward the ceiling. As the thrusting air hits the billowing cumulonimbus expanding overhead, the cloud spreads and begins to dissipate. In its place, a dense layer of mist falls to the floor, coating every exposed surface with a dewy dampness.

Including Trigger.

As he rigorously towels the water glistening on his tanned skin, his firm muscles ripple across his torso. I roll my lips together.

Soda and licorice.

Henry looks up, his goggles are spotted with water. "You know, lending Mother Nature a hand."

"Great. Then you can manipulate the weather and the Pioneer School will rule the world?"

When Henry touches the side of his safety glasses, two miniature windshield wipers clear the plastic. "Rule the world?" he snickers. "No, Triggs, nothing that dramatic." Henry snorts. "Just end droughts, drive tornados from populated areas, dissolve hurricanes, and stop tsunamis from coming inland."

"Oh," Trigger hangs his head. "Is that all?"

"At least that's my thesis project."

"Thesis?" Trigger tries to wring the experimental water from the air cloth, but oddly, it appears dry. Thoughtlessly, he slings the towel over his shoulder. "But you're only in high school."

"Pioneer Academy," Henry corrects him. "In order to complete junior year, each student must defend a thesis in their career concentration. In my case, present my findings in front of every professor in the science department." Almost immediately, creases stack like bricks on his forehead. "Did I mention my dad heads up the board?" Henry gulps.

"Golden. What dad would fail his kid?"

Henry starts to pant. His chest expands and contracts. Deeper and wider. Building like a thunderhead. As Henry's supercell-sized panic grows, he opens his mouth to let in more air. His body convulses, seeming to be on the cusp of a full-blown anxiety attack. Unable to control his short, unsteady breaths, he reaches for an inhaler and puffs twice. His breathing slows. And after a third hit from the inhaler, he says, "You haven't met my father."

Trigger weaves around the turbine engine, the humidifier, and the rows of Freon coolers to reach Henry's side. "You okay, man?"

I can't help but notice that Henry's panic attack coincides with the phases of his thesis project; building updrafts, emotional saturation, finishing with an explosive downdraft. I refrain from commenting, though. I wouldn't want to explain why I'm interrupting my classroom's heated discussion on black and white hat hackers.

"What if I can't figure it out?" Henry props himself against the sturdy steel engine. "What if I..." he fumbles for his inhaler. "Fail?"

I can only guess what accolades Henry's father has received. Considering his reaction, I estimate the list is long and distinguished.

"You're tougher than you think, Henry," Trigger says. "I saw the way you stood up to the Streeters. Fearless." He pauses, as if he's carefully selecting words. "No way. You won't fail. Besides," he reminds, "you've seen the future."

Even though Trigger and I have no idea what his new friend saw under the influence of the prophetic pill, one thing is obvious: Pioneer Academy wouldn't waste a minute on an unpromising student. Like Henry said, he was born part of a group chosen to protect the world.

The screen blips and I think I see Henry grin. His breathing stabilizes as he pushes away from the engine. Standing steady, he shakes his head.

"About the Streeters—"

Trigger interrupts. "You create bootleg frequencies, ones the administration can't listen in on, and sell them to the cliques for extra cash. You found a way to keep those stiff-necks off your back. Not by beefing up or selling out for protection. By outsmarting them. No shame in that."

Henry, however, doesn't look like someone who feels clever or even proud of his creative tactics. Maybe because, like Soraya's Information Security professor just said, "Hackers always get snagged." If he's right, then odds are good the Streeters will figure out how Henry broke through Pioneer's secure firewalls. Then, no longer valuable, Henry will become a geek with a target painted on his back.

"It's just self preservation," Henry exhales. "I really hate wearing a black hat."

Trigger doesn't respond right away. If he's anything like I am, he's busy trying to put himself into Henry's shoes. He seems to drift off in thought.

"What do you know about the aurora borealis?"

Divert and avoid. My favored weapon. Not only does Trigger distract Henry from his discomfort, he skillfully changes the topic to one that benefits us. *Way to go, my friend.* The first step in busting us out of Pioneer.

In the time it takes to throw a light switch, Henry's posture shifts from the hunched, cowering son of an mega-scientist to a straight-spined encyclopedia of weather facts.

"The northern lights," he moans, sounding like most guys do when the girls in school wear short skirts. Appearing inexperienced when it comes to anything without a power cord, Henry channels his social angst into his experiments. "The aurora forms when a solar flare shoots charged particles into the upper atmosphere, creating bursts of lights. Photons." His eyes cloud with intense concentration. "In order to see the crashing electrons," he explains, "a geomagnetic storm must push into the lower atmosphere."

I think about last night. Trigger and me slicing through the clear sky. The air, calm and smooth, mere moments before the mesmerizing ribbons of the northern lights appeared. Assuming Henry's theory is correct, we were swept into a geomagnetic event.

Now we're getting somewhere. Trigger feels it, too. I know, because I hear his words quicken.

"What kind of atmospheric conditions come with magnetic storms?" he asks.

"Excessive static electricity, strong winds, turbulence."

"Extreme turbulence?"

"From the solar wind."

Whatever phenomena were contained in the core of that monster cloud must have propelled us a massive amount of distance. What other force could have the power to move a plane hundreds of miles in a matter of minutes? More importantly, if the storm was our accelerated means of transport, could it possibly work in reverse?

Almost as if he's in my head, Trigger steals my next thought. "Is it possible to artificially create a geomagnetic storm? Maybe like the gust front you cooked up here in the lab?"

Trigger barely finishes the question before Henry starts shaking his head. He turns to the virtual chalkboard and scribbles some formulas.

"No," he says firmly. "Not possible. And as far as I know, no one has even tried."

"Trying is not enough," a husky voice booms from the lab doorway. "Succeeding is all that matters." Chief McDunney's frame tests the limits of the jamb. "Pioneer's mission statement."

"Stay away from McDunney." A memory of the voices I heard rattle in my head.

"What are you working on?" The chief examines Henry's electronic notes without reservation. Like he is familiar—way too familiar.

The chief has secrets…

McDunney glances down at Henry. "Professor Gu's period started ten minutes ago." The chief's eyes remain pegged on the complicated equations.

"Crap." Henry thwacks his watch and then scrambles for his electronic notepad. "We better go."

McDunney walks across the damp tile to help Henry gather his materials.

With the chief distracted, I notice Trigger scan the lab counter, holding for a second on Henry's desktop computer.

"Here's our chance," Trigger mumbles under his breath. "Hey, Henry? My dad might understand me staying out all night. I've done it a few times before. But no phone call. Or text?" He pulls his fried cell from a pocket and sighs. "He's going to wring my neck."

Decapitation may be the least of your worries, I think, wishing I could make the quip aloud.

Professor Flough is, without a doubt, a stickler for procedure. And when his son's plane didn't land as scheduled, with no call or explanation, there's no doubt in my mind he sent out search and rescue.

The good news is that if I'd had to pick one person who is capable of getting us out of here in one piece, it would be Colonel Lamar Flough. I'm banking on his son being just as resourceful. The bad news is that once Trigger contacts his dad, Flough is sure to tell my mother.

With McDunney and Henry preoccupied getting to class, my partner takes the advantage. "Mind if I send an email?"

"Go ahead." Halfway to the door, Henry doubles back and types in his password. "Don't be too long. My dad says only lazy people are late."

"Right behind you." Trigger launches Pioneer's server.

With the Chief and Henry out of sight, he drafts an email to his father: *Out exploring with Tana. Working through her issues with flying. Got a little turned around…*" He drums his fingers on the keyboard.

"I could tell him we're in trouble," he says out loud. "Pretty lame, though, since I don't know where we are. Then all he would do is worry." He strums for another minute and then finishes the message: *Think I've got it covered. See you soon. T. Xanthus.*

After Trigger hits send, the completion bar inches from half to full. "One out-all-night explanation on its way." Instantly, a reply arrives. In the upper corner of the screen, an inbox icon flashes.

"That was fast," I say out loud, catching the Information Security professor's attention.

"Candidate Lyre," he asks. "Do you have a question about the white-hat hacker code of ethics?"

"No, sir," I stammer and Soraya looks over her shoulder.

Rechecking Trigger's view, I read the reply message: *Mail undeliverable. Invalid address.*

CHAPTER 21

"Invalid address? Not possible." Trigger says, jogging to Professor Gu's classroom. "CodeNameMafia has been Dad's email since he left the Air Force."

Luckily, the end of period bell rings. I trail Soraya into the hallway.

"Could he have updated his address?" A question I meant for Trigger, but Soraya spins around and answers instead.

"You're chatting with Trigger, aren't you?" Her green eyes twinkle. "During class?"

I grimace and pinch two fingers to show just a little.

"For brother and sister, you guys sure are close." Soraya giggles and signals for me to follow her down the crowded corridor.

"Not a chance," Trigger clarifies. "That was his pilot call sign, his honorary nickname. Anyway, who the heck are you talking to?"

"Soraya," I shield my mouth, hoping to avoid further confusion. Beginning to realize how much skill it requires to conduct simultaneous virtual and face-to-face conversations. "Maybe if I invited Soraya to join us..."

"Careful what you say to her, T. We're still not sure who we can trust. Back to my dad." His breaths quicken. "There must be another explanation."

On screen, I notice him arriving at the far end of the meteorology wing. A digital board lists Dr. Gu's weather drone lecture as being in the main auditorium ahead.

"Soraya and I are about to go into Corporate Investigations. If I get a chance, I'll try to borrow her phone."

But who will I call?

"Good," Trigger ducks into Gu's classroom. "Going radio silent in three, two..."

"One," I shut my mouth, although we remain connected visually. I slip into a computer station next to Soraya and slouch behind the flat panel monitor. Splitting my attention, I stare at the former CIA case worker giving the presentation while I watch what's going on with Trigger.

Inside Professor Gu's domed theater, the lights are off, with the exception of desk lamps lit at each student's seat. A short pencil of a man dressed in an argyle sweater vest and thick glasses stands in front of a floor-to-ceiling projector screen. *Really? A movie?* Barely a few minutes into yet another hour long lecture, I can't help feel like maybe I drew the short end of the mentor stick.

Except for the straight black hair, the man on the stage is a copy of Henry. Professor Gu points his laser pen at the projector, activates the program, and "Property of the Department of Defense" scrolls on screen. After a page-long list of disclaimers, footage of unmanned flying drones appear behind him.

"Mr. Flough." Gu glances at his wrist and then motions Trigger to the front.

"Great. First day, and I'm on the radar." He moves down the stairs past the other students, who appear mesmerized by the slick planes gliding the entire length of the wide screen.

Far more interesting, if you ask me, than my current situation: reviewing the laws surrounding spying on employees' work computers.

"Please list all types of drones currently in production," the professor instructs the class as Trigger descends from the last step. Henry joins him and they approach the lectern. "Pleasure to meet you, sir," Trigger says. His mentor keeps uncharacteristically quiet.

"I met your dad once." Professor Gu smiles at Trigger. "A great man."

Here we go again. And I thought my parents' reputation was irritating.

"Yes," Trigger repeats mechanically. "He certainly is."

I envision his tormented eyes bulging as big as his head.

"He must be very pleased to have such a fine young man following in his footsteps." The professor turns to his son and sighs, heavy with disappointment.

Henry's shoulders sag.

How does Professor Gu know what kind of kid Trigger is? They've only just met. If he knew the actual facts—Trigger borrowing his dad's plane, flying through a storm, absent nearly twenty hours without even a note—would he still have the same opinion of him?

"The class is studying weather drones?" Divert and avoid. Trigger enlists evasive maneuvers and smoothly changes the subject.

Very well played.

A spark ignites across the professor's face as he turns to the screen. "With the speed at which weather patterns develop, any chance we have of planting our growing compounds in the clouds relies on drones." His voice amps. "The remotely operated planes are safer, more agile and incredibly reliable. Removing the human factor lessens the margin of error."

"Maybe you just haven't met the right flying human," Trigger says, elbowing Henry.

"Logical assumption," Gu replies. "Logical, but emotional."

For a second, his way of thinking reminds me of my mom's. Emotion equals weakness.

Gu continues. "But that's natural, considering your background. Regardless, the Department of Defense has contracted us to develop the next generation of pilotless drones."

"Pioneer has a military contract?"

"Contracts," the professor corrects. "Hence the heightened security, the private airstrip, and the jamming net blocking communications in and out of the immediate area."

The government? A high-tech shield? No wonder Professor Flough's email bounced back.

When Trigger says nothing, Gu shifts his focus to his son. Morphing into Henry's dad, he asks a very parental question. "Speaking of which, how is your research coming, Hengli?"

"It's Henry, Dad, how many times do I have to tell you that's how they say it in America?"

Gu smacks the lectern with a ruler. "Hengli is your birth name. If your mother were still alive, she would be..."

"Wha— wha— what, Dad?" Henry stutters as if he bit into a peanut-butter-and-cotton-ball sandwich. "How would she be?"

Gu squeezes his mouth so tight his face turns red. He cracks the ruler a dozen more times. Grips both sides of the stand and exhales. "The storm experiment?"

Henry throws his shoulders back and stands tall. "This morning I cooked up a sixty mile-an-hour gust front."

" 'Gust front?' " His dad mocks. "Child's play. I need anvil clouds. Supercells. A vehicle for the seeding mixture."

Visibly shaken, Henry spews information like a Super Soaker. "Yes sir, I'm getting there. Got it. The more unstable and convective the better. I'm working on some new angles." He says without taking a breath. "For example, what about geomagnetic storms?"

My jaw drops. Trigger's head comes around.

Careful, Henry.

"No, no, no," Henry's dad pounds fists on the lectern like a toddler. "Not possible, too high up in the atmosphere." His neck ticks. "Focus, Hengli. You know what's at stake here." Stomping away, he mumbles, "For generations, Gus have been born exceptional, with gumption. My son. Ah, I just don't understand."

Trigger rests a reassuring hand on his friend's slight shoulder. "Let me get him up in an airplane." Henry's eyes slant toward him. "And after a few minutes of loops and barrel rolls, we'd see who has guts."

Gallant as the effort is, it doesn't take the edge off the situation. Wheezing, Henry scrambles for his inhaler.

After two quick pumps, he turns to Trigger. "You better go to the rest of the classes without me." He sucks another hit. "Got to go back to the lab. I've a lot of work to do."

"Don't worry about me." Trigger checks the flat panel TV for the day's class agenda. "Physiology is next—effects of lack of oxygen on the body. Something I'm very familiar with."

"Go to the entrance near Assembly Hall," Henry says. "Security will take you out to the airfield." He frowns like it's Friday night and he's grounded for the big game. "Meet you later at the director's closing comments."

"Seventeen hundred hours," Trigger reads from the schedule.

"See you at five." Henry wraps his lips around the plastic inhaler one last time and hurries to the door.

"Hey, man," Trigger says. "No worries. You'll figure it out."

As Henry moves out of sight, I notice Trigger's view linger at the empty space.

"You okay?" I sink further in my chair and whisper.

"Just thinking about my dad."

"The email?"

"No," he hesitates. Then answers. "The way he is."

I'm not sure what to say. Definitely not an expert when it comes to relationships with parents.

Luckily, Trigger fills the gap. "How he pushes, demands perfection. Rides me until every flight maneuver is perfect."

"Tough, strict, and inflexible; believe me, I get it." Even though my words are meant to help Trigger, I suddenly realize I'm describing my life.

"Not a warm, touchy guy—not even close. But he never talks down to me, belittles me like Henry's dad just did."

"Perhaps being the great Lamar Flough's son isn't so bad."

CHAPTER 22

One positive attribute I get from my mother is a fast metabolism. According to the rumbling in my stomach, I gather it's lunchtime. With my head spinning, I leave Corporate Investigations with Soraya and head straight to the group dining room. Like me, my mentor is starving. Another thing I discover we have in common.

Outside the arched entrance of the cantina, the atmosphere shifts; colorful and festive, similar to a family owned Mexican restaurant. When the hostess greets us, Soraya chooses a table on the patio. We've barely sat when a uniformed server whizzes by with a pitcher of iced tea and two bowls of soup.

"They'll make just about anything you want." Soraya sips the tropical brew. "But the first course is always tortilla soup."

I feel a little queasy as I examine the thick chunks of chicken bobbing in the corn-colored broth. Last year, my parents insisted I join a leadership group that considered it a valuable educational experience to visit a pork slaughterhouse. Needless to say, after completing the tour, I no longer have any appetite for meat. At all. Fortunately, I missed the trip to the dairy farm and still seem to have a very strong taste for ice cream sundaes and banana splits.

"What do you think of Pioneer so far?" Soraya asks as she spoons the chunky broth into her mouth.

If I'm honest, I have to admit the classes are far more specialized than I expected. I can see how candidates at Pioneer graduate miles ahead of the average high school student. Throw in the military contracts and the weather-seeding program and, in another life, I might have even been tempted to attend Pioneer.

"Interesting." I use a coined answer, aware that I'm still connected to the intranet, avoiding what I suspect she's really asking. If attending a half-day of classes has swayed my decision whether or not to take the pill.

Although that choice is made, Trigger and I swore a pact. For a minute I allow myself to indulge in the idea of accepting Director Funkhouser's challenge, and I ask what classes are slated for the afternoon.

"International Politics, Cybercrime, and Behavioral Profiling," Soraya quotes from memory.

All subjects, I might add, I have never dreamed of, never mind had the chance to explore. And as far as Soraya? What can I say? She's upbeat, real, not to mention kind of funny. Truth is, I struggle to remember the last time I connected with anyone so easily. If ever.

Weighing the weirdness against the opportunities, I think of Ursula, the shot, an implant, the pill, the streaming voices and a chance to know exactly what I'm suppose to be. Right now. Not a hundred years in the future. From somewhere deep inside I hear a voice cry, "Yes." Yes, I want to know. Yes, I'd love to befriend Soraya, find a place to fit in, start fresh. But before I say another word, I visually flip the thumbnails on screen and tap three times on my lobe when I see Trigger's picture. With all chat windows closed, I speak freely. "I think anyone would be lucky to have a chance to be here."

Smiling, Soraya looks me in the eye.

"And now I know what a risk officer does."

"Keeping corporate executives in line," her words spike with excitement. "Digging for company secrets."

"Sounds very spy-like."

"A spy with no undercover work." Her gaze sinks to the table.

"Not a fan of dressing up?" I joke. Even though she wears a uniform, my mentor's designer shoes and coordinating messenger bag let me know that dressing up probably isn't the problem.

Soraya layers her arms. "I can't deal with lies. Any kind of deception whatsoever."

"Do all spies have to lie?" I ask. Since as far as I knew, I'd never met one in person.

"Not sure." She bunches her mouth. "When we lived in Lebanon my dad worked for the special police." As if the sun set, her natural glow darkens. "My entire life, he has warned, 'Never become me, Sora.' " She waves a scolding finger like I imagine her dad did. " 'Never compromise your values for work.' " Her eyes become glassy.

"He's not a policeman anymore?"

"No. He eventually got a job in the private sector. Head of security for a big pharmaceutical company."

"In London?"

Soraya blots the dampness with her sleeve and then scrapes the last bit of liquid from the bowl. "He went to night school and eventually got his PhD."

On cue, I do my thing. A game I play. Compliments of my upbringing. The basic negotiating tactic used when trying to read others. I guess what Soraya's dad studied. Business, law enforcement, corporate security? All logical assumptions. However, Chief McDunney runs Pioneer security, not her dad. Desperate for more information, I consider probing, but then quickly remember how respectful she was not to pry into my background or question my relationship with Trigger. The subject of her family and the past seems sensitive. I decide to wait and honor her privacy.

Borrowing a page from Trigger's playbook, I shift the conversation. "Where did you live in London?"

"In a small apartment near the shipping docks." Divert and avoid. Tried and true. Soraya's somber expression lifts. "You?"

"In a walk-up a few blocks from Green Park."

"Oooh, the ritzy area." Sparkling and bubbly, my mentor resurfaces. "You should come to my house tonight for dinner," she grabs my arm. "Meet my parents, we can swap stories about living in England."

Instantly, I feel tightness around my collarbone. Reach up and touch the neck scar. "Oh, well, I don't think..."

"My parents would love to meet you and reminisce about the UK. Please." Like Trigger, Soraya doesn't seem like the type to take no for an answer.

Guess I don't have to discuss my family, I think as I caress the smooth skin. I could deflect any small talk back to their time in Lebanon. The repetitive rubbing calms my nerves. It's not like I have any plans, and right about now a home-cooked meal sounds pretty good. As far as I can tell, there's no chance of going home anytime soon.

How bad could it be?

My ear warms. I imagine the glowing blue halo and lace my fingers tightly together.

"You're being paged." Soraya throws a look at my piercing.

Fairly certain who's calling, I press my palms together. A second wave of heat rushes.

"You going to answer?"

I nod, unfolding my hands. After tapping twice on my visual, I see Trigger.

"Hey, T, lost you."

CHAPTER 23

"Something is definitely not right about Pioneer," I hear after accepting Trigger's chat request. "I feel it in my gut."

Soraya mouths "Trigger?" and when I wince, she excuses herself and visits other tables.

Even though I'm certain he was offline, somehow I feel like he heard my inner thoughts. Perhaps even the dinner invitation.

"And it has nothing to do with the declining air supply in this pressure chamber." Trigger's attention shifts to the rest of the physiology class. Midway through a high altitude simulation, they all show signs of oxygen deprivation. Although Trigger sounds relaxed and coherent, the balance of students wander aimlessly around the airtight vessel.

The lack of muscle coordination, euphoria, and tunnel vision have set in, and once their blood cells constrict, hypoxia takes over. A reaction as natural as gravity. One that, if left untreated, leads to blackout and an excruciating death. But like fingerprints, every individual's genetic makeup is unique.

Particularly Trigger's. Gifted with longevity when it comes to low oxygen tolerance, his body has not yet succumbed to the stumbling, bumbling, drunken behavior of his peers.

"How long can you last?" I ask, sure he's aware of his body's limits.

"Six minutes," he glances at the timer on his baro watch. "My personal blackout limit is at twenty-five thousand feet." As valuable time ticks away, he rechecks his wrist. "T-minus two minutes, twenty seconds."

Time being of the essence, I ask, "Can you be more specific?" Since I can name a dozen things that seem kind of off about Pioneer.

Trigger's view tips right, then left, likely due to the onset of oxygen deprivation. "It's too perfect."

"What is?"

"This school."

He's right. On the surface, everything at Pioneer did appear utopic. Cookie-cutter. Like the students were copied from a template and pasted straight into a handbook on how to be a billionaire before turning twenty one.

The oxygen in Trigger's blood must be declining, because he now struggles to sit upright. Fighting the urge to slump, he straightens both arms and braces himself against the bench seat. Based on his actions, I'm certain he's rapidly approaching the euphoric stage. A state of incomprehensible bliss.

Barely lucid, he mutters, "Where are the independent thinkers, the rebels, the smoking-section kids who are determined to buck the school's rigid curriculum just for sport?"

"A rouge clique called 'The Individuals,' " I laugh, picturing a small splinter faction on lockdown, waiting for some sort of genetic reengineering experiment in Professor Gu's underground lab.

"Wouldn't be surprised," Trigger's hand circles his mouth.

"Ridiculous," I say, and I shake the nutty notion from my head. *Isn't it?*

When I see the sterile white ceiling of the chamber, I know Trigger's head has tilted back. "I can't stop thinking about Tana Lyre," he belts like a cheerleader over an air megaphone, and then pretends to toss the invisible voice amplifier end over end.

"Huh?" I knock my receiver. Must be a bad connection.

Did he just say... Nah, Trigger is crazy about Brooklyn Dehavilland.

Then I recall the remainder of Professor Flough's briefing, the short list of reactions once the body runs low on oxygen. Delirium, a sense of well-being, then the complete loss of all inhibitions. That's why he called out the wrong name, for sure.

When Trigger's view dims and narrows, I know he has tunnel vision.

"Put your mask on," I bark before he blacks out.

In no time at all, Trigger's groggy gaze shifts to his wrist and I hear his voice count down. "Five, four, three, two..." Fumbling, he reaches for a quick donning mask and pinches two red activation switches. Pneumatically, the flexible straps extend like a giant spiderweb and drape around his skull. The straps retract and seal against his head.

Drinking in the one-hundred-percent oxygen, he sucks and cycles a series of deep breaths.

Within seconds, his throttly voice returns. "Time of useful consciousness?" He squeezes the outside of his watch face and hits reset. "Six minutes on the nose." Exactly as expected.

"Done this before?"

"Hundreds of times."

"It shows."

His fellow students in the chamber have their masks on too, recovering at their own pace.

"Attention," the physiology instructor's voice pipes over the intercom. "Anyone interested in repeating the exercise, please remain in the chamber."

"Enough fun for one day, don't you think?" After examining the altimeter to make sure the pressure inside has normalized, Trigger removes his mask and leaves his seat. He crosses the room, which is no larger than a woodshed, and spins a steering wheel crank to open the exit. Once through the hatch, Trigger looks back to see if anyone else follows. Predictably, the group of alphas are still in their seats. "Suck-ups." He releases the heavy steel door and strides the length of the industrial hangar. Trigger reaches the door to the expansive Pioneer ramp.

"Hot as the exhaust pipe on a engine." He shades the unrelenting sun from his exposed forehead. Pacing over the tarmac, he assesses the weather. "Clear skies for miles." He spins on the heel of his worn work boots and spots one small dark cloud slightly south, hovering over campus.

"Henry," we say together.

"Does this baby cloud mean he's making progress?" I ask.

"You're on your way, Henry," Trigger says. "We're one step closer to getting out of this creepy place."

I say nothing. Unsure about this place, but not quite convinced I'm ready to go home. I use Trigger's eyes to look around.

During the day, the airport is changed. Similar, yet different. Consistent with last night, I don't see any regular operations. No fuel trucks, ramp workers or transient training aircraft; activities that are generally associated with airports. With the help of sunlight, I discover rows of identical hangars that I missed during our nighttime fly-in. Stacked one in front of another, they enclose a section of nondescript buildings that remind me of military barracks.

Trigger sniffs the air. He scans around. Almost as if he senses something familiar.

"Been here before?" I ask.

"Don't think so."

Tumbleweeds spin and crackle as they bounce across the flat, sandy surface.

His head comes around. "Maybe." His eyes move to the barracks. A long minute stretches before he turns away. "I don't know. I've been so many places. It must remind me of somewhere else."

Suddenly he comes about, like his brain catches up with the landscape. "Hangar B," he reads. I find myself mouthing with him. " 'The student aircraft are stored in Hangar B.' "

"According to Chief McDunney," I say.

"Why would he lie?"

Did I forget to tell him what I heard while still connected to all three intranet frequencies, after my physical? The conversation between

McDunney and Director Funkhouser, their interest in him, the antique compass, and the picture of us.

Before I have a chance to explain, Trigger trots to the side door. Disregarding the electronic key scanner on his right, he twists the chunky doorknob. Locked. He yanks on the metal handle to no avail. A beep chimes and a red light flashes on top of the card reader.

Although I only see straight ahead, something makes the hairs on my neck bristle. "Behind you," my consciousness shouts, but the actual words catch in my throat.

"Can I help you, Mr. Flough?"

"McDunney."

"Never get caught alone with McDunney."

Trigger twitches as the chief's heavy fist rests on his shoulder.

"Sir, hello," he spins to face the security officer. "I didn't realize you were here. Wait, hey," Trigger coughs. "You're choking me."

Static crackles. My view fuzzes. Trigger's visual disappears.

CHAPTER 24

Trigger

"Thought since I had some time," I cough. Chief McDunney's grip tightens around my throat. *What the hell?* I slam his forearm. "With the class still in the chamber, I'd go in and check on my bird."

"You need prior permission from the director, a pass, and a security escort to get into B," the chief grumbles. His nails dig into my flesh.

"What gives?" I try to wedge my fingers beneath his grip. I shout, "Let go of my neck."

"Are you uncomfortable, Mr. Flough?" McDunney unclips his security badge with his free hand and dangles a key card in front of my face. A ray of sunlight hits the plastic and reflects the outline of a holographic chip.

"Escorted access only, for everyone's protection." His lips split and I get a front-row look at a mouth full of rotted teeth.

"Protection from what?"

The chief yanks me closer, until my mouth is inches from his. His eyes slant down and he licks his lips.

"Back off man," I growl, clenching my teeth. The stench of burnt egg salad is making me sick.

The chief chuckles, releases a little tension and our faces separate an inch. Just enough room for him to flick the card off my chin. I swing wild fists against his midsection.

"It's not safe to have anyone poking around, potentially damaging other students' property. Don't you agree?" He speaks calmly. My blows seem to have no impact.

McDunney slides me into the notch on his arm. Steadies my fight by flexing a rock-solid bicep. He lifts me from the ground. Curls me against his chest. And breathes in.

"Are you smelling my hair, you sick bastard?" I punch, twist, and kick.

McDunney's heavy arms grapple down.

"Oh Lamar," he sighs and I feel a craggy thumb brush against my ear.

"Lamar?" I wail. "How do you know my dad?"

"Long story, little mouse."

I bend a knee and thrust it into his groin.

"Ohh," He groans. Sounding less like pain. More like ecstasy. Still upright, he spins me around and holds me tight against his chest. I rake knuckles over his forearm.

Without as much as a twitch, he slides the rigid edge of the badge down my chest and flicks the plastic on my belt buckle. "Is this what you're looking for?"

I feel the chief's badge drag over the front of my pants.

"Get— off— me— you— perv, and fight like a man." I throw elbows, head butt, and bite down on his hairy skin.

"Mr. Flough." A stern voice shouts from behind.

As one, the chief and I whirl around to see the Flight Physiology instructor's head poke from Hangar A's alcove. Ever so slowly, the chief unravels his crooked knuckles, relaxes his strong hold and lowers my feet to the ramp. He steps back and clips the get-out-of-Pioneer-free card back on his waist.

"Care to rejoin the class?" Straight-faced, the instructor's eyes lock solely on mine.

Saved by the professor in the oxygen mask. I answer with a hearty, "Yes, sir."

McDunney winces and adjusts his reptile eye patch "We were just catching up," he explains. "Trigger's dad and I have history. Old friends." He slaps me on the back.

"No way would my dad come within a mile of you," I snap.

"The class is waiting," the professor waves me over.

I glare at McDunney one last time and walk towards an opened hangar door.

A dark shadow casts as a puffy gray cloud drifts overhead. A clap of thunder rings and I flinch. Every muscle in my body shakes. A soaking rain falls. I pause and look over a shoulder.

Chief McDunney stands frozen. Not paying any attention to the water beading on his face.

CHAPTER 25

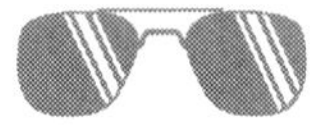

I wipe the sweat drenching my forehead and glance at my watch.

Five o'clock.

The end-of-day brief has surely started. *I should've skipped that last lap around the airport.* I pick up my jog. *I couldn't stop, though. After Flight Phys. class, all I want to do is run.*

"McDunney, that scumbag," I grind my teeth. "If he ever touches me again, I'll crush his skull."

My receiver burns from Tana's nonstop chat requests. She's going to want to know what happened.

Still a moment away from Main Hall, I tap on my piercing and Tana's thumbnail appears on screen.

"I've been trying to connect with you. What happened with McDunney? Are you okay?"

"I'm fine. Just a little late."

"I saved you a seat. You can explain when you get here."

I inhale and tighten my core. "There's really nothing to tell." On the edge of her view I notice Soraya smash cheeks and wave. Henry's stream piggybacks a second later.

"Be there in a sec," I breathe out and kick faster.

"You sure you're okay?" Tana asks. "You're breathing kind of heavy."

"Fine," I snap, even though I don't mean to. Slowing to a brisk walk, I fling open Main Hall's front door.

"You can listen in on any conversation on campus, right? Even the secure bandwidths?" Tana whispers across a vacant seat to Henry.

One chair away, Henry hugs his backpack to his chest.

"I know it's a lot to ask. Maybe even impossible?" Tana says.

What is she getting at?

"Not even." Henry opens an outside zipper and tears a magnet from his utility belt. Plunges the horseshoe into the opened pocket and retrieves a speck of metal. "Listening is for amateurs." He licks a finger and separates the two alloys. "Recording secure bands, however, is far better use of my talents." He drops the speck in Tana's palm, leaving a jagged disc smaller than a pinky nail behind. "You'll need this."

Miss Curiosity lifts her hand closer and analyzes the small, jagged disc.

Henry motions for Tana to put the speck near her ear. The metal shakes, then sucks from her palm, attaching itself to the stud.

"Another slice of earth magnet?" Tana says.

"Yeah," Henry snorts. "It's a booster."

More like the upgrade you provide for the Streeters.

A third virtual window opens in my view and when the status bar disappears, I hear that POS, McDunney. Audio only. No picture.

No. No. "Stop. Cancel. Disconnect." I shout out every command I know. *Tana can't hear this.*

"Yes, sir," the chief's voice thunders.

Is this live? No, must be a recording.

"I questioned him."

So that's what you're calling it? You chicken-shit pervert.

"Can't tell if he remembers." The line crackles, and when the static clears McDunney's voice returns. "Understood," he replies, like a soldier acknowledging an order. "Of course, sir, whatever you say. I'll make sure. Even remove the card from his compass."

What card?

"Got it— he's integral to the bigger picture." Shouting resonates over the recording and then the chief stammers, "I didn't touch him…"

"So sorry I'm late," I shout into the hall as I pass through a side door.

The entire assembly, including Director Funkhouser, turn their heads my way. "Sit, Mr. Flough," Funkhouser says. "We're about to start."

It worked. I notice Tana fidgeting with her add-on. Trying to revive the recording I interrupted. *I caught it just in time.*

I slide in and Tana's wide eyes meet mine.

"What happened with you and the chief?" She lightly touches my arm.

"Nothing, misunderstanding," I knock her hand away. *Why did I do that? She's just trying to help.*

"Trigger, McDunney's a creep," Tana whispers, her lips hovering near my ear. "I heard over the common stream that…"

"I don't want to talk about it."

She pulls back and focuses straight ahead. "O-kay."

"Did you borrow Soraya's satphone?" *Divert and avoid.* I change the subject.

Soraya pokes Tana from the other side. "Do you have plans for dinner?" she asks.

"Yes, and not really," Tana says, her attention bouncing between us.

"So?"

She shushes Soraya, giggles and faces me. "Soraya let me borrow her phone and… well… All the numbers I tried weren't in service."

"You sure?"

"*Annt, annt, annt...*" Soraya mimics a fast busy sound. "Can you say jamming net?" Tana's mentor wrinkles her nose. "Our intranet is self-sustaining."

"Meaning it's not connected to any other wireless or cellular networks," Tana adds.

She must have been paying attention in Cyber Security class.

"Yep," Tana answers as if she can read my mind. "Learned a few things today."

How does she do that?

From the corner of my eye, I notice Henry raise a brow above his chunky horned glasses. "Only security and administration have phones that can call outside the school network."

I'm about to ask about the inner workings, capabilities and range of the bootleg frequencies when Soraya interrupts.

"You're in, right, Tana? Dinner with my parents?"

Dinner at Soraya's? What's going on here?

"T, are you listening to me?" I clamp down on her forearm.

Her head whips around and her eyes narrow. She glances at my grip and says, "What's wrong with you?"

Holding firm, I lean over the armrest. "There must be a way to email or dial outside campus. This is a school, not a correctional facility." Her glare remains locked on my tight grip. My fingers twitch and unravel. "I just want to get out of here, is all. Our parents must be worried."

All the color drains from Tana's skin. *She looks really homesick.*

Tana wiggles and then sits tall in her chair. "I'm going to Soraya's tonight to see if her parents can help."

I sense an edge in her voice.

CHAPTER 26

"Did you enjoy the day?" Funkhouser's sweeping gaze meets rows of agreeing faces. "To be expected." His forced grin shifts to a more serious expression. "This next phase of orientation is critical. The rules surrounding the pill distribution. Listen carefully."

The director reviews the parameters. If, after shadowing our mentors, we've decided to stay and join the elite ranks at Pioneer, then we must complete one final step. Swear a sacred oath by taking the pill before going to bed. But if undecided, candidates must abstain. Delaying their glimpse at the future until they're ready to meet the honor bond. For the uncertain, the entire next day remained open to revisit classes, talk to professors and review the opportunities with our parents.

"Sundown tomorrow is the deadline," the director says. "The moment when every candidate will be forced to make a final decision. Take the pill and embrace your destiny, or return it and go back to your ho-hum lives. Your choice."

"See, we get to pick," I say to Trigger. "Stay or go. It's completely up to us."

Trigger's deep-water blues appear miles away.

Funkhouser continues. "Regardless of what you decide—a future of certain success or the whims of chance—there's a post-deadline dance to celebrate the beginning of the aurora season. The Spirit Dance."

Soraya puts her forehead against mine and releases a high-pitched squeak. "The dance. How exciting."

"Please," Trigger blows out.

"Not much of a dancer, Triggs?"

"Sure, I can dance, sort of..."

"It's nothing to be embarrassed about," Henry says. "Rudder toes are a fairly common condition, I've read."

"My toes are just fine." The sky surfer's eyes flick in my direction.

"What's stuck up his bum?" Soraya asks, not bothering to lower her voice.

I'd love to know too.

"Anyway," Trigger ignores her. "*You're* going to the dance, Henry?"

"Can't miss a chance to reconcile with the past."

"Huh?"

"When the aurora borealis appears," Soraya speaks as if telling a story around a campfire, "folklore claims that everyone has a chance to summon and make amends with the people who've passed."

I gulp. My fingers spider to my neck.

"No worries, T," Trigger draws my hand from the scar. "Probably another of Pioneer's drummed up rituals."

"It's real, Triggs. Native Americans call it the Spirit Dance. For the skeptics in the crowd," Henry throws a nod at his mentee, "think of the ritual as a chance to pay homage to the phenomenon that brings a new class of candidates each semester." Henry pats his wiry curls. "Way valuable research." He tugs at Trigger's sleeve. "In or out?"

"Out," says Trigger.

"In," I say without thinking.

Henry lowers his goggles. "What about the future pill?"

"No way." Trigger layers his arms, appearing not to be interested in getting ahead. Henry collapses in his seat.

"You think I'm making a mistake?" Trigger asks.

"Never mind." Henry shakes his head.

"I'm in, too," Soraya sings.

"Fantastic." Trigger sighs, leaning into my hair. "Who are you again?"

A question, I'll admit, I don't have the answer to either.

Trigger is about to stand when Henry straight-arms him back.

"I spent the entire afternoon thinking about what you said. About creating a geomagnetic event."

Mention of the words "create" and "event" captures our attention.

"Really?" Trigger bounces a foot.

I gnaw a thumbnail.

"I think I figured out how to get one started." Henry raises his bug goggles over his frames and cycles the mini wipers. "The rain event this afternoon—all me."

I had no clue that Henry had seriously considered Trigger's suggestion. That he would use his genius-grade brainpower to investigate a topic his father is so strongly against.

"Seriously?" Trigger acts excited, but his mouth frowns.

"What about your thesis?" I ask.

Henry avoids my question. "Hey, you guys want to see something really cool?"

Trigger looks at me.

"I already have plans," I say.

"You and me, then?" Henry asks. "Super top-secret scene at the airport."

"Okay," Trigger shrugs.

"Great. The weather lab at twenty hundred hours."

Trigger sets the alarm on his watch. "By the way, Henry, nice job on the supercell this afternoon."

When the scientist stands, I could swear he'd grown four inches.

Soraya and I wait patiently in the long line snaking in front of Ursula's nurse station, talking nonstop. As we move forward through the queue, my mentor discusses creative ways to accessorize school uniforms.

I laugh hysterically, as if Soraya is a stand-up comedian. I feel relaxed. Animated. My face tattooed with an ear-to-ear grin. There's no sense denying the facts. For the first time in over a year, I think I'm happy.

Near the front of the line Trigger wedges between us and offers to take us on a double date. Soraya cackles like a hyena and our trio shuffles forward, two spots away from the glimpse into our future.

When Trigger heads the line, he fashions his hands in front of him the way I'd seen people in church when taking communion.

Nurse H2O actually cracks a smile as she gently places a single pill in his palm. "Buckle up," she says, dishing me a matching gel capsule.

"Remember," Trigger yanks gently on my sleeve until I'm pressed against his solid chest. "We agreed not to take the pill."

I nod.

"I need to hear you say it."

"Double or nothing," I repeat through clenched teeth and tear away.

Stepping forward, Trigger bends over and presses his forehead to mine. "Remember, we're in this together."

CHAPTER 27

"Don't worry, my family's easy," Soraya says as she barges through a door painted the color of a blood moon.

A refreshing burst of evening air chases her into the warm, modest home. Soraya points at the handsome couple standing, hip to hip, arms intertwined.

"Tana Lyre, meet my parents, Doctors Abraham and Melina Harb."

The fading blue sky trickles through a set of vertical blinds, diffusing the unevenness of the dried clay walls.

Anxious, I hold my breath, step into the open living space, and offer a hand.

Soraya's father looks as if he's seen a ghost.

"Nice to meet you, Tana," the woman at his hip answers. Her olive skin and long, kinky hair are identical to her daughter's. She glances at her husband, whose face is pale and damp.

"Where are my manners," Dr. Harb finally speaks. "Welcome, Miss... What did you say your last name was?"

"Lyre," Soraya repeats with a hint of sarcasm. "Earth to Abraham Harb, where are you?" She places both hands on his temples. "Pay attention."

"Sorry, love, big project at work. Guess I'm distracted." His apologetic expression matches his words, but his eyes remain pinned on me as he ushers us to a sectional couch. "Please, sit down."

"Can I get you something?" Mrs. Harb asks.

"A cup of Earl Grey? I know it's weird."

"How funny, that's also Soraya's favorite," she remarks.

Soraya smiles and presses my hand.

As Mrs. Harb leaves for the kitchen, she brushes a light kiss on her husband's cheek.

"They lived in the UK, dear. Over there, young people drink tea, too," he calls after his wife.

"Ah, Daddy you're coming back to us now." Soraya and I squeeze closer and cackle. Giddy as soul sisters.

"Soraya hasn't stopped talking about her new friend, Tana. As she probably told you, we also lived in London."

Breathe. My palms sweat. *You don't have to say a word. About the UN, Dad, the accident or anything that happened in London. Deflect and redirect. Keep the focus on him.*

"Yes," I steady my voice. "Soraya said you were in security for a large drug manufacturer."

"A company called Bio Dynamics. Goodness, what a fantastic opportunity for our family."

Did he just say Bio Dynamics?

I knock the volume down on my ear receiver in order to lower the background voices. I shake my head, confident I misheard.

"As I was chief of security, they paid for my doctorate and my wife's medical degree." Dr. Harb fingers the picture on the end table where he stands dressed in all black, in front of a building marked BD.

My stomach cramps. Easily recognizing the company logo that is forever branded onto my frontal lobe. The same drug company named in the last lawsuit dad mediated.

A nausea geyser spews up my burning throat.

Keep your head, Lyre.

I touch the scar on my neck. With thousands of employees all over the world, I'm sure it's pretty easy to make a Bio Dynamics connection.

My stomach gurgles and I slide my hand over to soothe my roiling gut. *This is why I avoid social gatherings.*

When Mrs. Harb returns she carries a tray filled with cups, a light snack and a pot of tea. She sets the service on the coffee table, then leans on the armrest next to her husband.

After stretching an arm around his broad shoulders, she notices my discomfort. "Everything okay, dear?"

Embarrassed, I look down at my hand holding my tummy and quickly pull it away. "Just hungry, I guess."

Without another thought, Mrs. Harb passes a plate of cheese and olives.

"For so many years I was under the thumb of the secret police," Soraya's dad explains, helping himself to a teacup. Soraya leans over and takes the tea right out of his hands.

"Thank you, Daddy," she grins and wedges in next to me.

"This one," his chin falls to his chest. "Ahh, I never can say no to my girl." He looks at his wife. "Sorry, my love, being the heavy hand has always fallen on your shoulders."

"Yes," Mrs. Harb smiles at him. "Despite men's chest pounding, the women carry the heavy loads—preparing their children to survive in the world."

"While you and your dad were out flying around, I was home. Setting boundaries, enforcing the rules, protecting you." I hear mom's last few words and swallow. *Maybe she was just being a good parent.*

Soraya's dad kisses her hand. "Anyway, I did get out of the strong-arm business," he winks at Mrs. Harb. "And crossed into the private sector. That's my story." He prepares another teacup.

"How long did you live in London, Tana?" As Soraya's dad moves forward in his chair, his developed forearms flex.

Nibbling an olive, I run a series of calming scenarios through my head. Rolling waves, the pitter-patter of raindrops...

"On and off for years," I say, pretending I'm talking about a stranger.

"When did you return to the States?"

"About a month ago." I bite my lip as the shakes threaten to shatter my fragile exterior. I start to feel heat from the exploding plane blistering my skin. Tiny beads of sweat soak my hairline. I suck air through my nose in an attempt to steady my speech. "I live in Tulsa."

"Oklahoma?" Dr. Harb's baritone voice climbs two octaves. "Quite a culture shock, I imagine." He scratches his head. "Did your parents change jobs?"

Tears pool in my eyes. My heart thumps and I swallow a gag reflex. "Death in the family." I squeeze my ribcage. A time-tested tactic that usually curbs crying.

Soraya's dad avoids me. His gaze drifts to the snapshots on the fireplace mantel. He stops at the last frame, stares, his face turns solemn. The tattered snapshot looks to be of Soraya, much younger, with a small boy curled on her lap. Both children are dressed in worn clothes and wrapped in a frayed blanket.

The room is very quiet. Dr. Harb frowns at the shot of the young boy. "We also left our homeland because of loss." His lower lip twitches.

Soraya reaches and grabs my shaky hand. Oddly, she's trembling too. "Elias, my brother, died of malnutrition."

For the moment, the emotional floodgates hold, allowing a chance to step from my own grief and try on someone else's shoes. The Harbs'.

I'm not the only one who's stuck?

After a long moment of silence, Mrs. Harb speaks. "We are the American dream, Abraham. Born into poverty, we've worked our way into a comfortable, successful life."

"Yes, my darling." Soraya's dad takes her arm. "Education is opportunity." He turns to Soraya and me sprawled on his couch. "Go to the best school," he zeroes in. His eyes missile-lock on my face. "At any cost."

"Enough of the serious business." Mrs. Harb pretends to ring a dinner bell. "Our guest is starved."

Dr. Harb helps his wife from the armrest and then escorts her into the kitchen.

"Your parents are okay… Nice, actually," I say, as Soraya bounds to her feet. She spins in a circle and then offers an open palm. With a solid grip, Soraya launches me across the terra-cotta tile floor. Howling like coyotes, we scatter around the picnic-style table.

With my stomach somewhat settled, I swipe a carrot from the veggie plate, and share half with my hostess.

"By the way, what did your dad do in the special police?" I ask.

Soraya chomps down on the crunchy stalk and speaks like Bugs Bunny. "Ah, an explosives expert, Doc."

CHAPTER 28

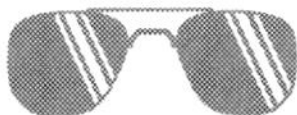

I shrink Tana's thumbnail to the bottom of my view. Although still connected, I see no point listening in on her and the Harbs battle through a virtual match of team dominos.

I hope she gets her hands on a satphone.

I pass through the open door at Henry's lab and find him dressed in camouflage and hiking boots, his backpack piled with a mound of camping gear.

"Going on walkabout?" I ask and slide past the barrels of Freon, squeeze in between the humidifiers, and duck under the tripod-mounted water cannon. *No way am I getting soaked again.*

"What do you mean?" Henry asks and I sift through the sleeping bags, flare gun, and night-vision goggles spread out on the lab table. Equipment to camp overnight.

"Sort of," he shrugs. "I like to be prepared."

"Prepared for what?"

"You'll see," Henry stuffs the gear into a huge pack. "I prefer to show, then tell." Henry grins and snorts. He heaves the pack over a shoulder and in the process timbers to the floor.

"Let me give you a hand." I trot over. Henry releases the stuffed bag, rolls on his side and agilely pops to his feet. I bend over and lift the gear pack.

"I've got this," I slide my arms through both handles and carry the supplies on my back.

"Follow me," Henry ushers me outdoors.

We hike about a mile on a dirt path. It leads to the base of a mesa that reminds me of my dad's flat-top buzz cut. We traipse through sagebrush and rocky terrain until reaching the top of the steep, isolated hill.

"Stellar view of the airport," I say, looking across the airfield. More specifically, at Hangar B. The four steel walls holding my plane hostage. I shrug off the backpack and drop it on the ground. A harvest moon moves up the eastern horizon, illuminating the rocky ledges that provide natural cover. "I've figured it out," I look at Henry.

"Really?" Henry unpacks goggles, a video camera and a portable humidity meter.

"Your top-secret reason for bringing me up here."

He shakes a napkin-sized sheet of his ever-expanding chamois towel and then drags his equipment over to a narrow slit between two boulders.

"That thing with McDunney."

Henry hikes an eye brow and removes his bug glasses.

"You heard what happened and brought me up here to bond. Man-to-man."

"Did you have a run-in with McDunney?" He waves me to his side and squats down behind the rocks. "I'd stay away from the chief. He's messed up, creepy, crazy. Rumor is he has dirt on Director Funkhouser. Otherwise, he'd likely be back in prison."

"What did he do time for?"

"Not sure," Henry checks his watch and peeks through the boulders. "It was back in his military days."

"The chief was enlisted?"

"Air Force."

Is that how he knows my father?"

"Take my advice," Henry tugs on his collar. "Stay as far away as you can from that whack ball," he shudders. "You know, since we're bonding and all."

If this isn't about the chief, then what are we doing up here?

I collapse on a small clearing in the sagebrush. "What are you looking for?" I ask.

Henry hands me the night vision binoculars.

I roll to my stomach and match the glasses to my eyes. From our position, a mile up on the hill, the entire Pioneer airport is visible.

"Focus just east of the runway." He sprawls, resting his cheek to the cracked earth. "A few miles above the surface. Should be any second now."

I stretch my neck to get a better look, but Henry swats my arm. "Keep your head down."

I flatten against the deck. "We're not suppose to be out here, are we?"

Henry closes his eyes. "I don't see anyone out here. You?"

I push the glasses back to him.

Henry splits his lids, adjusts the magnifiers and scans the airspace at the end of the runway landing to the north. "So, have you figured it out yet?"

I prop myself up on a bent elbow. "Figured what out?"

Lowering the glasses, Henry's expression reads, "Don't insult my intelligence."

I make the longhorn sign with my free hand, copying the two-finger technique Tana used in the plane to locate the North Star. Angling to the left, I trace the Big Dipper.

"The only thing I've figured out so far is that something about this school isn't quite right."

"Shame."

"What is?"

Henry exhales, "Guess I expected more."

"More?" I try to rise, but Henry knocks my anchor arm.

"You're not at all curious about how you got here?"

How could Henry know how we got here? What about going back? Does he have that information too?

"There are as many possibilities as there are stars in the sky," I say, being vague on purpose.

"Check it out." Henry jostles my shoulder. He aims the binoculars to the east. "Storm brewing, nine o'clock."

My head spins to see a neon, greenish-yellow ribbon snake over the horizon. On the tail end of each hairpin curve, the multi-colored band grows wider. "The aurora borealis."

"Right on, man," Henry takes measurements with a digital barometer. The brilliant light show shrouds the clear sky. He elbows me again. "One geomagnetic event in the making."

The wind blows stronger, kicking dust into the air.

Kneeling, I shout over the gusts. "This is exactly what Tana and I saw. Just before our plane was engulfed by a horrific electrical storm."

The rushing air howls.

Henry keeps scanning the distant airspace. "Then you woke up hundreds of miles away in the desert, right?"

"Yes… But how do you…"

The deafening sound of a high frequency whines. My eyes dash to the end of the runway. Before I know what has happened, the center of the dry lake splits. A mechanical door cranks open and two giant jet turbines miraculously appear. Whipping, the raw power echoes as the fan blades spin and the engines spool. I rub both eyes. "Is this for real?"

Roaring at full speed, the trailer-mounted turbines rip and blow away the sandy debris in what I thought was the remaining part of the dry lake. With the last grains of sand swirling in the air, a strip of grooved pavement begins to emerge. In the next thirty seconds, an additional 3,000 feet of runway surfaces.

"A hidden landing extension?" I hear my voice crack.

I must be dreaming. Or is this a side effect of the IV elixir?

The engine noise cuts and the turbines retract back into the desert floor. A buzz sounds, similar to the pop of a burning fuse. A spark flashes and the entire airfield lights up like a holiday display.

Just like Tana and I saw from the air.

The runway and taxi lights burn with high intensity. The rolling wave of lead-in rabbits paint a flashing path to the landing target.

My heart races.

"Over there," Henry shoves the binoculars into my chest and points to a fast-moving object breaking through the clouds.

With the lenses over my eyes, I hear him call out bearings. "090, 110, 130 degrees."

The ribbon clouds recoil and begin to dissipate. As the colored residue fades, an unobstructed sky full of constellations reappears.

"What in the world?" I stutter.

"This is the top secret part."

"Long wings, narrow hull, built like a dragonfly. Holy Chuck Yeager—what is it?"

Through the binoculars, I track the slick piece of technology soaring through the thermals, gliding, graceful as a hunting hawk.

"A very unique prototype drone." Henry answers.

By the time I hear the rumble, the stealthy drone is more than halfway down the runway. I blink and refocus, and a massive transport plane chases across the threshold.

The glasses drop to my side.

"T. Xanthus Flough," Henry makes the introduction. "Meet the WXP 5 Drone."

"You mean the drone that will eventually deliver the storm-seeding compound your dad developed?"

"The very one." Henry says.

"WXP 5?" slides from my lips.

"Yep, the beaut in front of you is fifth generation."

"Where are the first four prototypes?"

Henry shrugs.

"Why haven't I heard of the project?"

"Don't know, Triggs."

"Was the original test pilot Air Force? Does my dad know about this drone?" I stop. An incredible thought crosses my mind. The unthinkable. All the answers I seek are trapped in Pioneer's know-everything pill. I stuff my hand deep in a cargo pocket and dig until I locate the capsule. Rubbing over its smooth surface, I raise it overhead.

"Will I fly the next generation of fighters?" I ask the ordinary pill, which resembles a multivitamin. "Grow up to become a legend like my dad?" I angle it in the darkness to get a better look. The white contents shimmer in the moonlight.

"You going to take it?" Henry says.

Double or nothing. We're in this together… We agreed not to take the pill. My own words rattle around in my head.

"Test pilot, astronaut, experimental airplane designer. What will I be?" I thumb the pill into the meaty part of my palm. Dizzy, I thrust my hand to my lips.

The jelly-like coating has barely touched my lower lip when a bullhorn screeches. Henry and I both jump in the air.

The pill bounces from the edge of my mouth and tumbles toward the sand. I swing, catch the capsule mid-air and juggle it like a hacky sack. Finally, I trap the key to my future in my hand.

Henry sighs, shaking his head, then climbs to his feet. "Going to take a bio."

As he shuffles off in the bushes, I spy an army of fuel trucks, ramp workers and men dressed in lab coats step onto the tarmac in front of Hangar B. The tractor tug-chugs to the runway, hooks up on the drone's nose wheel and drags it into the hangar.

From my periphery, I catch two bobbing streams of light. I crumple into a squat and listen. In the distance, a sound grinds. An engine with manual transmission. Not just one, but two.

“Dirt alert.” Henry runs from the brush. He scrambles to gather up his pack and sprints to the side of the mesa. At the ledge, he leaps feet first down the backside of the steep, snarly slope.

Scooping up the binoculars, I take a few long strides and slide behind a boulder.

With the signal of security’s link coming in range, I pick up their audio feed. The rumble of aggressive power trains whine as four sets of all-terrain tires move over the flat mesa. I peek around the corner.

Number One leaps from the lead vehicle, appearing to canvass the area on foot. When his heavy utility boots kick something hard, he bends to investigate and then straightens with a sturdy leather case in hand. The kind made to protect binoculars.

Crap, we left a trail.

Wasting no time, McDunney’s minion hustles back to his vehicle.

He grabs his satphone and hits a number stored in speed dial. “Chief,” his no-nonsense tone rumbles through my receiver upgrade. “We have a problem.”

I roll flat and slide, following Henry’s lead.

CHAPTER 29

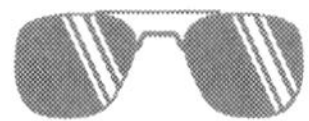

Ahead, Henry's small frame maneuvers tight and fast like a human toboggan until his feet collide with level ground. He flexes his knees and squats to absorb the momentum before standing.

I, however, bounce out of control over the stony surface, less like a luge and more like a lead sled. Hitting bottom, my ankles roll and I tumble to my back.

"You okay?" Henry inquires, hovering over me.

"Not sure." I heave. "Cloud-seeding drones, hidden landing strips, top-secret facilities in the desert." I rub my temples.

"Kind of a lot to take in for one night." Anchoring a heel, Henry offers a hand.

Back on my feet, I dust dirt from my mouth. "There's still one thing I don't understand."

"Only one?" Henry moves forward, tracking alongside the dirt road.

"I think I get how we got here." I slow to match his short stride. "The aurora borealis, right?"

"Yes…"

"If the solar wind pushes the protons and electrons into the lower atmosphere," I say.

"And…"

"They eventually collide, and, like a neon sign, we see the spectacular display of northern lights."

"Yeah, baby, keep it coming."

"But if the storms are random acts of nature, how can they be scheduled like departures on the airlines?"

Henry's head bends back, and he stares at the stars. "What direction are we walking?"

I locate Polaris. "West."

"You sure?"

I recheck the most consistent light in the sky. "Yes."

"What if it's overcast? How would you find direction without the stars?"

I dig in a cargo pouch and pull out my pocket compass and hold it up for Henry to see. "I'd use my compass."

"Your *mag-ne-tic* compass?"

"I always carry two. One in the plane and one on me, for backup. Hold up." I knock a fist to my head. "Is it possible that the compass has some connection to the storm?"

"He gets it," Henry steeples his hands. "The storm activates the compass."

"Hold up. I'll admit I've seen a lot of remarkable things at Pioneer, but weather-activating flying instruments? Not on this planet."

"Proven fact, Triggs. During the First World War, the government contracted an up-and-coming biotech company to develop a new generation of compasses."

"Seriously?"

"When the war ended, President Woodrow Wilson awarded veterans, businessmen, bankers, athletes and politicians—anyone who contributed greatly to the war effort—a compass, as a token of appreciation."

I shake my spinning head.

"What the recipients didn't know at the time was each compass was wired with a basic, first generation, three-dimensional tracking chip."

"Now you're suggesting our government is spying on its citizens?"

Henry pauses, looking a little surprised. "Didn't take you to be so naive. Anyway," he shrugs. "If the military ever needs to mobilize the most influential people in the country—for a natural disaster, World War Three, or an invasion from outer space—" he bumps my shoulder. "All they have to do is activate the compass chips and they would know exactly where to find their patriots."

"Sounds pretty smart. A stretch. But smart. Considering it only took about twenty years to start another world war."

Veering off the sandy shoulder, Henry cuts into an area covered in dense sagebrush. "With our government's worst nightmare realized, not just once, but twice, the military's top brass developed a strategy." He lifts his knees high and smashes the prickly bushes with his boots. "One to protect the future of our nation."

As we walk the last half-mile toward campus he tells me the rest of the story. How an offshoot of the compass initiative created the idea of a place where the children of patriots could learn and excel. There, they could be trained to keep the nation strong, safe, and on the cutting edge. As a result, Pioneer was built and has since been protected, hidden in the desert.

"Technology has evolved over the years," Henry explains. "The next generation of compasses were fitted with a GPS chip that includes the latitude and longitude coordinates of Pioneer's campus."

"Its homing signal is activated during geomagnetic activity, I'll bet." *Fall and midwinter. Each of Pioneer's semesters begins during heightened visibility of the aurora. The geomagnetic storms during this time activate the GPS compasses, summoning the chosen candidates.*

"And the pill?" I ask.

"A Pioneer graduate who went on to work at a biotech company developed the future pill to give a competitive edge."

And perhaps a way back to Oklahoma?

"Henry." I stare ahead at the amber glow from Pioneer campus. "You up for a challenge?"

CHAPTER 30

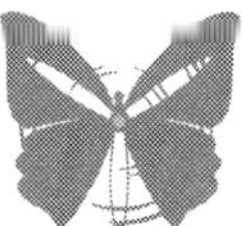

Create a geomagnetic storm and break into Hangar B while evading McDunney and security. By sundown today. That's what we're up against if we want to get out of here.

Leaning closer to the oblong mirror hanging on the back of my dorm room door, I wonder if the dawn's rays are responsible for making me look different. Better. Softer. The crescent frown lines that surfaced shortly after Dad's funeral seem to have smoothed out and disappeared. Even in the dry air, my temperamental skin radiates a clear, dewy texture. But as much as I want to believe the old wives' adage, I know the transformation is a result of something else altogether.

For the first time since I can remember, I'm not simmering with anger. Is it possible that twenty-four hours have passed without the urge to search for that wretch who killed my father?

I think of Soraya. Her normal family. Consider how comfortable and safe it felt to be in her house. A home filled with love. Completely the opposite of how I feel in Tulsa.

Rolling my future pill across the wooden dresser, I seriously consider my options.

Stay or go?

There is a knock at the door.

After a quick time check, I hurry across the tile. Still moving, the capsule rolls to the edge of the bureau and falls to the floor.

"You're early." I open the latch, expecting to see Soraya. Trigger stands opposite me, leaning on the frame. I touch my ear. No pending request from T. Xanthus Flough.

"Expecting someone else?" he asks.

"Going to class with Sora." I motion Trigger in, and he sits on the edge of my bed. Bending, he pinches the white capsule from the floor and maneuvers it between his fingers. "Did you find a way to call home?"

"What?" My attention is drawn to his hand.

"Get any help from Soraya's parents?"

"No." I try to drag my gaze from the mesmerizing capsule. "I forgot."

When the pill has cycled to his pinky, Trigger allows it to drop into his palm. "If I didn't know better, I'd think you weren't in any hurry to go home." Although his words sound casual, I hear a serious undertone of doubt. "You still want to go home, right?"

I don't answer. Not to be annoying or stubborn, but because I really don't know.

"Soraya's parents, what are they like?" Divert and avoid. Trigger changes the subject.

"Funny, nice." I'm sure my face lights up. "They came from humble means. Her dad was in the secret police in Lebanon and later fled with his family to London."

"London?"

"Like my family, the Harbs moved there for work. We overlapped for a year, but never met. Isn't that crazy?"

"Wild," he says, even less excited. "What kind of work?"

"Soraya's dad was head of security for a drug company. Bio Dynamics."

"Bio Dynamics?" Trigger repeats. Loud and exaggerated.

"Then he went to night school and earned a PhD."

Trigger's mouth looks axle-deep in mud. He mumbles to himself. "What did you say your dad was working on before he died?"

My voice becomes unsteady. "Lawsuit against a big drug company."

"Was he winning?"

Even though I know the answer, I revisit that morning. Our kitchen in London. The day Dad took off work so I could solo.

"Yes," I say with confidence. "He said the company's back was against the wall and a big settlement was imminent."

Trigger sits silently with his thoughts.

"Strange coincidence, right?" I say.

"I guess."

"I don't understand." My voice starts to escalate. "What does this have to do with the Harbs? They're just regular people."

"Sure," Trigger snaps. "Working-class citizens employed at a hidden compound in the desert with its own special school that can't be found on any map."

My body temperature rises. I clench my teeth and tighten my fists.

"What do you really know about these people, Tana? What is so interesting here that you're not sure you want to go home?

"I know what I feel." My tongue lashes.

"The same sort of desperation you had in my plane? The answer to all your troubles? Another easy way out?"

Doubling over like I've been stabbed, I hold my side as pain shoots across my chest.

"How dare you?" My vision blurs and I purposely bite my tongue.

Don't cry.

I tighten my rib cage and suck a substantial breath. When air finally funnels through, I arc upright and storm across the room. I fling open the door and glare at Trigger.

A few silent minutes pass, and then he speaks, "I think Henry's found a way home." From the expression on his face, I sense his goals are clear. Leave Pioneer ASAP.

"Out," I yell.

"I'll work on the specifics. Meet me at the dance tonight." Trigger launches off the bed and holds the future pill in front of my face. "Here. Your choice."

An aura of energy spins around the capsule, pulling my fingers towards it; closer and closer, until the centrifugal force slaps the pill against my hand. I grin.

Vectoring around me, Trigger hesitates, like he has something else to say but keeps it to himself, and walks out the door.

I lean against the cool metal frame, relieved he's gone. Still, Trigger's harsh accusations swirl in my head. I bite a thumbnail.

When the door latch clicks again, I hope he has come back to apologize and tell me everything between us is all right. Securing the pill in a pocket, I hold my breath as the round knob twists.

"Yes, I want to go with you," I practice.

But when the door cracks open, Soraya's bushy head pokes around the corner.

"Hey, girlfriend." She jumps like a skydiver onto the twin bed. I notice her brightly colored knit dress. Motorcycle boots and textured tights. The cutting edge of fall fashion. "Ready for the day?" She flips over and catapults to her feet.

Wiping the dampness from my face, I glance down at my own outfit. Same cargo pants and white blouse as yesterday. I lie to myself and say that if I had actually packed for this trip, my choice might be more stylish. The truth is, however, yoga pants and sweatshirts, navy and black, have become my unofficial uniform. After smoothing the wrinkles, I tuck in my ordinary blouse.

Probably noticing my discomfort, Soraya kneels down and rummages through my duffle. "Are these all the clothes you have?"

I turn to my reflection in the mirror and examine my fingernails that appear to have been mauled by a colony of termites.

My friend watches closely. "I have an idea," she says. Her emerald eyes seem to shine from the inside out. "Let's go shopping."

Oh, God, no, I start to say, but then stop. I hate stores. Despise overbearing salespeople. And most importantly, don't have any money.

"What about classes," I say, analyzing my hopeless get-up.

"Ah, pish," Soraya blows from her lips. "I feel a migraine coming on."

My eyes meet hers. We smile. Matching devious grins.

"That actually works with your parents?"

"Of course," Soraya messes her hair and makes a sullen face. Retrieving a satphone from her purse, she dials home. Impressive. Is it possible that corporate risk officer Soraya Harb could also be destined for the stage?

As Soraya speaks to her mom, she moans, adding an occasional wince, and just for effect, holds her head tightly, as if stricken with unbearable pain. When she hangs up, a satisfied expression covers her face. Apparently her mom bought the story, without a single question. Mission accomplished. The day just became our own.

I revisit my own attempt to fake a headache and stay home. Amateur, compared to Soraya's Oscar-worthy performance.

I feel for the pill in my pocket. Consider that each of us may have more than one viable future.

CHAPTER 31

When my receiver vibrates, I shut my eyes, hoping when I open them again, the message request is from Trigger. But it isn't. Henry's mug pops on my visual.

"Hey, Tana," Through his view, I see the inside of the weather lab. Notice the back of Trigger's sun-stained head, standing next to a turbine engine.

"Awkward," Henry states unnecessarily, sliding his windshield goggles over his eyes. "So my suddenly-silent friend over there tells me you guys want to blow this sandbox."

His view shifts to the whiteboard and in a blink, a super-sized projection of his face stares back at me. His voice turns deep and raspy, as if speaking through a ventilator. "You do want to go home, don't you?" In the next breath, however, he shifts philosophical. "Blame you not, I would, if you wanted to stay."

"Hey," Trigger twangs Henry on the ear. The footage streaming on the white board disappears.

"Nice," I say referring to his latest upgrade. "How did you..."

"Are you two through?" Trigger snaps. He marches to the workbench and begins to straighten Henry's cluttered equipment. "Because unless I'm missing something," he separates the beakers from the test tubes, "boosted piercings, fortune telling pills and special effects aren't going to get us back to Oklahoma."

Although pointless, I glare at Trigger's virtual image.

Buzzkill.

He's right about one thing, though; the pill's deadline clock is ticking.

"Back to Tulsa it is," Henry checks the timer winding down on Trigger's wrist. "Less than eight hours until sunset."

Scrambling like a man gone mad, Henry ricochets around the lab gathering supplies. Additional beakers, flare guns, glass tubes, and a dozen or so containers marked "liquid accelerant."

"You already know my assistant." He points at Trigger and murmurs, "Pretty face, but a little light in the IQ arena." He snorts twice. "Not even close to genius. If you know what I mean."

Expressionless, Trigger slugs his shoulder.

"Right, back to work. Let's see…" Henry reads the pen scribble on his palm. "First item on the to-do list— Steal one of security's satphones." Transcribing on the electronic white board, he assigns task number one to Trigger.

"Two," he shrugs as he reads the barely legible handwriting. "Get Tana." His eyes slant to his partner. "I'll put you in charge of yourself, T."

"Three, break into Hangar B," Henry pauses. "The hangar can only be accessed with a keycard, but once inside I'll need reinforcements." He sighs, clearly calculating best use of available resources. "Number three will be a team effort."

"What about the leaky fuel tanks?" I ask, assuming that's next on the list.

Henry and Trigger exchange a look. "Plug fuel leak," Henry writes in bold letters. "Still thinking on that."

The fifth and final item is obvious. Create a geomagnetic event. "This one is all me," Henry volunteers, and in no time at all, the storm maker moves from the board and ignites the turbine engine.

When the fan blades crank to maximum potential, a strong, sustained wind blows, creating a narrow funnel above Trigger's head.

He duck-walks a few feet and then squats beneath the gusty current. "Brace yourselves." Henry picks up a flare gun modified to hold a test tube of red-hot accelerant. "Enough of the tell. Time to show."

With no further explanation, a shot is fired.

Trigger jumps, I shudder, but when the liquid in the clear tube hits the air stream, an epic combustion occurs. First, a fiery flame ignites. Then, hundreds of colored particles collide, glowing in the shape of a candied ribbon. The neon lights ebb and flow, rippling like clean sheets on a clothesline. A second shot blasts and a hot flash lights the stream. Another curtain of lime-green afterglow appears.

"Off the charts, killer." Trigger springs to his feet, his torso now mingling in the first ever man-made aurora. Henry brings the flare barrel to his lips and blows the tip of his smoking heat gun.

I gulp.

"Unbelievable, man." Trigger jogs to his mentor's side and taps his fist.

When Henry attempts to return the celebratory gesture, he whiffs and unleashes another signature snort.

"But how?" I swallow the tension building in my throat.

Pushing his safety goggles up on his head, Henry cuts power to the wind machine. His eyes are wild and defiant. Pretty brilliant, even slightly appealing if you're into that sort of obscure, nerdy chemist kind of thing. Pioneer's future pill hit the target with Henry Aska Gu. This is living proof that he's becoming exactly what is destined.

Straightening his thick glasses, he scratches a dent in his helmet hair. "I reconfigured the gun to simulate the heat of a solar flare," he says, as if describing how to make a peanut butter sandwich. "After mimicking high altitude winds with the turbine, I injected an elixir of electrons and protons and KABOOM!" He waves his arms like a wizard casting a grand spell. "A geomagnetic storm."

"Wait." I intervene. "Yesterday you stood in this very lab and said creating a geo event was impossible. Not a chance, no way."

"That was before."

"Before what?" Trigger asks.

"I spoke to my counterpart at Bio Dynamics."

"Huh?" Again, Trigger says the very thing I'm thinking. Almost as if we are not just virtually linked, but have some other connection altogether. "Bio Dynamics?"

"Their tech specialists are buff," Henry grins with admiration. "Lending cranial muscle whenever I give them a call."

One mention, probably a coincidence. Twice is slightly suspicious, but three references to the biotech behemoth? *Uh oh.*

Now I need more information. "So you've worked with them before?" I ask over Pioneer's wireless.

"Anytime I'm stuck on a meteorological plateau. Their R&D has been integral to my thesis."

"You do realize Bio Dynamics paid for Dr. Harb's PhD?" Trigger fishes.

"Common knowledge." Henry shrugs. "Kind of a Cinderella story. Sad start. Happy ending."

"I'm not all that familiar with fairy tales, but I assume the happy part of the Harbs' ending meant opportunities at Pioneer?"

"Bio D is known for investing in its employees, Triggs." Henry starts to mix another batch of liquid storm enhancer for the flare gun. "Education, training and advancement. In return, they create a very loyal work force."

"How loyal?"

"Fiercely."

"Maybe even to the death?"

Death? Where's Trigger going with this?

With his eye protection back on, Henry carefully stirs the volatile fluid. "To the death? Not sure. But Dr. Harb owes a great debt—his career, his home, his daughter's invitation to the fast-track at Pioneer."

"Yes," I interject, now understanding what's Trigger's getting at.

Call me suspicious, but I can't help but wonder how loyal a man would be to a company that provided opportunities and security for his family. More importantly, what do corporations like Bio D expect in return?

Ugh. What am I thinking?

Disgusted, I shake my head. This is Soraya's father we're talking about. A hard-working man who still mourns the loss of a son. Isn't it entirely plausible that Dr. Harb feels a sense of duty to the company? Similar to the unwavering commitment Trigger pledges to the military, our country and his dad.

Not everyone has ulterior agendas, Tana.

Sticking to what I know for sure, I propose a more rational question. "How did Dr. Harb wind up here, when Bio D corporate headquarters are in London?"

The brilliant young scientist grips a steaming beaker with a pair of forceps and tilts his liquid concoction into a tray of test tube capsules. "Since the compass contract, Bio D's management has been heavily invested in the success of Pioneer."

"Invested how?" Trigger helps steady the tubes.

"They manufacture the future pill."

Trigger's hand flinches. The test tube tray jolts, allowing a few drops of propellant to splatter on the workbench and burst into flames.

"As a matter of fact…" Henry unhooks the chemical fire extinguisher from the wall and doses the blaze. Light flakes of fire-retardant foam float in the air. "The prototype of the pill nearly bankrupted Bio D. An undisclosed side effect caused seizures."

"Were they sued?" Trigger finds a sheet of the expanding chamois and tosses it on top of the smoldering foam.

"Ten deaths in the first year. Rumor is the company settled with the families."

If I want, I could attribute the thick bulge in my throat to the dry desert air. Or deny the fact that when I reach for a bottled water it is my intention to swallow its entire contents in one elongated gulp. But that would be a lie. Because whether he knows it or not, Henry just revealed a piece of the puzzle. Something, I suspect, that forever changes Trigger's perspective. And possibly mine.

"Anyway," Henry puts on heavy rubber gloves and then soaks the bench with water. He spins the turbofan blades to help the fire retardant evaporate. "The settlement agreement was all but signed when a consultant for the prosecutor, their mediator, was killed in an airplane accident."

What is he talking about?

Those court records were sealed. I know, because I used every one of my daughter-of-a-diplomat privileges to get them reopened. Then, as if fast-forwarded, my brain caught up with his words. Mediator. Airplane. No. Could it be…

My father?

Trigger coughs and reaches for some water.

"With the advocate for the families gone, the settlement agreement fell apart and Bio D was allowed to pay the families in private."

"The case was dismissed?" I choke out the words, realizing the answer.

"Dr. Harb's expert testimony was so convincing at the grand jury, they ruled there was not enough evidence to hold the company accountable without a reasonable doubt." Henry clamps giant forceps on the remaining beaker and carries it over to a HAZMAT cabinet. "After that, Dr. Harb and his family were transferred to Pioneer."

"That can't be true," I say, recalling that all my inquires were stonewalled. "Soraya's dad's testimony saved Bio D from bankruptcy?"

"It's in the court record."

"How did you..."

Breathe, trust facts, not emotion.

"Where are these records?" My lips quiver.

"Here, in Pioneer's library."

Trigger clears his throat and looks at Henry. He opts to divert. "Do you really think there was any connection between the pill and the seizures?"

Henry gazes into the hazy air. His head bobbles from side to side and finally, his neck centers. "All I know is that when the next generation of the pill was distributed there wasn't a single side effect." He raises a cautionary finger. "Did I forget to mention Dr. Harb was in charge of the entire second gen. pill production program?"

Predictably, Henry sticks to the facts. More likely, the case studies published by independent research companies. After all, the only thing you can really count on is science.

My nerves settle, and I breathe a huge sigh of relief, believing Henry's analytical conclusion.

It's the only thing that makes sense.

Regardless of the unexplained parallels between Bio Dynamics, Dr. Harb, and my father, there isn't any proof. Just a bunch of unfortunate coincidences that, if indulged, might appear to be a complicated web of conspiracy. From what I can tell, Dr. Harb is heroic, a survivor. A man willing to stand up for what is right at all costs.

A man just like my father.

CHAPTER 32

Stepping through the French doors outside Soraya's bedroom, I move across the wide balcony, lost in thoughts about my dad. Leaning against the sandstone railing, I smell the sweet fragrance of cacti flowers. I hear the sprinklers tick. See the snow-like shower appear as the wet spray hits the sun's beams. The late afternoon heat fizzles as our solar system's brightest star sinks closer to the horizon, leaving a rosy pink glow in its wake. Its vividness highlights every crevice of the campus town.

The dorms, academic buildings, and the "village," the section of the complex designed for residential homes, grocery stores, and restaurants. A mile-long block where the people who work at Pioneer actually live. The very street where Soraya and I ditched school and spent the day prospecting in a few well-stocked boutique shops.

Funny, I think, how it reminds me of my old signature color. Warm, optimistic, hopeful. All the characteristics I used to naturally emit.

A gentle breeze swirls and lifts the hem of my A-line sheath. Hibiscus pink. The dress Soraya convinced me is perfect for tonight's dance. I agreed, since it had pockets to hold my lip gloss and pepper spray. And I only put up a slight resistance when she insisted on the color. A choice I expected to wear uneasily, since I'm no longer that naive, lighthearted girl. *But I'm not a dark, angry person either. Maybe there's some way to be a little of both.*

I smooth the silky fabric and entertain the thought that emotions have nothing to do with clothing color. Behind me, the window shears billow, grazing my calves. A string of patina bells chime Soraya's mourning dove hymn.

I close my eyes and listen.

"Princess in a castle, right?" Soraya's voice comes from behind. "That's how I feel every time I stand here." With her hips pressed against the smooth rail, she waves like royalty addressing her court.

Oh, what the heck. I smile and then thrust a hand in the air. "Queen of a nerd herd."

A tiny yellow butterfly swoops down, flutters its wings and arcs whimsically in front of my face. I'm about to swat it with my royal fingers when a screech comes from Soraya's lips. "It's a sign."

"A sign?"

"The symbol of joy and sweetness."

I face Soraya and exhale out loud.

"Seriously," she says. "When a butterfly crosses your path, it's a reminder to stop taking everything so seriously. Express yourself by wearing colorful clothes," she tugs on my dress hem. "See, you're right on track."

"Is this from another one of Pioneer's special studies courses?" I say, shaking my head.

"No," Soraya giggles. "My Sitti—grandma—taught me animal speak. She was a healer in the village where we lived in Lebanon."

After looping an arm through mine, she turns my attention to the flitterbug. "It's time to break out of your cocoon, and in spite of your current challenges, hope is just around the corner."

Is it possible? Hope? Even for me? I look at Soraya and for some reason I believe her.

"This is so exciting, I feel like I could fly."

"So you're feeling better, are you?"

Startled, we both lift in the air.

The sound of two heavy soles stomps closer.

"Dad," Soraya squeals, and throws her hand to her chest. "You nearly scared us over the edge."

"Sorry, honey." Dr. Harb comes closer and wraps his arms tightly around his daughter. "Your mom called and said you were suffering through another migraine and asked me to come home and check on you."

I admire the ease with which the actress shifts into her role. "Luckily, my BFF shared her gran's home remedy and within an hour," Soraya snaps her fingers, "the headache was gone."

Dr. Harb glances at his daughter, forehead wrinkled, like perhaps there's more to the story. But when Soraya flashes her daddy's-little-girl grin, he seems to buy the iffy explanation.

"I guess we owe your friend a great debt of gratitude." He winks at me. Practically saying with his eyes that we'd keep her fib between us. "Let me guess, since you were feeling better, you went back to school and finished classes?"

Unable to maintain her cover, Soraya bursts out laughing. "Something like that." She lovingly hugs her dad.

"I'm sure you two enjoyed a free day," he says, and eyes the tag dangling from my dress. "Sora, can I talk to you for a second?"

"Sure, Dad." She brushes against my shoulder. "I'll be back in a minute. Go through the chest on my bureau and find earrings to match your outfit."

I nod, and before joining them inside I take one last glance at the spectacular view.

A yellow butterfly loop-de-loops and flies a low pass, grazing my chin.

"Hello there, fella," I say and trace its path with my index finger and then fill my lungs with the dry, feverish air. Exhaling slowly, I take in my surroundings. Peaceful. Calm. Absolutely perfect.

When the last wisp funnels through my lips, I split the shears and walk into my best friend's bedroom.

Thick Persian rugs tickle my bare feet. I see the lacquered jewelry box centered on the dressing table. The one, I assume, holding Soraya's earring collection.

Sitting on the silk, tufted chair, I crack the lid, and dozens of sparkly pairs glisten in the box. I pick through the pile, trying each style against my ear.

As I stare at my reflection in the oval mirror, I notice the back of a handcrafted picture frame propped behind the ornate box. I reach over and angle the plain wood mounting in order to see the snapshot. The image shows Soraya and her dad standing in front of a small airplane.

"London City Airport," reads the sign over their head. My chest clenches.

The same place Dad and I used to fly.

I study the terminal sign. Read it again. To make sure my eyes aren't playing tricks. They're not.

Bells chime. The wind blows. Window shears surge. A burst of light glimmers, reflecting a piece of metal buried against the side of the plush jeweled box. Frantically, I dig. Poke. Pinch. Burrow through the layered beads until I see which earring caught my attention.

I stop.

Every ounce of air punches from my lungs. I ease a hammered earring from the pile and see a very familiar cross dangling before my eyes.

An exact match to the pair I got for my fifteenth birthday.

"Did you find something?" My periphery catches Soraya's bubbly reflection. My hand twitches, and the cross I thought to be destroyed in the airplane explosion falls to the floor.

"Tana?"

I hear my name. Read confusion in Soraya's expression. Flushed with adrenaline, I scramble to my feet and dash across the carpet.

Sprinting, I spread my arms wide. Collide with her torso, tackling her to the floor. On her back, Soraya squirms beneath me.

"Liar, manipulator, deceiver, accomplice, cheat." I straddle her girth, hold her wrists in my hands and pin down my ex-friend's elbows with my knees.

"What are you doing?" she wails, her face terror-stricken. I could care less. She is about to get what she deserves. Jamming my knees further into her flesh, I reach for a lamp sitting on the floor.

"Stop!" A familiar voice screams from the doorway. I don't have to look to see who it is. I raise the metal shaft and dangle it over Soraya's head.

"I know what you did." I snap around, thick swag of bangs swinging, and I see Harb straddling the evidence. Footsteps rivet over the floor. His arms reaching for his daughter.

"STOP," I shout, the heavy lamp shaft wavering. "Or I'll hurt her like you hurt my father."

"Wa-it, please. Sora has no idea what I've done."

"So, you admit it," I growl, using my other hand to collar Soraya's neck.

"Noooooo." Harb thrusts towards me. I wind up and swing the metal shaft like a ball bat. Mid-stride, I crack his temple and his head whips back. Dazed, his knees buckle. He squats and holds his head.

A surge of fight fires and I tighten my grip on his daughter's throat.

"Where is Ed Stiles?" I scream as Dr. Harb comes to. I ratchet the lamp shaft again.

"Ed Stiles didn't kill your father," Harb bubbles. "I did."

Liar.

That's not possible. "I was there. Saw him set the bomb off with his cell."

"Such an observant girl. Have you considered that events oftentimes have more than one point of view?"

I move the hovering object closer to his daughter's head.

"All right, yes, your companion Eddie held up his end of the deal."

"What deal?" I seethe, resisting the urge to crush Soraya's skull.

"Providing the location and time you and your father would be at the airport in exchange for a very important piece of information."

"I knew it, that traitor." I inch my fingers further in Soraya's fleshy neck.

"Another emotional conclusion," he tsks. "I expected more of Benjamin Lyre's daughter. Ed Stiles was completely loyal to your father. When asked, he brokered the exchange of information."

"Don't even—"

"Your dad was going to lose against Bio Dynamics."

"I've got them backed into a corner, T." Dad's words echo. Eddie's follow. "*Your father won, made the drug company pay to the tune of billions.*"

"You're wrong, he beat them; he'd never lost a case."

"Miraculously, right? At the last minute?"

Forgotten memories surface, interrupting my train of thought: grueling hours, heated conversations, Dad absent from his seat at the table. *The break-ins...*

"Now who are the liars?" Harb taunts. "Think of the hundreds of comatose kids whose wasted lives would go unavenged. An unacceptable outcome for someone like your father. So he used every resource he had to get justice—both above-board and illegal."

"He would never..."

"Really? What wouldn't Benjamin Lyre do to settle a score? Your dad knew, Tana. Accepted that if he brought down a multibillion dollar company, he would pay with his life. When he got the proof he needed to win, he canceled his personal security detail and went to the airport."

I think back. I can't remember seeing any guards but Eddie.

No, no, no. Divert and avoid.

"I know what you're doing. Don't try to distract me with nonsense." A tsunami of tears washes down my cheeks. "If what you say is true, then why was Bio Dynamics never prosecuted?"

"Modest settlements were made, quietly, out of courts. Funny, despite his reputation, your dad was surprisingly naive, emotional, almost as if something about this case hit close to his heart." He looks at Soraya, flat on her back, skin purpling, flapping like a fish snagged in a net. "Benjamin Lyre belonged to a dying breed. One I admired. Wish I could have measured up to; but I couldn't. I had to look out for my family. I did what I had to do to get us here."

"My dad died for nothing." My voice vibrates with the same horror it did that day when I ran, full force, into the fury of ash and fire.

But I'm not there anymore. No longer stranded in the past. I'm here, alive and about to punish my dad's killer. I release the lampshade and it topples to the ground. With all my might, I clench both hands and strangle tighter.

"You ruined my life."

"I had no choice," Dr. Harb leaps and clamps on my shoulders, screaming in my ears. "If Bio D bankrupted, I would have lost everything."

Soraya's emerald eyes bulge. Their bright light dims.

He tries to yank me off his daughter. I spin and use a defensive combo Eddie taught me to escape the grips of a powerful man. Clasping the back of my head, pointed elbow in front of my face, I rhino Harb in the chest and thrust my free hand square into his windpipe.

Stunned, he coughs, clawing his neck, stumbling backward. Before he's out of arm's reach, I crack his nose with the butt of my hand. Now on autopilot, I slap his ear with my left, stomp on his foot and shove him down.

"He was everything to me." I reel, then fall back on Soraya and concentrate every ounce of pain I feel into this single act of vengeance. I lace my hands around her throat and wail, "And now I will take all that matters to you."

Dr. Harb scurries to his feet. He hurls his bulky frame forward. I feel his knuckles graze my skull, and I clench even tighter on his daughter's throat cords.

Helpless, he drops to his knees. "Please," he folds his hands in prayer. "I cannot lose another child." He sobs. "Can never forgive myself for the pain I've caused you. It was your dad or my family."

I'm not sure why, but tears track down my cheeks. Could it be the aftermath of a year of pent-up emotion? Or is it Dr. Harb's pathetic plea about loss and broken families? Confused, my mind runs a hypothetical. To what great lengths would my dad go to protect my mother and me? The answer comes fast and I lessen my grip, cringing. He'd go to the edges of earth. Even to the death.

"Believe me, I know." Dr. Harb's voice softens.

"You know nothing," I shout, grinding my teeth.

"If you take Sora, you will have your revenge. Pain and suffering will be inflicted on me. But remember her mother. Her friends. Their lives will be changed forever."

Almost as if summoned, my eyes draw to my gran's hammered cross laying on the floor. My heart pummels, a year's worth of anger pumping through my veins. "What's that, then? You sick, twisted trophy hoarder. A prize to give your daughter?"

"Not a trophy, a reminder," Harb touches his breast. "My heart never hardened enough to take a life lightly—thank goodness. Ever the curious cat, Soraya found your earrings. With Soraya I'm a weak man; I never could bear to say no to my daughter. Perhaps like your father."

"The plane, Tana, it's yours."

The ceiling seems to shrink, the walls close in. My attention returns to Soraya. Her red skin starved of oxygen. About to be another innocent victim of circumstance. This time, by my hand.

I can't.

As quickly as they'd gripped, my hands fall slack. I push to my feet and tilt back on my heels and climb unsteadily. The room seems to spin. Wobbling, I trip to the dresser. Swipe my future pill from the bureau and hurry through the doorway. Stumbling down a flight of winding stairs, I barge through the heavy wood door and run.

Blocks away, I'm still sprinting. As fast as my legs will carry me. I reach for the center of my receiver, touch Henry's bootleg speck of earth magnet, and open our private stream and discover that Henry's and Trigger's thumbnails are already active in the remote corners of my view. I touch my ear and at once, the visual enlarges and shows my friends' whereabouts.

CHAPTER 33

Hauling like a rocket, I round the block at the Harbs' home, kicking hard, mumbling every swear word I know.

Steps from the front door, I slow to a steady walk and straighten my shirt.

Bang, bang, bang.

I pound with a clenched fist. My heart thudding, testing the limits of my chest. When no one answers, I cock a hand and prepare to strike even harder.

Just before my hand hits, the door cracks open and Dr. Harb's murderous mug appears.

"Where's Tana?" I growl, my vision blurred. Otherwise, I would have known she was no longer there.

That witch Soraya peeks from behind her father, with splotchy marks on her neck. Bloodshot eyes. Cheeks stained with tears.

Sniffling, she says, "Tana's gone."

I can't even look at her. I drag my eyes over Dr. Harb. "It was you."

When Harb says nothing, I lose control. Feel the force of a missile build in my shoulder. I cock my arm and my fist flies forward. After grazing his cheek, my clenched hand collides with the door frame. Stucco pieces crumble.

I shift my focus back to Soraya. "Did you know?" I ask. "Tell me this whole BFF thing with Tana wasn't an act."

Soraya falls to her feet. Sobbing, she steps away from her dad.

"You cowards." My racing heart throbs. "Where did she go?" I grab Harb's shirt collar.

As if in severe pain, Soraya holds her stomach and chokes. "Don't know." Tears roll. She bawls.

Shut up.

Nose to nose, his shirt wadded in my hands, Dr. Harb says the very thing I think I've suspected all along. "They'll never let you leave here." His threatening tone makes him seem less like a remorseful man and more like a desperate killer.

"We'll see about that." I turn, hesitate, and then glance over my shoulder. "You'll never get away with this."

Harb smirks, "I already have."

Spinning, I rub my eyes and touch the upgrade on my receiver. "Tana? Where are you?"

Now able to see her view, I recognize the dirt road lined with tumbleweed and sagebrush.

The path I took last night to the airport with Henry.

My legs move swiftly beneath me, as if I'm gliding through the air. Down the Harbs' front walk, slowing only at the sound of Soraya's weak words. "Trigger— She has the future pill with her."

My thighs cramp. I skid to a stop. My eyes cast skyward, and I cry, "T, please don't."

CHAPTER 34

I run full bore. Non-stop from campus, through the desert, down the only road that leads to Pioneer's airfield. The place where this whole nightmare began. I'm not sure for how long.

Dad lied. Why did he lie?

All this time I blamed Eddie.

While processing what happened at Soraya's, I've lost track of time. The sun has set, dusk has come and gone, and the once clear sky is now cluttered with gray, gauzy clouds.

Arriving at the edge of the airport, my legs wasted with fatigue, I taper to a brisk walk, and track straight ahead. I know exactly where I'm headed.

Minutes later, I stand at the base of the beacon tower and stare up at the rotating light. Green and then white. The beam flashes across the otherwise dark airfield. When the light cycles again, my gaze drops to my sweaty palm. The powdered key to my future.

Time's up.

The decision deadline is long past. I latch onto the tower's metal ladder and climb.

I crawl up each narrow rung until reaching the maintenance platform and hoist myself to the catwalk. The alternating colors splash against my face.

I weigh my options.

Take the pill and move forward.

The beacon's grinding motor labors in the background.

Or go home and remain stuck in the past.

A rigorous gust blows. Goose bumps crawl across my bare legs.

My broken heart shatters to pieces. And for this reason, I make my decision.

"Show me my future."

My cupped hand moves to my mouth. My lips split and I stick out my tongue. With a quick snap of a wrist, the tiny white capsule passes between my teeth. I thrust my neck aft, securing it against the roof of my mouth.

I scale the remaining four rungs to the tower's second level. At the top, I turn backward and scoot up on the jungle-gym-style rails. With both hands gripped on the thin metal, I inch back and hang by my knees. Arch my spine, allowing my head to dangle freely in the wind.

Heat from the beacon's candelas scorch my thighs. The future pill's coating begins to dissolve. A rush of sugary flavors floods my mouth and every thumbnail in my view fuzzes. Lightheaded, my eyes slam shut.

My lids still closed, I find myself in a cavernous tunnel. Similar to a darkroom designed for developing print film. I hear a familiar sound. The gentle hum of giant propellers spinning in sync.

I'm on an airplane.

My senses scramble, and the sweet powdery taste on my palette is chased by a bitter bite. In a flash, I'm seated on a hard bench, tightly secured by canvas harnesses. Straps and loose buckles clang noisily against the exposed steel airframe.

Looking down, I notice my hands. Thinner, wrinkled, covered with protruding blue-purple veins.

I'm older.

My skin has aged beyond my current years. Disoriented, I touch the heavy helmet squeezing against my skull. Listen over the intercom as voices speak a variety of languages, most of which I understand. Dim, red aviation lights shine over army-green walls, affording me a look into the cockpit. Up front, I see two pilots wearing oxygen masks.

A loud thud jolts, and the back of the heavy transport plane opens like the mouth of a mighty gray whale. Freezing air rushes the cargo bay, but I don't feel cold. I pinch my legs. Discover that they're covered in synthetic black fabric, the thickness resembling a scuba diver's wet suit. Once the cargo door extends, a motor grinds, locking it into place.

In my helmet, a single garbled voice rings louder than the others. I recognize the dialect.

Church Slavonic. A language I somehow understand.

Turning to the cockpit, the man in the right seat signals a thumbs-up. Without further communication, I release the five-point harness and face the back of the plane. I stand tall and tighten the parachute attached to my back. Adjust the night-vision visor and consult an oversized, chunky altitude watch.

After two clearing breaths, I lunge back into a sprinter's stance, raise a bent elbow, drop my chin to my chest. As if a starting gun fires, I push off a heel and stride to the opening. At the end of the platform, I plant both feet, half-twist in the air, stretch both arms over my head and dive, headfirst into the darkness.

A cyclone of air pelts my second skin. Just beginning to enjoy the thrill of knifing through the air, I hear the echo of Trigger's voice. "Come on, T, this isn't the way out."

From the darkness I feel two fleshy hooks grapple around my waist.

My body separates from the monkey bar railing and eases down onto serrated grates. I sense him try to spread my eyelids. Heavy, they remain shut. He must be lifting me to his chest, because muscular pecs brush against my back. Bear hugging beneath my ribcage, I feel him close a hand around a fist and up-thrust against my sternum.

My body contracts.

I lie still.

Please just let me be.

He bears down a second time.

After the third hefty compression, my chest convulses. My throat flexes, and when he executes one final thrust, my eyes pop open and a soggy white pill shoots from my lips. The unabsorbed powder from the broken capsule sprinkles white dust into the moist air.

My head falls forward. I cough. Spit. Raise my chin to see a ratty eye patch.

CHAPTER 35

"You don't belong here." Chief McDunney barks, tightening his hold on my waist. "Do you have any idea how many families would donate an organ to have their kid on the candidate roster?"

The stench of rotten eggs drifts up my nose.

"You were legacy, missy. Your dad graduated top of his class. But *nooo,* the mighty Linnea Lyre thought her daughter was too good for Pioneer." He grunts. "Yet here we are."

Dad went where... and Mom knew what?

"Stupid girl," The chief pries my jaw open and swipes the inside of my mouth with a bent, calloused finger. "What did you see?" He shakes my limp limbs.

Groggy, my eyes shoot around, still uncertain of my surroundings. The air is still. Overhead, thin clouds dissipate.

I touch my thighs and pinch. *Bare.*

"How long was the pill in your mouth?" McDunney asks.

Heavy, my eyelids flutter. My body stirs. I pat at my head with both hands, expecting to feel a helmet. When my fingers sink into wavy strands, my eyebrows draw together. Squinting, I try to recall. "I saw..."

"You saw what?"

A streak of fear rips through my body. I shudder. The chief steadies my shoulders.

"Nothing," I snap and stare into the cloudless sky.

"Over here," McDunney's number two shouts from below. He shines a flashlight and I crane my neck to see his team spread in a grid pattern. The chief and I raise together, me locked against his hip.

"Sir," he says, and then wedges his flashlight in his teeth. He kneels, and searches the dry ground with both hands. Sifting through the sand, a loose, jagged piece pokes through his fingers.

"Found something." He narrows the light beam, revealing a crushed capsule. "A future pill, sir." The guard stands at attention. "Or at least what's left of one."

Ka-boom.

A shotgun sound fires, sending us both to our knees.

Sha-boom.

A second noise blasts across the airfield. We pancake. McDunney commando-crawls over the narrow metal grate, dragging me with him. He crouches behind the base of the beacon, touches his lobe and says, "Round it up. Storm's coming. Reroute all teams to Hangar B. Trigger Flough is about to run."

CHAPTER 36

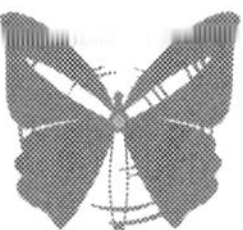

Laying flat, hands bound behind my back, I'm trapped beneath the canvas cover stretched over the trunk area of McDunney's Jeep.

Where are they taking me?

My chest pounds, breaths shorten, teetering on the edge of a full panic attack.

Think, Lyre. How can you get free? My mind goes back to the compound break-ins.

I need a weapon. Something sharp enough to cut a hole in the tarp overhead.

No purse, no cargo pants. I take mental inventory recalling I traded my regular garb for a silk sheath.

What was I thinking?

I bicycle my knees until the dress bunches up near my waist. I twist on a side to better position my hands to search my pockets. *Mini hand sanitizer, lip gloss, pepper spray.* Nothing with a blade or ragged edge. After another quick pat-down, I realize that's all I have.

I shiver.

Don't give up, Tana. Toss the net wider—check your surroundings. Wait.

I wiggle across the metal floor until I butt up against rubber. A spare tire. I allow myself to hope, if only for a second: *Where there's a spare, there's a tire iron.* Inching like a worm, I touch every bit of the covered space with my feet. Crossing fingers that before completing a full circle, I will kick something solid and metal.

I'm not that lucky. After one complete rotation, my heart beats faster, aware that my chances of escape are nearly nonexistent.

Try one more time.

My subconscious rallies on, and I wiggle closer to the Jeep's frame for a better angle to reach every crevice and corner. I'm about halfway when my toe hits something small and round. Definitely round—because whatever it is rolls away across the floor. I spin faster, the soles of my boots running along the inside edge until the paper tube hits my nose.

" 'Tire repair kit,' " I read from the label. " 'For all rubber repairs. Container includes: A set of cut-to-size patches and a single-use tube of rubber cement.' " I sigh. "You have got to be kidding me."

Hopeless, I roll flat on my back. *Don't waste resources. Be creative, Tana. Use your noodle.* Eddie used to coach me on resourcefulness. *Even the simplest items can be repurposed.*

I twist my neck to the seemingly useless patch kit and blow bangs from my eyes. "All right, I'll take it with me." I thrust my hips in the air and allow the cylinder to drift to my hands. Curl my knees to my chest and stuff the tube, shaped like a travel-size toothpaste, in my pocket. I want to *make* a hole, not patch one up. Speaking of holes…

With my body 180 degrees from where the chief set me in the Jeep, I notice a glint: a flash of green light. Then a white one.

The beacon tower.

I crunch my abs, lifting my torso enough to match an eye to a tiny tear in the canvas. From the slit, I see the star cluster of Orion's Belt. Confirmation that we're traveling southward, towards the hangar complex.

"Storm Chaser, this is the Weatherman, over."

Henry? Although garbled, I hear Henry's words crackle over our private stream. The first sound I've heard since loosing contact on the tower catwalk.

I exhale. “Guys, it’s me,” I tap my piercing against the cold steel floor. “I’m in trouble.” I blink my eyes, but still nothing appears on my visual.

“Storm Chaser here,” Trigger responds.

“Cold front is approaching, nine o’clock. I’m hacking the security stream now.”

“Henry, Trigger, can you hear me? It’s Tana. I’m with McDunney. Not by choice. I’m being held prisoner. Over.”

Dead air looms.

Then I hear Trigger. “I feel the pressure rising.”

“Roger, Storm Chaser. Twist the upgrade ninety degrees to increase range in order to pick up security’s position.”

I flounder like a fish. Trying to cock my add-on without the use of my hands. My view remains the same and I press my ear harder to the floor. I still only see through my view.

“Come on, you piece of junk magnet,” I say and give the ragged disc one last crack. Henry, Trigger and McDunney’s visuals pop up on my view.

Yes.

“Hey, you two—missing anyone?” I ask.

Again no reply. As I watch all three streams at once, I conclude the connection is one-sided.

“Time to make like turbulence and bounce,” Henry transmits. “Operation Get Out of the Sandbox initiated. Weatherman over and out.”

“Meet you at the rendezvous in five.” Trigger creeps down hangar row.

CHAPTER 37

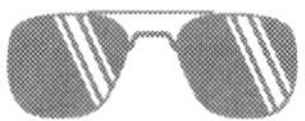

I press flat against the hangar wall, shuffling my feet over the asphalt until I find a big enough rock. When my ankle rolls over I squat, pick up the loose stone and then whip it at Hangar B's security light. The rock smashes glass, and the narrow space goes dark.

I continue to shimmy along the wavy steel wall until reaching its side door. The exact spot where McDunney rushed me earlier.

Rotten breath, clammy meat-cleaver hands. Snapshots of hours earlier flash like strobes. I start to sweat. *That will never happen again. I won't let it.* My jittery hand jiggles the door knob. Still locked. Crap. *I thought we'd get lucky. I know better.*

A hinge creaks, and from across the narrow corridor between buildings, Henry barges through Hangar A's ramp door.

"The Weatherman has the solution." The weight of the huge pack on his back shifts, knocking him off balance.

"Right on time." I steady Henry's arm. Once stable, he lowers his pack on the ground and pushes his night vision goggles back on his head. "Where's Tana?"

"Isn't she with you? Before I lost her visual she was on her way to the airfield." I feel sweat trickling down my forehead. "If separated, she knows the plan is to meet at the plane. I just assumed…" *Divert and avoid.* "I assumed she would do what I would." *Do everything in her power to get out of here.*

Wipers swipe across Henry's goggles and he sniffs the misty air. "Something's wrong."

"Tana's missing." I say, my finger-tapping on my receiver. "Tana Lyre."

"That, but the humidity shouldn't be rising." A burst of wind blows and the air temperature drops.

"It's not you?" I ask, referring to the shift in weather.

The gusts blow stronger.

"Not me, not yet," Henry's four eyes show concern.

"Get us in the hangar and I'll keep trying Tana."

Henry digs through the expandable pack and pulls out a Pioneer access card.

"Professor Gu," Trigger reads off the ID. "Your dad's?"

The weatherman's mouth curls. "I've got some catching up to do." He hurries over and waves his dad's electronic key over Hangar B's lock scanner. A green light shines and the deadbolt cycles open.

"We're in." Henry snorts and enters a six-digit access code. The box beeps twice and the lights click on. A yellow-green hue shines on the glossy white floor.

"You open the main door and I'll find our bird." I splinter towards the rows of parked planes and Henry bee-lines for the door's motor.

"Hey, Gu," I say and jog back towards Henry. His eyes are fixed on a speck of dust on the otherwise perfectly polished floor. At his side, I tighten the heavy pack over his shoulders. Straighten his workman's utility belt, equipped with every weather-measuring device he could carry. Then rest a hand on his shoulder. "You, my friend, are all right."

Henry's chest swells, but a second later, a frown cracks his bold facade. He raises his eyes to mine. "Think we'll ever see each other again?"

I press my lips together, but can't resist the urge to grin. "I have friends all over the globe. If there is anyone who can find a way to get us together, you can."

Henry's confident posture returns. He lifts a sealed plastic jar from his pocket, shakes the single pill inside the amber-colored container. "In case," he offers.

I take the tinted plastic, raise it to the light and see my unused pill. I look at Henry.

"Maybe someday you'll want to know if our paths cross again."

I clasp Henry's shoulder and bury the answer deep in my cargo pocket.

Henry stiffens. Adjusts his goggles to the night vision setting. He licks a finger and holds it in the air. "Feel that?"

I laugh, catching on to what he's getting at. "Feels like a little gumption building in the air."

As prepared as a special forces unit, Henry pats his gear. "Sayonara," he salutes and struts at the hangar door.

"Cessna. Mooney. Beechcraft," I jog past rows of single-engine planes.

"Whoa," I slide to a stop. Lose my breath. My hand flies over my heart. The entire back of the hangar is lined with the WXP 5 cloud-seeding drones. I count at least a hundred. How many tsunamis, hurricanes or tornados happen every year? Way less than the number of drones parked here.

If they're not all being used for seeding, then what?

CHAPTER 38

In the back of the Jeep, tires screech to a stop.

I release my cramped stomach muscles and walk the sidewalls until I'm lying as McDunney left me.

The engine quits. I hear footsteps.

Hand sanitizer, pepper spray, and a tire repair kit. I take mental inventory of my available resources.

The tarp peels off.

Leaning over the frame, Number One and Number Two lift my crouched body from the floor. Once clear of the Jeep's frame, they tilt me upright and recheck that my hands are secure.

McDunney approaches, squats, and hurls me over a solid shoulder. He shifts his weight and stomps over the tarmac.

Onscreen, I see Trigger climb on the wing of a prop plane and scour the rows of aircraft for our bird. Leaping from the wing walk, he hauls, full speed, toward the red and black tail.

The chief slows, lowers my feet to the ramp. He hooks his bulging biceps around my neck and lurks in the shadow beneath Hangar B's roof overhang.

On the right side of my screen, I see Henry at the control box. Fingers inches from the dial.

"Don't!" I belt.

McDunney's hand slaps over my mouth.

The weatherman hits the green button and the door motors open.

When the gap is wide enough to clear our plane's wings, Henry releases the power button. He leans over the threshold and twists his head to check the tarmac.

Like a hunting tiger, McDunney surges, ambushing from around the corner.

"Trigger," I shout.

Pioneer's muscle blocks the exit. Me in one hand, Henry in the other.

"What's it going to be, Mr. Flough?"

Without hesitating, Trigger shows both palms and then climbs from the cockpit. "Let them go," he offers before McDunney insists. "I'm the one you really want." He steadily walks ahead.

Never get caught alone with McDunney. The chief was in prison. He's a perv.

"No, Trigger, don't. Who knows… *what he's done…* what he'll do with you."

McDunney sneers.

Trigger steps outside the hangar, stops a foot away, and hooks his thumbs on his belt loops.

"Let her go." He stands solid as a steel post.

McDunney wedges his hands up my shirt and brushes both breasts. After licking his lips, he hurls me into Trigger.

"Dirt bag," I grunt.

With my cheek against the sky surfer's pecs, he drapes a comforting arm across my back. Snuggled against his chest, I hear his heart pounding.

"You okay?" he asks.

My eyes meet his. I nod.

He bends to get something from his pocket. A second later I hear a sharp *snap, pop,* and feel my hands free behind my back.

Separating, he closes the pocketknife. Touches my neck and whispers, "Go get the plane ready."

"Got it," I say, lost in his ocean blues.

"Now," he shoves me away and I sprint to the opened gull door. About to climb on the left wing, a glint of light reflects off the floor. I squat to see two fuel puddles beneath either wing. I sag back on my heels. *We're never getting out of here.*

"Tana…" Trigger yells, his voice unsteady.

Resources? I scan around, searching for something to plug the leaks. The floor is immaculate, with not as much as a single speck of dust. *Great, now what?* I stuff my balled hands in my dress and punch my thighs. *Hand sanitizer, lip gloss, pepper spray and…* My fingers sift through the hidden pockets. *A tire patch kit.*

I yank out the tiny cylinder, tilt on all fours and crawl to the source of the drips. Flip the top off and dump the contents between my knees; a sheet of thumb-size rubber strips and single use tube of rubber cement.

I've got this.

I twist the lid off the glue and puncture the seal. Tear off a square size patch and feel the bottom of the wing for the source of the leak. A drip hits my scalp and I look up to see the source, then peel the sticky back off the rubber strip. I glob on some cement and cover the hole the size of a pinhead. I hold it in place for a count of ten, and then let go. The patch falls to the floor.

You have got to be kidding me. I knock my head. My entire body trembles. Tears fill my eyes. *Stop crying.* I brush away the dampness. Push to stand, and my foot kicks the kit's serrated lid. "*Rough up the surface before you add another layer, Tana.*" Dad's words emerge from my subconscious. "*If you want the carbon fibers to stick.*" That's right, when we were building the wing we needed to sand first.

I swipe the cheese grater lid and scrape it back and forth, roughing up the paint surrounding the pinhole. Rip another rubber square and squeeze out a drop of cement. I thrust the patch to the wing's underside, shut my eyes and press as hard as I can. Slowly, I let go, open an eye, and see my make-shift fuel plug hold. *Yes!* I stand and smack my head on the wing, scurry to the opposite side and fasten another patch.

I run around the propeller, jump on the wing walk and swing into the pilot's seat.

I grab the ignition key, grip the throttle. My heart pounding like a marching band.

I can't do this. My confidence wavers.

I bend my leg over the center control console, and scoot comfortably in the right seat. "Before starting engines checklist," I stammer in my student pilot voice. "Fuel—full rich, throttle—cracked one quarter, engine start."

After completing the last line item, my arms freeze. My brain scrambles searching for some sort of motivational chant. But no pre-game one-liner comes to mind.

"I can do this." I repeat the old standby, even though I don't believe it. Not a bit.

Paralyzed, I stare through the windshield.

"I'll deal with you later," McDunney taunts and releases Henry's elbow. The weatherman scurries across the ramp and disappears into a retention ditch.

The chief turns to Trigger. "Held up my end, and now, I'll claim my prize." He curls a crooked finger. "Come to me, Mr. Flough."

"Tana, start the engine." Trigger hollers and then plows head first into the chief's midsection.

McDunney's arms swim and then lock around Trigger's svelte frame. The chief squeezes, Trigger wiggles, shimmying like a crocodile until he fights his way free. Settling into in a wrestler's squat, Trigger flattens his palms, feet shuffling, and just before the chief gets within arm's reach he fakes to the right; stutter-steps in place and then spins like a top. Corkscrewing, he winds by his oversized opponent, unraveling only to snatch something from McDunney's belt.

By the time the chief realizes what hit him, Trigger's tight funnel blows past and shoots crosswise on the ramp toward a parked tug.

The chief swipes at his utility belt to discover his satphone missing.

"We have an outside line." Trigger grins. The smile disappears, though, as his ankle twists. Tripping, he falls forward. The phone slips from his grip, bounces once and rolls into the sagebrush.

Off-balance, his body crashes onto the tug. He claws his way to the steering wheel and hoists himself up to the driver's seat. Trigger flips the ignition key and shifts the tractor-like machine into low gear.

"Oh, no." Henry's head pops from the berm. A fuzzy halo settles around the ramp lights. Henry grabs a portable barometer from his waist and thrusts it up amidst the moisture. When the mercury settles, he reads off two numbers. "The temperature and dew point spread are less than five degrees apart."

"Hurry," I yell, understanding why he's concerned. At the edge of the airport, a dense fog layer builds.

"Not a chance, Dad. Not this time." Henry jumps to his feet and holsters his measuring equipment. "I won't let you win."

He beelines and borrows a Jeep.

Circling the chief, headlights approach from every direction. With too many to count, Trigger points his tug to the narrow lights in the center.

"Ah, Tana…"

CHAPTER 39

Crank the engine.

I remain frozen. "Dad, please, help me…"

Quivering, I bite down on my lower lip, recalling what Dr. Harb said. Empty words, broken promises, my father's righteous legacy.

Revving their engines, the line of Jeeps move closer. I see Trigger idling, perched on the tug, expecting that at any second I'll come shooting through the door.

He did his part; now it's my turn.

I collar the black throttle handle and curl rigid fingers around the yoke.

"Please." I set my sights on the sky. "One last time. Get me through this. Then I promise…"

"Girls your age can do anything, Tana," Reassuring words seem to whisk in with the wind. *"You have choices, resources. All you have to do is step up and take them."*

Can it be?

I recognize the voice. Not Dad's or even Eddie's.

She wasn't lecturing. I see that now. They were honest and loving words. That—unbelievably—came from my mother.

Have I had it wrong all along? Did my self-reliance, determination, and even my defiant streak come not from Dad, but from my mother?

Tears spill down my cheeks, wishing I could tell her how sorry I am. But I already know what she would say. "Stop making excuses and kick it into high gear."

On it, Mom.

Envisioning her fiery spirit, I hunker down on the seatbelt, check over both shoulders and shout, "Clear."

The ignition fires, the starter cranks, and when the prop turns over I waste no time advancing the throttle. Clearing the other airplanes, I jam in the power and launch through the split hangar door.

Once the main wheels reconnect with the ramp, I taxi to Trigger's side and face the looming stand-off. At the opposite end of the ramp, McDunney and the security convoy hold a tight line.

My partner, seated on the clumsy ramrod tractor, pretends to wipe a swag of sweat from his forehead.

"Nice of you to join me," Trigger cracks a smile and then focuses on the caravan.

"Double or nothing, right?" I reply.

Like clockwork, a second flare rockets through the air. A spray of neon showers the looming fog bank. I glance at the sky and see the green aura begin to appear.

"Now." Trigger stomps his foot to the floor and steers the tug straight at the center Jeep. Number Two follows suit. Head to head, they tear toward one another.

McDunney's driver holds steady, his turbo-charged engine rumbling with the power of 350 horses.

The gap between the two vehicles narrows. Neither driver shows signs of blinking. In trail, I jockey the rudder pedals and chase closely behind the tug. Both vehicles rattle and squeal. Labor and vibrate. Tracking an unwavering course straight ahead.

A second before impact, Trigger stands, throws his arms in the air and leaps from the driver's seat.

Hitting the ground, he barrel-rolls down the side of a ditch. His tug, however, continues ahead, smacking McDunney's vehicle dead center. Security's Jeep lifts into the air, flips on its side, and glides across the ramp, spinning in a circle.

As all four men dangle from their seat belts, the remainder of the convoy splits, one Jeep breaking formation to rescue their leader. The final three arrow relentlessly in my direction.

Off in the distance, a hollow shot fires. From up on the mesa, a blazing red flare bursts through the fuzzy air. Neon lights spark.

Henry Aska Gu strikes back.

CHAPTER 40

"I'm owning it," Henry's thumbnail moves to the front of my view.

As expected, the protons and electrons he fired combust like a green glow stick. Again, he drops to one knee and piston-pumps his arm. Although it's a success on his end, his dad's overpowering fog hinders further development of the storm. No geomagnetic activity equals no energy to activate the compass, leaving us with no accelerated portal to get back to Tulsa.

Henry retrieves night vision goggles from his pack and sprawls out, GI Joe-style, on the gritty ground. From his makeshift command center, the very spot he and Trigger staked out the night before, he has a clear view of the entire airfield. The synthetic smoke screen, the crown jewel of his dad's research, rolls over the mesa, threatening to obscure his view.

"Think," I hear Henry say to himself. "What busts up fog?" He runs the eye wipers and mouths out the possible solutions. After a few minutes of calculating, he blurts, "Eureka."

Kneeling, he spins his workman's belt around his narrow hips. "We need to warm the air just above the ground."

He reaches for the second-to-last flare, appearing confident the custom design packs the heat required. Leaning on a heel, he adjusts his ear protection, grips the gun butt with both hands and unleashes a fiery blast at the center of the airport.

The gray sky lights. A stream of blazing rays cuts through the fog and heats the desert soil. Layer after wispy layer, the opaque bank dissolves.

Henry hops to his feet and pounds his chest. "Ha." He releases a roar worthy of a jungle king. "How's that for a little gumption, Dad?" Henry pounds his breast. Then, like any science purist, he starts to collect data.

As the fog clears, I'm able to see McDunney's Jeep on its side in the ditch. With the chief's remaining crew in rescue mode, I pop the cockpit door, motor down the taxiway and search for Trigger.

In less time than you can say supercell, the security squad commandeers their vehicles and resumes the pursuit.

"Looks like you could use a hand, T." Henry scrambles to his feet, dumps his backpack, and searches through the contents. He discards the measuring instrument and the to-go cups filled with cloud seeding concoctions, and then he finds what he's looking for.

"A bullhorn and a chamois?" I twist over a shoulder to see the Jeeps gaining. "That's what's going to save us?"

Activating the emergency horn causes a screeching siren to vibrate through the air. After that, I need no further explanation. Everyone on the ramp cringes and covers their ears.

At that moment I notice a pair of hands reaching over the side of the sand berm. A head pokes up and scans the immediate area, to make sure, I think, the guards are distracted by blocking the nerve-shattering sound.

They are.

Seizing the tiny window of opportunity, Trigger springs to his feet, running parallel to the taxiway.

I catch his awkward trot and tap the plane's brakes, slowing to no faster than a brisk walk. As his shoulder parallels the wingtip, I hold steady, and with one final burst, he dives and belly-flops across the slick surface. Crashing against the door opening, he transitions onto his feet and then ducks into the cockpit. All in one motion he latches the door, adjusts his headset, powers the pressure seal and connects his seat belt.

Now securely inside, Trigger looks out the back window and sees the remaining Jeeps tracking like heat-seeking missiles. He pushes the mike to his lips.

"What are you waiting for?"

Jamming the throttle, I speed down the taxiway.

CHAPTER 41

"Check your six," I warn over the stream.

The hairs on my neck spike. I sense the three Jeeps getting closer.

"Hit the gas, Tana," I shout.

She shoves the power lever to the panel.

The plane accelerates further, lifting the nose wheel from the ground.

"Golden," I say over the intercom.

As we shift onto the main wheels, I fasten the knee board to my thigh. I skim the before-takeoff items and then toss the to-do list in the backseat.

"Two bogies, nine and three o'clock," Henry reports, like an air traffic controller. With the benefit of his view, I can see the Jeeps drafting along each wingtip.

I recheck the door lock, lean forward and point at the end of the runway. "Ready for takeoff?"

"Ready? Me?" Tana stammers.

With no time for second-guessing, I take the yoke. "I have the controls."

"You have the controls," she says. Probably disappointed. Or relieved? I can't tell.

I feel her foot pressure leave the rudder pedals and notice her shoulders slump forward. Definitely disappointed.

With no time to waste, I cram the right rudder pedal to the floor. The tires squeal. The airplane angles off the paved surface and cuts across the rugged brush.

"Hold on," I say as we jerk and bounce.

"Off-roading?" Tana asks. From my periphery, I see her clench her shoulder straps.

"A straight line is the fastest way between two points."

"Remind me if we get home to swap to all-terrain tires."

After one final jostle, we climb back onto the pavement. Tearing over the painted threshold markers, I spin and align the propeller with the center of the runway.

Coming about, all three Jeeps split and speed partway down the pavement. Crossing the three thousand feet markers, they park bumper to bumper, forming a barricade. Blocking our departure.

"Operation geomagnetic storm, phase three," Henry clicks his mouth like a walkie-talkie. I see him shoot the final flare in the air.

That's the signal.

I shove the throttle full forward and steer the plane down the asphalt like a sprinter vying for Olympic gold.

"One thousand feet," Henry reads the distance markers.

I use forward pressure on the yoke, holding the nose wheel down to build more speed.

"Two thousand feet."

The second marker flies by. The guards and their impenetrable roadblock grow larger on the windscreen.

"Twenty-two hundred."

I hawk our speed. *Only ten more knots.*

"Twenty-four… twenty-five…" Henry reports.

High beams from the vehicles blind. I glance off to the side.

"Twenty-six, twenty-seven, twenty-eight hundred feet."

I hold my breath.

"Eighty knots." Blow out. Yank back on the stick.

The plane lifts in the air. Our tires bump the spotlights on top of the row bars.

"Hoorah!" Henry cheers as we climb beyond reach of the chief's blockade.

I suck up the landing gear, and like a freed bird, our homebuilt soars through the night sky.

"We did it," I crank my head around to see McDunney's crew, fists air-punching.

"Was there ever any doubt?" Tana asks, pinching my arm.

I smile my best jet-jock grin.

She utters a pretend walkie click, since we're still connected to the in-skull network. *Although not for much longer.* Approaching the limits of Pioneer's jamming net, I'm sure we'll lose contact.

"Love you, Weatherman," Tana yells, to be sure to be heard over my transmitter.

"Shucks." I imagine Henry's face flushing red.

"Think I'm losing you…" the weatherman adds. "…*crackle, buzz, crackle.* Can you hear me now?"

Tana smiles wide. "The geomagnetic storm is brewing."

I bank ninety degrees, turning due east, towards the wild prism of the northern lights.

"Weatherman, I don't know how to thank you," I say to our friend on the ground.

"No worries, Triggs, I'll collect the next time we see each other."

An awkward silence settles. The sort of quiet that occurs when something is said that can't possibly be true and no one wants to admit it.

While the three of us struggle thinking of what to say next, my screen splits and I see a terror appear on the boosted security feed. McDunney's sightline comes into focus. He appears to be scaling the mesa. A third stream joins. Number Two is on the trail, less than a step behind.

"Henry," I holler. "Behind you."

"Dirt alert," our friend utters. At once, his eyes drop. Through the static I see Henry reach for his hip, retrieving the camouflage chamois. He fans the cloth in front of him and then stretches it over his body. His view goes dark.

"Where is he?" the chief crests the slope, huffing. His view pans around—sagebrush, sand, and piles of red rock. No sign of Henry. I'm guessing he pancaked, his desert camo print blending perfectly with the rocky terrain.

Number Two hurries forward, shuffling his feet over the grainy surface. He drags his boot sole like a backhoe clearing land. In the top corner of my view, I see a bit of earth shudder. I squint, now knowing where to look. Amongst the rocks, the outline of Henry's covered body becomes visible.

"Lie still," I whisper over the stream, even though our private band is secure.

Number Two approaches the seam of Henry's cover.

I trap the air in my lungs.

He shuffles closer.

Tightening my grip on the stick, I ready to turn back and help.

Number Two's boot hovers on the edge of the camo fabric, thick treads about to crush what is likely Henry's hand, when McDunney whistles. "Bring it in. We're wasting time."

Number Two teeters on a chunky heel, centimeters away from striking gold. "Thought we had him cornered, sir."

McDunney's gaze drifts over to his second. Lifts his patch and rubs a cloudy eye. "Clever kids. Resourceful." He touches the empty holster where his satphone used to hang.

"No excuses, sir." Number Two stands straight. "I take full responsibility."

The chief reaches over and clasps his subordinate's shoulder. "Relax, Sam." He retrieves a tiny silicone compass card from his pocket and holds it in front of both of them. "We'll deal with Henry Aska Gu later. But more importantly, Trigger Flough will never find his way back to Pioneer."

With that, McDunney and Number Two fall back and descend down the mesa.

"All clear, guys." The chamois floats to the ground. His view lights again and he acts as if he hasn't heard the chief's threat. "Go commit aviation. Weatherman, your flag carrier, your friend, over and out."

"Watch out for yourself, Henry." A sinking feeling settles as I realize we're leaving Henry alone. "Steer clear of McDunney—at all costs."

Reluctantly, I walkie click my tongue twice. Swallow and point the nose straight into the eye of the storm.

CHAPTER 42

There's no doubt which way leads home.

Ahead, the geomagnetic monstrosity grows as a transport portal forms deep within its core, surrounded by the serene shower of effervescent light. Regardless of the imminent danger, the lightning, power loss and treacherous turbulence, turning back is no longer an option.

"Piece of pie," Trigger says with his everything's-a-molehill perspective. "All we have to do is fly into the aurora, pick our way through the magnetic activity, fight to hold level, and stay awake."

He shrugs as if the monumental challenge blocking our path is just another training exercise.

I keep quiet. Think of my tire patches. Not feeling so optimistic.

"I'll admit…" Trigger glances at the streaks of heat lightning veining through the aurora's colored ribbon. "It's more like a mound of carrot cake."

In short order, the propeller pulls our plane past the majestic northern lights into rougher air.

"Here comes the turbulence."

Trigger begins to wrestle with the control stick. The wings level for a second. Then, the plane pitches and rolls like that rickety dinghy hopelessly traversing ten-foot swells. Every piston in the engine hammers harder. All the brilliant colors of the spectacular light show blur as our bird porpoises, slicing hash marks in the developing overcast.

Scared, I lock my eyes to the instrument panel.

Ragged clouds cover the wings and an opaque film molts over the windows, blocking any visual references of up or down. Hypervigilant, Trigger scans the instrument panel. Orientated solely by the directions on the digital screens.

A massive bolt of lightning thrashes and lights the muted sky. The electronics in the cockpit dim. Burn bright. Blink one more time. Then go black.

"Power's out," I steady my voice, remembering that we experienced the same malfunction two nights ago. The joyride. The unexpected flight that catapulted us to Pioneer. Not quite calm, but far from hysterical, I twist on my mini-flashlight, and shine the narrow beam a few inches above the panel to highlight the floating card on the antique magnetic compass.

When the indicator settles in the fluid-filled case, I call, "Heading 090."

Another updraft lifts the fuselage and sloshes the viscous fluid. The direction card bobs like a buoy, resembling the answer window on a temperamental Magic 8 Ball.

"Roger." Trigger has barely uttered the confirmation when a pothole pocket of turbulence spikes the plane toward the ground.

A blot of lightning strikes the wing. A spark skates across the leading edge and burns a hole in the cabin door.

The panel momentarily lights and Trigger reaches for the radio. His hand jerks as a shock jolts. His body spasms and collapses against his seat straps. The left wing dips. Nose sinks into a shallow dive.

"No, no, no," I belt over the intercom. "This can't be happening again." Surely he'll come to any minute. I begin counting in my head. A subtle hiss sounds, similar to a leaky bicycle tire.

Bang.

My ears pop. The door seal splits and in an instant, the cabin depressurizes.

I hyperventilate. Puff as the airplane's nose falls further. The engine whines, rapidly gaining speed. I turn to Trigger for help, when another wicked downdraft tosses me forward against the dash.

As I hang taut against my safety harness, Trigger's chunky barometer watch catches my eye.

Time of useful consciousness. I picture his class in the pressure chamber. As oxygen decreased, what did they do?

Put on their masks.

Reaching in the side pocket, I don my oxygen mask. After taking a couple of long breaths, I adjust Trigger's tightly over his nose and mouth.

Breathing somewhat normally, a wild thought comes to mind. Last year, I was ready to solo. I repeat the facts I'd known and forgotten. With my head bumping against the side window, I take the thought a step further. Just because I hadn't soloed didn't mean I couldn't.

My thumbs hook over the shoulder harnesses.

I'd flown many hours in an airplane, just like this one.

Sitting upright, I sweep bangs from my eyes.

Lightning cracks and I can see the backup instruments. The vacuum-driven dials show the airplane in a steep left dive.

Aggressively, I commandeer the controls. My left hand eases the throttle to idle, while my right slowly pitches the nose toward the artificial horizon—until blue and brown are split equal. As the airspeed slows, I tip the yoke to the right and carefully level the wings.

Despite the fact that we're still bouncing through air pockets, the airplane returns to straight and level. Ahead, one more obstacle stands between me and getting home. A massive thunderhead.

Bring it.

I eyeball the erupting supercell and hunker down on my seat belt. Narrowing my view, I analyze the core of the storm and map out a path. I lean forward, lower my head, and squeeze the side stick. As the gap between the wall cloud and the plane closes, I inhale and enter the eye of the storm.

The propeller tears a hole in the festering mass. I remain steady; hold the eastbound heading at all costs. Trusting in the hours of my rigorous training, I shoo any doubt from my mind.

I can fly.

CHAPTER 43

When the windscreen finally clears, I see nothing but blue, tranquil skies. Unobstructed, the sun casts a blinding glare over the instrument panel, warming my cheeks. Shading my eyes, I scan the flight instruments. Like before, all electrical power returned. My sight line darts to the GPS screen. "KRVS."

"Experimental 111X, do you read? Over," An authoritative voice comes through the speaker. My head whips around for visual confirmation. Off the right wing tip another single-engine plane parallels my path.

I key the mike and transmit, "N111X reads you loud and clear."

"Tana, is that you?" Relief rings in Professor Flough's voice.

Ahead I see the dam, the Arkansas River… And then, the most delightful sight. The Riverside Airport. Our home field.

My fingers relax, allowing the stick to rest loosely in my palm. "We're back," I scream and rock the wings like a seesaw.

The abrupt maneuver flings Trigger's body upright in his seat. Magically, his eyes open and he reaches for the controls.

"Are we dead?" he asks, and gently rubs his fingertips together.

"Look," I angle my neck at the airplane rocking its wings back at us.

"Let me guess, my father." Instead of an exasperated sigh, Trigger rushes to press his thumb on the mike. "We've got the field in sight—Dad, it's good to hear your voice."

"Tower says you're cleared to land one-niner-right, son," his heavy drawl cracks. "Switching to essential conversation only now."

"My landing," I call out with a confidence only found in seasoned aviators.

I finally get it; understand Trigger's cocky smile and easily muster one of my own. I suspect he recognizes his own reflection because in a flash his mouth curls into a similar smug grin.

Slowing the plane, I lower the gear and configure for landing.

From the corner of my eye, I see Trigger readying to offer help. But when I align the nose right on the centerline of the runway, he slips his headset on and moves the mike boom to his lips. "Okay, Ace, you're cleared to land."

A mouse-like squeak is music to any pilot's ears. Especially when you hear it just as the main wheels grease the ground. With constant backward pressure on the yoke, I hold the nose off. Showboating a main gear wheelie down the remaining runway.

"Show-off," Trigger teases, and I can't help but smile; wingtip to wingtip.

Wondrously, a full-grown butterfly with wide yellow wings marked with black hashes, soars gracefully ahead of our path.

CHAPTER 44

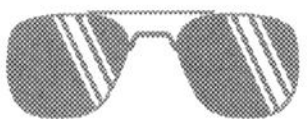

"So I guess you can fly," I say to Tana while keeping an eye on our hangar door until it seals. I hop into my hand-me-down pickup, stretch across the bench seat, unlatch the passenger door then and whistle at her. "You coming?"

She bends down in order to see through the open window.

"So I guess you can drive?" she says, thrusting a hip to the side.

"I've been known to maneuver a tug or two."

She checks out the beat-up sidewalls of my ride. The car jolts when she kicks a tire. "You got a license to drive this heap?"

Since when is Tana funny? I rub my hands over the steering wheel and laugh. "Same kind of license you have to fly planes."

"A special permit of sorts, then?"

"Something like that." I reach over the front seat and offer a hand.

"Sounds like you're more than qualified." Tana looks like she's about to accept my gesture when something at her feet grabs her attention.

"Hello, pretty boy," she says. "Check this out, he's rubbing against my shins."

I scoot over, look down, and see an orange cat weaving in and out of her ankles.

She squats to stroke him and misses, because at the exact same moment, the wiry striped tabby jumps and plops right onto my lap.

He rolls on his side and purrs like a rotorcraft. "You're a friendly fella." I scratch the amber tabby behind both ears.

The fuzzy critter rubs his whiskers against my cheek and kicks his purr machine into high gear.

"What do you think?" Tana asks. I'm guessing she's already decided to keep him.

I scratch the kitty's chin. "He doesn't have a collar, and I felt claws when he jumped."

"You think Jenks is a stray?"

"Jenks?"

"Appropriate, don't you think? Since we found him at the Jenks Riverside Field." Tana nudges us over and climbs into the passenger seat.

I buckle the cat in with the middle lap belt. "It's a pleasure to meet you, Mr. Jenks." I say and move the shifter into reverse. A strange twinge tickles over my skin and shoots the length of my spine. Throwing an arm over the seat, I face Tana. "I don't know if you noticed," I pause to caress the cat's smooth fur. "But your new owner is wearing a very pretty dress."

Tana's cheeks blaze. She tilts her head and twists a strand of hair.

I feel my chest pull to hers. *Does she feel it too?* I touch her hand and she doesn't move away.

Jenks purrs.

CHAPTER 45

When Trigger stops at the curb in front of my house, Jenks and I hop out and watch as his pickup coasts down the tree-lined street.

I blow out, calculating how much trouble I'm in.

At the edge of the tiled walk, I look at our historic house. For some reason the old place looks different. Brighter. Like it's been touched up with a fresh coat of paint.

Inviting and welcoming on the outside, sure. But what kind of reception looms on the other side of the stained wood door?

Worry? Relief? Anger? Not necessarily in that order. One thing is for certain. I'm indefinitely grounded. Regardless of the potential consequences, I tuck my bangs behind my ears, straighten my wrinkled dress, and start up the long pavers walkway.

Jenks trails closely behind.

Moving past the century-old oak trees and the rows of manicured boxwood bushes, I circle around the tiered stone fountain, drinking in the warm fall air. Perhaps it's the gentle breeze or the light-hearted chirps of the cardinals and blue jays, but not only does the house look different, it feels different. The quaintly-aged neighborhood I used to consider sleepy and boring suddenly seems to draw me with the appeal of a soft, cushy couch.

Taking one last deep inhale, I face the grand pillars, likely the gateway to a perpetual life sentence.

I'm about to climb the wide concrete steps when the front door creaks open. My foot catches the edge of the stair. After steadying myself, I look up to see my mother's blank face staring down at me.

"Mom, I… I can explain." I cross my arms over my chest, stalling to come up with one viable reason why her sixteen-year-old daughter disappeared for two nights without so much as a text message.

Before I can state my case, something incredible happens. From behind the maple door steps the man I once knew as my protector.

Eddie.

My heart sinks to my stomach as the wrongfully accused steps onto the porch.

"So it's true."

Eddie nods.

Mom starts to speak. "Your dad—"

"I know," I interrupt Mom and she looks at me. About to reach for my neck scar, I pause, and I fold my hands instead. "He made a choice."

Joining us on the stoop, my mom smiles and then opens her arms.

"Mom," I skip up the last stair and crash into her embrace. "I'm sorry." Tears drip from my eyes. "I didn't mean to… should have… I know you were just trying to protect me… I've missed you."

"Shhh," Mom says while stroking my hair. Easing me from her chest, she looks into my wet eyes. "I also owe you an apology. I let you down," she says, wiping my cheeks. "We both lost the most important thing in our lives, and I got scared."

Sniffling, I suck a couple of short breaths and swallow. "Dad is gone." I watch as my mother starts to cry. "But we're still here."

Mom hugs me, closer than I can ever remember.

Eddie moves and drapes his long arms over our shoulders. "Your dad would be so proud."

"When you went missing, Eddie came."

I lift my head and lock eyes with my protector.

"A promise is a promise."

Later that night, as a gentle breeze lifts the shears around my bed, I get a call from Trigger. No longer connected to Pioneer's in-skull network, he uses his cell, puts me on speaker.

"So, what's the verdict? Life imprisonment without parole?"

"Nope," I laugh. "The judge let me off with a warning. You?"

"Same, except I got a really long lecture about avoiding unpredictable weather. His voice sounds distant. "Strange…"

"What do you mean?"

"When I told Dad about the storm, how it forced us to land unexpectedly, leaving us stranded with fried phones, he really didn't ask any specifics. Seriously, it's not like the Colonel to be so understanding…" Trigger trails off like he has more to say, but decides against it.

I wait quietly for a minute, just in case.

"I know what you mean; maybe we should take off more often," I say to break the silence.

Trigger chuckles.

"Sure feels good to be home," I say, flipping and then burrowing in the soft sheets.

"Guess so." Mixed in with his words, I hear a constant ticking, a fan, and a cycling, pump-like sound.

"Are you at the hangar?" I ask, recognizing a noise that could only be made by hydraulics.

"I was so happy to make it out of Pioneer, get home and go back to being just an average high schooler, that I lost sight of the bigger, more important picture."

"Created a man-made geomagnetic storm, broke into a super secure hangar, escaped from a psycho security chief and navigated safely through a high-speed portal. Call me wacky, but it seems like you covered the gamut."

"You're the one who actually plugged the wings and got us through the portal."

"And you prevented me from making the biggest mistake of my life." I swallow.

"But we left Henry." Trigger says solemnly. "Alone, with the chief, to face the consequences of us not choosing to stay and keeping our future pills."

I picture McDunney hovering over our friend in Director Funkhouser's office. Think of Henry's dad and how disappointed he already was in his son. My mind skips from son to daughter, daughter to father to Soraya and her dad.

A sharp pain slices my gut.

"And what about Dr. Harb?" Trigger adds, almost as if he hears my thoughts. "I don't know about you, but I just can't go back to business as usual knowing that man is getting away with murder."

His words rekindle a feeling inside me, one I haven't felt since I choked Soraya's neck. Agony, rage, and the burning need for retribution.

"How can we go back?" My body trembles. "We don't have the location, remember?"

"It's you who's forgotten," Trigger says. "Think back to when we landed, right before McDunney inspected the cockpit. I grabbed the notepad and copied down the identifier."

He's right.

I think, recalling him pushing past the chief, tearing the sheet and crumpling it in his hand. "We have the airport's coordinates?"

"The white cursor is flashing on the GPS and I'm entering the lat/longs now." Excitement rings over the receiver. "XTA is set in and…"

"And?" I scoot to the edge of the bed.

"Seriously?" His voice shifts. "No such airport in database?"

"You probably mistyped. Try again."

A second later, I hear fists pound and then paper tearing. "Why aren't you working?" Trigger says, his words followed by another heavy thump.

"Gone radio silent?" I use his words.

But before he speaks I hear a rattling noise. A clack like something solid knocking against plastic.

"What's going on?"

"Considering Henry's contingency plan."

I realize the sound is Trigger's future pill jiggling in its amber jar.

"Just in case." Henry's words repeat in my head.

In case we ever need to find him again.

Are you out of your mind? I think, sitting comfortable, safe, and secure in my bed. Go back to that messed-up place? No way. Right here is where I belong.

But after the initial frenzy subsides, like Trigger, I sense a familiar angst simmering beneath my homecoming bliss.

Justice. The sentiment I mistook before as plain and simple revenge. I've learned vengeance never evens the score. It only perpetuates pain. Justice, however, is something far nobler.

"I'm in," I state, confident in my decision. "How will we find our way back? The pill reveals the future. Not flying directions."

"Don't know." Trigger jostles the prophetic capsule. "But one thing is for sure. We're going back to Pioneer."

Read on for the first chapter of E.L. Chappel's second book from the *In The Eye Of The Storm* series.

CHAPTER 1

Tona

"Wall cloud, twelve o'clock!" I shout to the team.

I scramble from the passenger side of the storm chasing rover, angle between the bucket seats, drop to my knees, and shimmy like a chimpanzee along a narrow metal catwalk.

I clench the thin side rails of the gangplank.

Don't look.

I will my eyes away from the bottomless floor, unsure that if I lose my balance, the crisscrossed net fastened to the frame will keep me from a fate worse than roadkill.

An epic bolt of lightning cracks.

The back of the mobile weather center lights up.

An electrified bolt strikes the wet road.

"Hold on," our meteorology professor yells. The rover swerves, and my fingers slip from the rails. My chest crashes against the catwalk. Wide-eyed, I stare at the two-lane rural road.

The world tilts as the asphalt blurs past. Nausea climbs my throat. *I'm not afraid of heights. I'm not afraid of...*

The rover's thick treads swerve over the solid yellow line, and when the vehicle jerks back, I cannon from the walkway.

Heights.

I soar—Superman style. The road markings below smear. I tense my muscles. *Any second now.*

The stiff hatches of the woven safety net snap against my skin.

After two loosely tucked rotations, I roll to a stop, belly up, gravel pelting like BBs against the back of my waterproof jacket.

Couldn't have stayed in the lab and written a paper on temperature and dew point spread, could you, Lyre?

I exhale with the force of a violent gust front and grip the nylon straps, knowing that the temperature/dew point project would earn me, at best, a C midterm grade. KC was right; with this professor, the safe route is a guaranteed GPA sinker.

I blow my bangs from my forehead. The question is, are the risks that come with chasing tornados worth the chance to get an A grade?

Clenching my fists, I squeeze my eyes shut and silently thank the engineering club for spec'cing a heavy-duty harness when tricking out our school's weather-hunting Hummer.

"I see it. I see it," Trigger calls from the Doppler station. My lids split to see my best friend secured in an ejection seat salvaged from a fighter jet. "Epicenter building…three miles, dead ahead." His sky-blue eyes glom on to the radar.

Bright-red scallops forge across the screen, pulsing with green thunderheads. Outside, tornado sirens shrill.

"Spotter…report." Professor McVie's voice climbs a notch, and I hear the rover's big-block engine rev faster. "Tana?"

Wiggling like a bug on its back, I pull my knees to my chest, rock to regain my footing, and then push to a wide-legged squat. I thread my wrists through the overhead subway lanyards and clench the leather loops. "Searching, sir."

A blustery gust lifts the rear tire in the air, and my thick rubber boot soles dig into the cross straps to maintain balance.

I paste my face against the picture window and scour the gray-black cloud mass until I spot the thunderstorm's pointed ledge. "Got eyes on the anvil," I shout over the howling wind. I release one overhead handle and trace the sharp point of a cloud resembling a miner's pick.

Golf-ball-sized hail pelts the shatterproof glass.

"Pressure readings, wind speeds." Our professor weaves, dodging another lightning assault. Undeterred, the weather hunter redirects the rover straight into the storm's path. "KC, any rotation?"

Along the back width of the vehicle, the fourth member of our team hangs upside down from the ceiling, strapped in a recliner, swiveling side to side like a bombardier gunner. My second best friend, KC, rides the semicircle track, unaffected by McVie's erratic maneuvers, and cycles from one end of the vehicle to the other as if she's at home on the couch, dominating in a virtual game jam. "Pressure's falling; dew point's steady," she says, viewing at least a dozen isobar maps.

I scurry across the remaining walkway, well aware of what's coming next. I revert to my monkey bar ways, swinging from overhead harness to looped harness, my feet grazing the gangplank grate. I stretch over the last two handholds and drop into the second ejection seat welded next to Trigger's. With my shoulder harness fastened, I tilt my head back and stare into the belly of the billowing storm monster that hovers over our pitted moonroof.

Crack.

Flash.

Thunder rumbles. In its wake, a rainbow of color burns.

A neon-green band of ribbon shoots from the festering supercell.

Shuddering, I nudge Trigger.

His surfer tan pales.

"The aurora borealis." I blink, and the majestic curtain of light vanishes. "But how?" I mouth, aware the northern lights aren't associated with this kind of weather. My earlobe tingles, and an image of blood, spit, and phlegm sprays in front of my eyes. "Aaaaaah."

"T?" Trigger's perfectly arched eyebrows spike.

"It's nothing." I shake my head. As quick as it came, the gore flash goes away, and I divert my view to the rover's side window.

"Nothing? You look like you've…Tana, you aren't seeing—"

"No," I snap, well aware of what he's about to ask. I'm not having visions from the afterlife, and I'm *not* hearing whispers from my dead father.

The howling winds fall off. Soaking rain lightens into a foggy, eerie mist. The roaring charcoal monster seems to have retreated. But it hasn't.

"I've got rotation!" KC screams.

"Incoming!" McVie bellows. "Brace for impact."

I want to look away. Seal my eyes tight. Cower with fear. But for some reason, the beast's greatness calls to me.

Thrills.

Entices.

Terrifies me beyond death.

My heart pounds like hail on pavement.

Water seeps from the cracked moonroof and splatters across my forehead. I stare as a decrepit funnel finger extends from the churning wall cloud. The wretched spindle whirls, pointing like a parochial school nun. Its punitive funnel spins and engulfs our armored rover.

"Brace, brace, brace! Cover your heads!" McVie hollers.

I hunker down on my shoulder straps.

"Lift-off in three, two, one…"

··· *Coming Soon* ···

The Surge

Book No. 3